THE LAST
CHANGELING

CHELSEA PITCHER

THE LAST
CHANGELING

Woodbury, Minnesota

First Edition
First Printing, 2014

Cover design by Kevin Brown
Cover photo © M. Pallas
Cover art © iStockphoto.com/6524824/©ANGELGILD

Flux, an imprint of Llewellyn Worldwide Ltd.

This is a work of fiction. Names, characters, places, and incidents are either the product of the author's imagination or are used fictitiously, and any resemblance to actual persons living or dead, business establishments, events, or locales is entirely coincidental.

Library of Congress Cataloging-in-Publication Data
Pitcher, Chelsea.
  The last changeling / Chelsea Pitcher.—First edition.
      pages cm.
  Summary: "When Elora, the princess of the Dark Faeries, meets Taylor, a seventeen-year-old exile in his own home, they form an unusual friendship, and Elora immerses herself in the mortal world while plotting to overthrow the Dark Queen"—Provided by publisher.
  ISBN 978-0-7387-4084-3
  [1. Fantasy. 2. Fairies—Fiction. 3. Friendship—Fiction.] I. Title.
  PZ7.P6428Las 2014
  [Fic]—dc23
                                                    2014025038

Flux
Llewellyn Worldwide Ltd.
2143 Wooddale Drive
Woodbury, MN 55125-2989
www.fluxnow.com

Printed in the United States of America

For my parents,
who took me in after the wolves tired of me.
Thank you for everything that followed.

1

ELORA

I was seventeen when death crossed my path. Before that, I'd only dreamt of twisted limbs and blood as bright as poppies. But late one night, death offered me an opportunity. She whispered dirty secrets in my ear and pulled back my eyelids with curling hands.

"*There*," she said, and pointed.

I did not recognize her voice then. I did not know who was leading me into the darkness.

I followed.

Down below, a girl traveled the highway alone. She carried a hefty knapsack—the staple of the runaway. Her hair was red like mine and we might have been sisters, if not for the obvious difference.

She was a mortal.

As I followed the runaway along the darkened street, I thought about mortality. Perhaps a part of me knew what was to come. When a chariot of iron pulled over to the side of the road, and the girl climbed inside, I feared the worst.

Then the buck stepped out into a pool of light, and I realized death would not be satisfied with one life tonight.

Buck and car collided. I closed my eyes, hoping to block out the worst of it. But the sound of the tires and the scent of blood did not escape me.

Try as we might, we cannot block out everything.

After the sounds had died down, I heard a whisper on the wind: "*Go*," it said to me. Was it death, or had I imagined it?

I approached the scene with caution.

A crack in the front window spiraled out like a web. Before this moment, I'd thought only spiders could create such things. But the girl's skull had collided with the glass and the result was this strange artistry. Curious, how beauty exists beside horror. Now her body lay slumped against the door. There was only a smattering of blood, there on her forehead. But even in the dim light, I knew she was dead.

Not so for the man in the driver's seat. His breath came out in little rasps. I reached in through the window and touched his head; just a jolt, to blur his memories. When he came to, the scene would tell a story his mind could not place. He would see the front of the vehicle smashed in, and the body of the buck sprawled out before it.

And he would know what had happened.

As for the girl, the one who had come into his life a few miles back, well ... He wouldn't even remember her.

I carried her body into the woods. Even in the darkness, she was a wonder to behold: once a living organism filled with possibility; now a bag of skin containing sharp secrets. Her blood stained my gloves.

I stripped off her clothes. Underneath, she was as pale as I am. Her hair was a duller shade of red, but that was no surprise. What human could have hair like mine? If I wanted to pass as one of them, everything about me would have to be dimmed.

My wings rustled at the thought of it.

I peeled off my gown, not bothering to unlace the bodice. Ribbons tore in my haste. Then we were free, clad only in the skin we were born in. Two little girls about to switch places.

Who would have thought it—a changeling at my age?

Changeling. That word had power behind it. That word could transform me. Surely, a loyalist of the Dark Court would never wear the mask of a human, but that's why my plan was so perfect. I would be in and out of the human world before my family could track me.

I had to be.

Still, my heart raced as I pulled on the mortal's clothes. In the pocket of her pants I found a stack of paper bills and a little card with her information on it: Laura Belfry. Age sixteen.

A year younger than me.

In the eyes of my mother, I was still very much a child. Reckless. Irresponsible. Incapable of creating any real change.

I'd show her.

I laced up Laura Belfry in my gown. At the last minute, I decided to keep my gloves. Those gloves, along with the pouch I wore around my neck, would serve as a reminder of who I was. When I lifted Laura's corpse from the ground, her head rolled toward me. Eyes open, she asked silently: Why?

Wrong place, wrong time, my dear.

I carried her deeper into the woods. Already I could feel the power of our exchange. Even glamour, the simplest of magic, gave me a rush. My skin buzzed as I lay her down on the ground. Together, our bodies began to change: my features softened while hers grew rigid. Within seconds, I looked positively mortal, and a crumbling log sat where she had been.

My little homage to the stories of old.

I almost laughed.

But I didn't. The girl's blood speckled my skin. It seeped into the creases, staining me. As I trudged back to the road, legs heavy in her boots, I summoned the rain to wash me clean. A quick wave of my hand disguised the crack in the chariot's window. By the time my magic faded and the log turned back into a girl, I would be long gone from this place.

I walked in the direction of the next town.

2

TAYLOR

The minute I walked onto the soccer field, I knew we were going to cheat. The signs were right in front of me. The guys on the opposing team looked like they'd shot up over spring break, and Coach was too busy ogling the cheerleaders to give us any valuable direction. But worse than anything was the look in Brad Dickson's eye, the one that said: *Win or go home in a body bag.*

What does that spell?

S-C-R-E-W-E-D.

See, Brad was on our side. He was supposed to be our lead defender. But he was better at skirting the rules, and the guys on the team tended to follow him—*if* nobody called him out. So I had to decide if I wanted to keep quiet (as usual) and let Brad cheat, or speak up and get punched in the face. Every day. For the rest of the year.

Isn't high school great?

I can do this.

In this corner, with 170 pounds of skin and bones... Wild and Wiry Taylor!

I can probably do this.

And in this corner, with 220 pounds of muscular madness … Brad "The Beast" Dickson!

Maybe I should just duck and cover.

The first half of the game passed in a blur. Our guys just couldn't make a shot. Meanwhile, Carson High's players scored goal after goal. The score at halftime was four to zip.

I'm royally screwed.

When the halftime whistles blew, Brad beckoned us into one of his infamous huddles. I tried to think about palm trees and breezes. If I could slip into a state of Zen, maybe it wouldn't hurt so bad to have my teeth knocked out.

"Listen up, guys." Brad draped his arm over my shoulder like we were buddies. With his bulging eyes and spiked-up brown hair, he looked like he had the bad habit of sticking forks into electrical sockets. "Keller's our biggest problem."

"Our problem is crappy coordination," I muttered.

Brad acted like he hadn't heard me. He was too busy glaring across the field at Carson's dark-skinned, goal-scoring god. At six-foot-seven, Jackson Keller was everything stocky Brad would never be.

"We remove Keller, we control the game," he said.

"Remove him?" I asked.

Are we going to levitate him off the field? Are we wizards now?

"Don't worry about it." Brad squeezed my shoulder. I think he was trying to get me to pass out.

Nice try.

"I'm not worried about it." I eased out of his death grip. "I'm worried about winning with integrity."

"*I'm worried about winning with integrity,*" Brad mimicked. "You believe this fairy?"

The guys laughed. Of course they did. Assholes.

"I just don't think we should give up yet," I said.

Brad looked at me like I was the town idiot. "We're not giving up. We're in it to win it!" He was practically barking now. And that, the guys responded to; they started cheering and pumping their fists.

I felt like I was in one of those old TV Specials of the Week.

Everyone's doing it, Taylor.

Just try it and see if you like it, Taylor.

YOU WERE JUST FOLLOWING ORDERS, TAYLOR.

I took a step forward. "Hold on," I said, fully prepared to get knocked on my ass. But maybe I'd get a shot in before Brad put me on the ground. "We're not doing this. This is pathetic. And anyone who thinks it's a good idea is pathetic."

Dear God, if ever you were to listen to me, please let me survive this.

I waited for the blow.

I kept waiting. I realized my eyes were closed, and I opened them.

Now Brad was laughing. "Nice speech," he said, giving me a slow clap to illustrate my powerlessness. "You guys believe this shit? Who knew we'd be getting a game *and* a show?"

Now they were all laughing.

I'd never felt more humiliated. Then Brad slapped me on the back. "Thanks for giving us a laugh," he said. "Guys, get back to your places. If anyone sees a clear shot, pass me the ball."

And that was that. My heroic moment had come and gone. Brad would find a way to win, and the victory would be all his.

I would lose.

We all would.

I walked back onto the field. Brad was already in position, conspiring with Guillermo Martinez to take Keller out. I knew the play: Brad would charge Keller while Guillermo came up behind him. When Keller jumped back and to the left—his signature escape move—he'd trip over Guillermo. Twist the shit out of his ankle. Maybe break his neck.

I had to stop them.

But how?

Then it came to me. God, it was so obvious! I just had to play *really well*. If I scored enough points ethically, Brad and the rest of the guys wouldn't need to cheat. They'd get their victory, and the glory, and no one would suffer for it. Of course, I'd been playing my best all game, and we were still losing. But I was getting desperate, so I put my heart and soul into my plan.

Race, dodge, kick. Race, dodge, kick. Good God, it was actually working. I scored two goals in the next ten minutes, and Keller managed to outrace Brad. Everything was falling into place, for the first time in, well, *ever*, until Brad shifted his attention from Keller to me.

Shit.

He looked like Old Yeller did after the guy got rabies. He may have actually been foaming at the mouth. And he came running up to me, yelling, "Pass the ball to me, pass the ball to me," because winning the game wasn't enough for him.

The victory had to be *his*.

Too bad I ignored him. The guy was clearly a psychopath. He was also a purely defensive player, and right then he wasn't doing his job, because he was running after me. And the rest of the team was watching, just waiting for a fight to break out. When Keller stole the ball from me at the last minute, there was *no one* to stop him from going for the goal.

So he did. And as the ball flew past our goalie, this wicked smile spread over my face. I actually felt happy. For the first time in longer than I could remember, I experienced joy.

Because we didn't deserve to win.

Then Brad fell to his knees, and my smile turned into a laugh. Coach was shouting at us to huddle up, but I wasn't about to listen. Where had he been all game? I gave Jackson Keller a high five and headed to the gym.

The farther I got from my teammates, the better I felt. I was in and out of the locker room before the first of them arrived. Then it was just a quick jog to my car. I called her Sue. She was my secondhand sedan. She had a long history of malfunctioning, usually at inopportune moments, so when the door didn't open right away, I didn't think much of it. I just wiped my hands on my jeans and tried again.

Again, the handle snapped back without unlatching. *What the hell?*

Crouching down to get a closer look, I reached for the handle a third time, then stopped. On the other side of the park, someone had made a sound like laughter, the kind that jumps from your mouth when you're trying to hold it in. Not for the first time that week, I got the feeling that I was being watched. But I wasn't in the mood to cower—the game had knocked that out of me—so I put my keys into my pocket and walked toward the sound.

I had a feeling I knew where it was coming from.

On the outskirts of the grounds was a swing-set, which people liked to say was the portal to another dimension. In reality, it was the sad remainder of a rickety wooden play structure, a structure that died so our second parking lot could live. But the swing-set was saved—we "kids" needed somewhere to play—and I liked to sneak away there when things got too typical at school.

I approached the swings slowly. The girl sitting there was anything but typical. Her hair was fiery red, and her skin looked stark white in comparison. In the blue light of dusk, I could make out a black T-shirt and jeans, which seemed out of place on her, though the long black gloves didn't.

She looked up. "Have I stolen your secret hiding place?"

She had a hint of an accent, maybe Italian or French, but it was too subtle for me to place. I hadn't exactly traveled to many places.

"No," I said, stepping up to a vacant swing. "I mean, it's fine."

I could feel this wild energy radiating from her, the way it feels in the middle of a storm. My hands buzzed, wanting to brush the tips of her fingers, her shoulder, anything.

I had to get myself together. "Aren't you cold?" I asked, sitting beside her.

"Yes." She smiled slowly. Seductively. "But I like it."

"Are you sure?" I would've given her my coat. Possibly the shirt off my back.

Whoa there, buddy.

"I'm sure," she said, holding my gaze. I couldn't believe how bright her eyes looked in the shadows—like the hottest parts of a fire, like blue and green flames dancing. "But you changed the subject."

"I did?"

"You most certainly did. And I wasn't finished with it yet."

"Sorry."

"Oh, how can I blame you? First I intrude upon your secret hiding place, and then I intrude upon your privacy."

"It's fine," I said. Over in the parking lot, car doors closed and engines turned over, but here in the park I felt far removed. I had only to glance at the girl and the headlights disappeared.

"Truly?" she asked, and the sound of the cars became a memory.

"Sure."

"You don't mind?"

"I don't mind."

"Oh good. Then you won't mind telling me what it is that you're hiding from?"

"I'm not hiding from anything. I heard a noise, so I came to investigate."

Like Sherlock Holmes. Sure, that's sexy.

"But this is not your first time here," she said.

I froze. It sounded like she was confessing to spying on me, and I probably should've bailed right then. But I didn't.

I told her the truth. "Sometimes I come here to get away."

"From what?"

"My family. School. Life, you know. All of it."

"It weighs heavily on you," she said, eyes widening in surprise.

I turned away. It was amazing how I could spend hours,

days, even weeks ignoring parts of my memory simply by keeping busy with unimportant things. Yet the minute one memory squeezed its way in, there was a flood.

I ran my hands through my hair. I'd recently started growing it out, and I liked the way I could hide behind it when I needed some space. My mom had other thoughts on the matter: each time we came into contact she shot me veiled, disapproving glances, like the daggers in her eyes would transform, midair, into scissors and give me a much-needed trim.

"Same as what weighs on everybody," I finally said, searching for a way to shift the focus away from me. What was she doing here anyway, swinging in the park by herself? "What about you? Did *you* come here to hide?"

"I came here to escape," she said, and her lips twitched. Her skin was so pale, and her lips so red, it reminded me of that story of Snow White. Of blood in the snow.

"Escape what?"

"The repetition of history."

I chuckled. "So we have that in common."

"I suppose we do." Her tone was casual, but I could see caution in her eyes. It occurred to me that she was using humor to mask vulnerability.

I should know. That was my favorite trick.

She held out a hand. "What's your name?"

"Taylor," I said, sliding my fingers over her gloved hand. She was warm, easy to sink into like water.

"Call me Laura," she said. At the last second, she added, "With an O."

"Lora," I repeated. "What brings you to Unity High? Did you just transfer?"

"Transfer?"

"You know, change schools?"

She licked her lips. "I guess you could say I'm checking things out."

My face flushed. For a second, I could've sworn she was using innuendo. But girls were different from guys. They didn't go around making hints about sex in casual conversation.

Did they?

"So what do you think?" I asked, both fearing and needing her answer.

"I haven't decided yet." Her upper arm grazed the swing's chain and she sucked in a breath, like she was in pain.

"You okay?" I wanted to touch her arm, to soothe the place where the chain had shocked her. I couldn't understand the intensity of my feelings. Sure, she was beautiful, but it wasn't just that. There was something about her fear, and her refusal to give in to it, that made me feel perfectly at home.

For once.

She leaned in. "I might consider ... *transferring*," she said slowly, like she'd just learned the word. "I think it would be useful to meet more people. But I don't know what to do, exactly. I've never gone to a traditional school before."

Ah, that was it. She was home-schooled. Well, it wasn't anything to be embarrassed about. "You can still register," I told her. "You just won't have transcripts from old schools. Can't your parents—" I stopped as the moon rose above the trees, illuminating her face. The look in her eyes killed me.

"I don't live with my parents," she said.

"Me neither," I quipped, before the reality of her words sank in. I waited a beat before asking, "Did you run away?"

"You might say I flew."

I smiled involuntarily. It was like my body was rebelling against the seriousness of the situation. "Do you have a safe place to stay for the night?"

"Not exactly."

"Do you need a place? I live above my parents' garage—"

"What would you ask in return?"

"Nothing," I said, and my body felt hot. She looked so distrustful then, I wanted to hurt whoever had taught her that kindness always came with a price. "I just want you to be safe."

"Why?"

Because I'm a good person.

Nope! Try again.

Because if I help her, I'll become a good person.

Not quite, but we're getting close.

Because I'm a terrible person, and I need to atone.

There you go.

"Because the park is dangerous at night. Someone could

harass you, or worse…" I tried to subtly look her over. She was almost as tall as me, and by no means scrawny. I was pretty sure she could hold her own in a fight. But if someone caught her unaware, or had a weapon, would any of that matter?

"Just try it for one night." I stood up, holding out a hand. "Please?"

"I guess I could take a look," she said finally, taking my hand.

I could feel her pulse through her glove. I focused on the feeling of it. "Really?"

"Yes. *If* you promise to help me transfer."

"I do. I will." I helped her to her feet. Up close she smelled like the forest, like earth and rain and berries. I resisted the urge to taste her cheek. "Come on."

———

I turned off the lights as I pulled into the driveway. To the right of the yard, the house was dark. This time of night, it would take a full-scale alien invasion to get my parents out of bed. I had no reason to feel worried as we hurried into the garage.

But I did. My nerves were in a tangle. My heart acted like it had something to prove, always racing, sometimes jumping over hurdles.

Lora had that effect on me.

Now that we were nearing my bedroom, those nerves were making me jumpy. The garage felt like a minefield of boxes. Sleeves spilled over the tops of the cartons like abandoned limbs, but they gave me an idea. I reached into a box, searching with my hands as much as my eyes. My fingers trailed down the fabric of a nightgown. A minute later I was climbing the stairs to my room, balancing the box in front of me. It took me a minute to locate my keys. And once I had them in my hands, I still managed to miss the lock twice. Finally the key slid into the lock.

I flipped on a light.

Oh no.

What had happened to my room? Hours earlier, it had seemed like a perfectly acceptable place to sleep. Now it looked like a pigsty; the last place you'd ever want to bring a girl. I tried to very casually pluck clothes from the floor and toss them into my overstuffed closet. I had to leverage my body against the doors just to get them to shut.

Way to look like a badass.

At least the bathroom was dark.

"Are those school books?" Lora asked as I gathered stacks from the floor.

"Some," I said. "Do you like to read?" The question was stupid, something I might have asked in kindergarten, but I wanted her answers to everything.

I needed them.

"I love to read." She grinned, sitting on the edge of my bed. I have to admit, it felt good to make her smile like that. "But I haven't had the chance to read … modern things. The books back home are much older."

I nodded, picturing bookshelves stacked with multi-colored Bibles. I set some of my favorite books beside her. Then I just stood there, feeling out of place in my own bedroom. "You can change if you want." I tapped the box of clothes with my foot. "And feel free to sleep in the bed."

"All right," she said, almost dismissively. Her hair spilled over the books as she flipped through them. It was so bright, and her lips were so red.

Yeah. I was staring. "I'll just, uh…" I took a step back. "I'll be back in a minute."

Turning away, I felt the blood seep back into my brain. Then it was three short steps to the bathroom. It hadn't really occurred to me that the bedroom was barely big enough for me to live in.

Now it was too late.

I rushed through my nightly ritual, brushing my teeth like my life depended on it. I practically fell over trying to get into my pajama pants. I went through T-shirt after T-shirt, searching for one that didn't smell like sweat, *but they all smelled like sweat*. Then I started to panic. I felt increasingly cornered, like I'd been given far too little time to transform into the man I wanted to be.

Man?

The thought made me laugh. Most days I still felt like a clumsy kid. Other days, I was an old soul drowning in disillusionment. But that elusive essence—the essence of being a man—was something I'd yet to drink. Except when she looked at me.

God, when she looked at me …

I had to get back to the bedroom. What if she'd already left? I checked my face in the mirror (twice) and hurried out the door.

Lora looked up when I entered. She was dressed in a full-length flannel nightgown my mom had worn when I was a kid, and her cheeks were pink, like she was up to something. She might've passed for a cherub if not for that hair.

She hadn't taken off her gloves.

"Are you sure you don't want to sleep in the bed?" she asked.

I didn't know if she meant *with her* or *alone*. I shook my head, lying either way, as she thumbed through *Othello*.

"I've heard of this man," she said. "He wrote about faeries."

I sat down on the edge of her bed. My bed. "You like fairy tales?"

Her hand stopped in mid-flip. "Some."

"Yeah," I said, thinking of the cheesy movies I'd loved as a kid. I wanted to tell her about them, maybe share a laugh, but the look on her face stopped me from joking around. I realized we were skirting the conversation we needed to have. "Hey, Lora?"

She lifted her head. She must've noticed the change in my voice. "Yes?"

Don't ask now. There's no reason to ask now.

"Are you in any danger?" For a fleeting instant, I saw

myself as the hero who would save her from the villains of her past. Then I realized that inventing some danger, just so I could save her from it, wasn't heroic at all.

She sighed. When she said "Yes," my eyes closed. "There are those who would do terrible things if they knew I was here. They would force me to return with them. They would hurt me." She watched me as she spoke. "They might hurt you as well. I should have told you before I let you bring me here."

I fought to keep my emotions off my face. "Do you think they'll find you here?"

She started to shake her head, but stopped. "They dwell outside of society, surrounded by acres of wildlands. They would not expect me to come here." She braved a smile. "To the city."

She took my hands. Smooth currents shot up my arms, jump-starting my heart. I realized I'd been holding my breath.

"If you wish for me to leave, I will do it," she said. "Right now. I won't hold it against you." She scooted toward me. The nightgown bunched up beneath her, revealing long, curvaceous legs.

I willed myself to watch her face. A nice pair of legs would do me no good if some asshole mobster came and broke mine, not to mention my face. "I'm not going to throw you out in the cold."

"I appreciate that," she said, staring into my eyes.

Studying me. "And do not worry that I will stay too long. Inevitably, I must return … "

"Wait. What?" Now I was totally lost.

"Not to rejoin them," she said, and I thought she was choosing her words carefully. "But there are those I left behind … "

"I see," I said, though I didn't really. But I wouldn't push her on it, not tonight. "Why don't we get some sleep? I'll be able to think more clearly in the morning."

She lowered her eyes. It was like she knew the effect they had on me. "That sounds fine."

I turned off the light on the way to my futon. It felt good to stretch my limbs, in spite of the narrow space. It wasn't like I was going to miss out on my normal good night's sleep. Usually I was lucky if I fell asleep before three a.m. With Lora lying so close, I doubted I'd sleep at all.

Then, just as I'd accepted that I'd probably be up all night, her voice pierced the silence.

"I need to … purchase some things."

I started to laugh. I couldn't help it. "You need to go shopping?"

"Yes."

I grinned into the darkness. I'd never been so happy to hear something so mundane. "What do you need?"

"I'm not sure exactly. But it looks as though I've come into some money—"

I wasn't going to ask. No matter how much I wanted to, I just wasn't going to ask.

"—and I was hoping to find something I could use to contact a friend back home. Something that would be confusing to one who lives outside of society. Something h—" She stopped herself, breathing heavily.

"High tech?" I offered, my eyes adjusting quickly. Moonlight filtered in through the window above my bed. I could just make out the outline of her face as she said, "Yes. High tech."

"Disposable cell phones," I said, unfazed by the feeling that she wouldn't know what the hell that meant. "I could get you some, and you could mail one to your friend or something."

"You wouldn't mind?"

"No big deal. You can just pay me back whenever." I didn't really want to take her money. I wasn't sure what she'd gone through to get it.

She nodded slowly, like she was mulling over the offer as she agreed to it. Then she smiled and I was certain—*certain*—the moonlight spilled directly over her head. When she spoke, she spoke in the voice of a person in a trance: "It feels as though my power wanes with the passing of each breath. But power shifts like changing seasons, and when it waxes once more, I promise you this: in exchange for true kindness, I will do everything in my power to grant your heart's greatest desire."

My body flushed, a multitude of emotions filling me with warmth and shame. First, the thought that my greatest desire was to crawl onto that bed, climb over her like an animal, and draw her lips into mine. Then, the fear of what could be interpreted if I read between her words. What if she was a teenage prostitute run away from some crazy cult? I wasn't naïve. I knew these things happened. I tried to imagine myself using a baseball bat to ward off a gun-toting preacher pimp.

I pressed my face into my pillow. If Lora wasn't a prostitute, she wouldn't be thrilled that I'd allowed the thought to enter my head. And if she was ... well, if she was, I'd do the best I could to help her begin a new life, and if she wanted to thank me carnally, I'd smile, give her a brotherly hug, and politely decline.

Then I wondered, with a new wave of shame, how I was supposed to use theoretical morality to resist the most beautiful creature I'd ever met. My cheeks were so hot I thought my capillaries were going to burst. I lifted my head, peering at the outlines of my belongings: books stacked on my desk; the accordion-like shape of the lampshade; and my soccer jersey hung over a chair. But these familiar, inanimate objects failed to tantalize my *very* active imagination, and my eyes found themselves trailing Lora's barely moving form. I studied her from across the room. When the sound of her breath grew even, I knew she was sleeping. When she started to twitch, I knew she was dreaming.

Hours later, I slipped into sleep.

3

ELORA

Liquid moved like honey through my dreams. Ravens took wing and blanketed the sky. I could almost taste the air of Faerie, sharp and sweet like the forest after the rain. Then I awoke and these things slipped from my mind.

I was on my knees in an instant, staring out the window above the bed. The moon drifted behind webs of clouds like a secret the sky was not ready to reveal.

I know the feeling. I kicked the tangled sheet from my legs. *If I could just slip into the sky for a moment, I might be sated for the remainder of my trip.*

See, that is the thing about faeries and lies. We can lie perfectly well in our own minds. It's the passage of the lie from the lips that is forbidden.

One short flight, and I'll be fine.

I pulled myself onto the windowsill.

It's dark, and I'll be quick. What is the danger?

Of course, I knew the answer to that. The mortal lay so close I could hear him breathing. He needed only to glance up to see me climbing through the window. He might banish me from his bedchamber, or worse: see a glimmer of my true nature and try to trap me.

Make me bargain, like a villain, on my knees: *I'll grant ya three wishes, or me pot o' gold.*

I never could do a believable Irish accent.

Slinking back into the room, I moved onto the bed and then the floor, creeping across the carpet like a sulking pup. The mortal was sleeping, his breath unsteady as chirping sounds escaped his mouth. His tawny hair spread out around his head. In the dim light I saw his resemblance to a young forest elf, before age slants the cheeks and points the ears. His eyes were closed, fluttering little wing beats against his cheeks.

Taken in by the illusion of innocence, I lifted a hand to his cheek.

He is a killer.

I stopped in midair.

All of them are.

Taylor laughed in his sleep, as if he had heard my thoughts and found them faulty. He turned on his side, away from me.

I took it as a sign.

I was back at the windowsill in an instant, crawling through the frame and out onto the little ledge. My wings, tucked neatly beneath the loose, billowy nightdress, began beating against the cloth before I had even set them free. The night air swirled around me, undoing the buttons on the back of the gown, and within seconds my wings burst from their bindings.

Then I was off.

Calling on the night to stain my skin, I soared into the sky, beating back the cold with ecstatic wings. The beauty of that moment knocked the breath out of me. I did not dare try to steady my heart, but let it beat against my chest as a reminder of how much flight meant to me.

Held in the embrace of the cool night air, I was truly free.

Higher and higher I flew, chasing the moon, pulling back clouds with my hands. I dove into a burst of rain, came away soaked to the skin, and felt the bumps rise upon my arms in silent tribute. The scent was intoxicating.

Then, something odd: I seemed to be shedding stars. Drops fell from my skin toward the earth, catching each glimmer of moonlight. I touched my face with cold fingers and brought them away covered in tears. Giddy with the wildness of it all, I licked them from my hands, tasting the salt of the sea. Sea, earth, air, darkness: I was a part of them all, and all of them resided inside of me.

Slowly I became aware of other things. Glowing bulbs of light suspended in the sky. Tree trunks sprouting wire branches. A honking, unlike any bird, came near and then faded away. My glamour flickered, responding to my unease, and I knew I should return to my little cage.

One more minute.

I did a flip in mid-air. My stomach dropped, unable to

catch up to my body. I laughed, feeling reckless and free. There was a part of me that knew I was risking too much, knew I needed to lower myself from the sky. But my happiness in that moment kept me in flight.

Until Taylor screamed.

The fearful sound echoed throughout the sky. I could scarcely think. I dare say I forgot how to breathe. And though it seemed highly illogical, my instinct told me to lower myself back to the ledge of the garage.

What will he do to me? What will they all do?

I was terrified.

Yet the strangest thing happened when I lowered myself to that little ledge. No raging mortal awaited me there. No torches, no knives. No guns to tear my wings to shreds. I peered inside the window, my stomach aching with nerves. Still, silence. A simple glance to the left showed what my heart dared not hope.

Taylor lay sleeping.

Had I imagined the scream? Or had someone else spotted me in the sky? I'd been certain, at the time, that the scream was his. But how could I be sure? Here in the mortal world, men of a certain age might all sound alike.

Squeezing back through the window, I moved quietly into the bathroom to dry my skin and clear my mind. Clothing formed pyramids on the floor, accompanied by the occasional towel, but I passed them by. Drawing upon my waning strength, I drew quick circles above my head until the room was spinning with warm air. I tucked my wings against my back and set to work buttoning the night-dress. I hated the confinement, the feeling of being held down in my own skin. But what choice did I have, here?

Now my clothing was dry. My desire for flight was temporarily sated. Yet I did not leave the room immediately. Instead I walked across the tiles, feeling their strangeness with my feet, and touched the glass of the mirror.

Reflections hold a deep fascination for the fey. Often we steal glances at the surfaces of lakes, just to see if our reflections will do something silly without our bodies' permission. But staring into this looking glass, at the two-dimensional, trapped version of myself, all I could see was the lie.

For a moment I let the glamour slip, freeing the glow that lived within. Dark symbols flashed and faded beneath my skin. My hair curled over my arms like tongues of flame. But I did not let out my wings, now that I had tucked them away.

I did not want to see them.

When I was a child, many in the Court mused that the Queen had mutilated my wings as some form of punishment. Indeed, they appeared to have been sliced along their thickest curves. But no such punishment ever occurred; I was born with the abnormality.

At least here, I could pretend I was normal.

I reapplied the glamour slowly, watching my reflection as it changed. Smaller eyes, smaller mouth. Everything proportioned and uninteresting. A little knob rested on the side of the mirror, and I opened it to find a cabinet built into the wall. I was pleased to learn that humans had secret compartments just like faeries did, even if they were quite easy to find. Armed with this new discovery, I continued to poke around the room. I pulled back a curtain hiding a long, white basin and picked up a bottle, turning it over in my hands. It slipped.

The bottle crashed against the basin and slid toward the drain. I placed my hands over my ears, as if that might somehow drown out the noise.

It didn't.

There came a tentative knocking on the door.

I opened my mouth, but only the tiniest sound escaped.

Taylor knocked again. At least, I thought it was Taylor. Considering my limited knowledge of the human world, it could have been anybody.

"Lora?"

It was Taylor. That should have put me at ease. But upon hearing his voice, my heart began clattering around the way it had when I'd been in flight. I felt nervous, joyful, and panicky.

"It's me," I said through the door, though, upon immediate consideration, this seemed an improper response.

"Are you okay?" His voice was soft, muffled by fatigue.

What could I say? I felt, in that moment, a great many things, but "okay" was not among them.

I opened the door.

Taylor stared through the darkness. "Were you in there without the light on?"

Yes, but it's not a problem, as I can see in the dark.

"I didn't want to wake you," I said.

"What were you doing?"

Again, I searched for an acceptable answer, all the while growing more anxious. In the end, it was a tiny tuft of hair that saved me, sticking up from the top of Taylor's head. It was not the sight of it that disarmed me, but rather the fact that he regarded me with the utmost sincerity while, unbeknownst to him, that tuft rebelled.

"I'm just trying to get used to"—I gestured grandly—"this."

He took a step toward me, his mouth contorting in a yawn. He looked like a roaring lion. "Is there anything I can do?"

He wasn't looking at me. I got the distinct impression he didn't want to, though I could not guess at his reasons. Even more interesting was the fact that my heart had resumed its pounding the moment he'd come nearer.

"I don't know that there's anything anyone can do," I said, shifting my gaze to the floor. I couldn't stop noticing the emptiness of the room: the floor devoid of soil and insects, the ceiling of neither sky nor trees. My whole life, I'd lived with the possibility of losing these things, yet it was an entirely different thing to actually be without them. To miss them. "Back home, things are just … different."

"They must be." He looked at me then, his eyes kelpie green in the darkness. "You said you live out in the country?"

"Far from here."

"I used to want to live outside the city." He lingered in the doorway. "Have dogs and horses. Climb trees."

I smiled faintly, and it seemed to encourage him.

He placed his hand on the doorframe. "I drew up these plans for a city in the trees. It was basically a bunch of tree houses with bridges connecting them, but ... " He paused, and in spite of his smile, there was an edge to his tone. "I was *convinced* it could happen, if we just moved out of the city. My brother, Aaron, and I—" He stopped, busying himself with a fraying corner of the door. "We thought we could make it happen."

"You have a brother?" I asked.

Taylor stepped past me toward the sink. He turned on the water, running his hands under the stream. "He's not here anymore."

"Oh."

Back home, much had been said about the discon- nected nature of human families. Now I had the chance to learn about it firsthand. But the scowl on Taylor's face, reflected in the mirror above the sink, told me I daren't ask him now.

I stepped up behind him.

For a moment, he was too busy touching the water to notice me. It seemed to put him in a kind of trance, and he closed his eyes, feeling.

When he opened them, his scowl had lessened. "I would go into the bathroom and pretend I was running my hands through a stream," he said, turning off the faucet and shaking droplets onto my arm. Before I could respond, he was walking out of the room.

I followed.

"I would stand at my desk, or my dresser, and pretend I was touching tree trunks." He ran his fingers over the surface of his desk. "Sometimes I could even convince myself I was feeling that buzz, that energy you get from touching trees."

I stepped up beside him, in a trance of my own, and touched the desk. The wood was smooth, glossed over with a substance I did not recognize, but the pattern could still be seen.

I closed my eyes.

When Taylor's arm bumped against mine, I nearly opened my wings. The energy I had been hoping to find in the desk emanated from his skin. For an instant, I couldn't breathe.

Then, just as suddenly, my wings settled against my back and my breathing returned to normal. I was simply on edge, I assured myself, lifting my hand from the desk. He'd caught me off guard.

I looked up to see him staring.

"I don't know if that helps," he said, sitting on the edge of his bed, "but it used to make me feel better whenever I felt trapped. It helped me to think that the things you find out there"—he gestured toward the window—"are in here too. Just in different forms."

I sat beside him. "Taylor."

He turned to me, and the look on his face said he would grant me three wishes.

"Words fall short," I said. Ignoring the fire burning in my chest, I placed my hand over his. "But, yes. That helps."

4

TAYLOR

If Saturday was weird, Sunday was royally messed up. I woke up at dawn and snuck off to the cemetery, just like usual. After that, I stopped off at the mall to pick up two disposable cell phones, because, you know, covert ops were a part of my life now. Things didn't really go wrong until after I got home.

It was close to ten-thirty, and Princess Sleeps-A-Lot was still in bed. *No biggie,* I thought, *I'll just program her phones before she wakes up. Everything will be great!*

Oh, the lies we tell ourselves. I'd barely emptied the blue plastic bag when the knock came at my door. The knock of horror. The knock of death.

"Taylor? Honey, are you in there?"

No, worse. The knock of my mother.

"Shit, shit, shit," I whispered under my breath, because moms are more scared of swear words than they are of video games where you get points for killing prostitutes. My gaze shifted to the bed, where Lora-the-possible-teen-prostitute lay sleeping. She looked so innocent, curled up into a ball. I thought I would do anything to protect her.

"Taylor?"

"Just a second!" I yelled as Mom jiggled the handle. Thank God I'd remembered to lock my door. Now I just had to remember to *think*. I sprinted across the room and knelt beside the bed. The blankets were all tangled up around Lora's legs and some of them had dirt streaked across them, which was strange. I didn't remember her being covered in dirt when I'd brought her home. Then again, it had been dark and I'd been in a daze.

I was in a daze now. "Code red. *Code red*," I whispered, though it probably sounded like gibberish to her. But she must've understood, because her eyes popped open and she sat up.

"What happened?" she asked. Her cheeks were red, like she'd been sitting in front of a fire, and her hair was everywhere, and *how does she look this good when she's just woken up?* Nothing about the morning felt fair.

Nothing about the morning felt *right*.

But now I had her full attention, and the handle of my door had stopped jiggling. For one perfect moment we just stared into each other's eyes.

"My mother," I mouthed, "is at the door. I'm so sorry."

Without a word, Lora slid the blankets off her legs and climbed out of bed. She pointed to the bathroom, tilting her head to the side, but I shook my head.

"She goes in there sometimes," I said. "She pretends

that she's looking for clothes, but really she's just snooping. I do my own laundry—"

Lora frowned, and I realized I was rambling. Who cared why my mom went into my bathroom? I needed to get Lora *out of here*. But how? It's not like she could go out the window.

I swallowed, unprepared for the heaviness in my chest. Meanwhile, Mom was knocking again, and Lora was looking at me with those big, frightened eyes.

Okay, I can do this.

I bolted to the bathroom. I was leaping over mountains of clothes, evading tall moms in a single bound. Kneeling next to the shower, I twisted the knob that was notorious for spitting out freezing-cold water. Still, I whispered, "Warm up, warm up, warm up," because sometimes, when you really want something, it just happens, right?

Icy spray assaulted my face. My lungs constricted and certain parts of me probably turned blue, but I didn't pull my head away until it was soaked. Reaching blindly across the tub, I added a little shampoo to the mix, because authenticity is important when tricking your parents. Then, with the door only partially closed, I stripped. I took off everything except my boxers, and once I had a towel around me, I took those off too. I couldn't risk the towel falling and my mom realizing this had all been a scam.

Of course, if the towel fell off now, my mom would see me naked, and that was just as horrifying. So basically, I couldn't risk the towel falling down, period. Holding on to the ends with one hand, I clutched it tightly to my waist and hurried back into the bedroom.

Lora was standing by the window, her hand on the half-open sill.

I shook my head. There was no way I was letting her climb onto that ledge and risk falling to her death. Sure, we were only two stories up, but if she tripped and fell headfirst, that wouldn't make a difference. Then she'd be lying there, in a pool of her own blood, silent as a stone, and—

Stop.

I held Lora's gaze, pointed toward the bathroom, and made a motion like I was opening a shower curtain.

She nodded.

Then, with a heavy heart and a sudsy head, I turned to face the door. Using my free hand, I undid the lock, yanking the door open with more force than intended.

"*What?*" I said in my best bored-but-irritated voice.

"I . . . " Mom stared at me, in all my half-nakedness with suds on my head, and heaved a gigantic sigh. "Oh, honey, I'm sorry." She brushed past me into the room. She was wearing this flowery blue shirt you'd expect to see on a Sunday school teacher, with TV-commercial khakis, and her silver-streaked hair was pulled back in a braid. "I thought something was wrong."

"I was just about to rinse," I said.

She nodded, looking around real causal-like, but her

nostrils were flared like she could *smell* the deception. She was dangerously close to noticing the dirt on my sheets.

"Mom. I'm getting shampoo in my eyes," I lied.

Her gaze snapped back to me. "I only need a minute," she said, searching my face for wayward suds. "I received a call from—"

"Ow—fuck!" I squeezed my eyes shut.

"Taylor Christopher Ald—"

"What? It *hurts*." I wiped at my brow, which only managed to spread the shampoo around. "I have to rinse *now*."

I turned before she could say anything else. I'd almost made it to the bathroom when I realized she was following me. Which meant I had to stand there, with shampoo actually in my eye at this point, or get into the shower with Lora and *take off my towel* so Mom wouldn't think something was up.

Um. *Seriously?*

I started to panic. It's the only explanation for what happened next. I stumbled to the sink, splashing water into my eye to try to cool the burn. It helped until my mother said, "What are you doing?"

"You said you wanted to talk."

"But ... " She pointed to the shower, and the water that must've been pretty hot, because the bathroom was filling up with steam. For a second, I wondered if Lora was standing in there in the scalding hot water because she didn't know how to cool it down.

Okay, no one was *that* clueless. Right?

Still, a terrible feeling settled into my chest. I needed to get in the shower, even if it meant humiliating myself in the process. Lora could actually be hurting herself for me, and my mother was pretty close to calling me on my bullshit anyway. As stealthily as I could, I slipped through the crack between the shower curtain and the wall, prepared to bare all.

What would she think when she looked at me? Would she be horrified, thinking I was going to hurt her?

Would she laugh?

My hands shook as I struggled to open the towel. With shampoo dripping down my face, it took longer than it should have for me to realize what was wrong with this picture.

The shower was empty.

I mean, *I* was in it, but Lora wasn't.

She was gone.

Outside.

Gone.

The truth hit me like a fist to my gut. Why would Lora go stand in the shower and risk getting caught when she could just go out the window instead? My heart thudded as I reached into the scalding water and turned the knob to the right. I jerked it too hard, and the water came out too cold, but I didn't care. It actually helped to numb my fear as I rinsed out my hair, panicking all the while.

Had she run away? Would I never see her again?

Or worse, had she...

"Honey, I got a call from Hal Munskin," Mom said, breaking into my thoughts. "The guidance counselor—"

"What?" The heat of shame prickled over my skin, making me dizzy. I turned the water to freezing. "Hackneyed Hal called—"

"*Mr. Munskin*, Taylor, and he said you've stopped going to your sessions—"

"I don't need to talk to him."

"You need to talk to somebody. It hasn't been that long since—"

"I know how long it's been," I spat, fury bleeding into my voice. It was bad enough that she'd pawned me off on a counselor instead of talking to me herself. But a high school guidance counselor? "His job is to help people with their college essays. He's not equipped to deal with … "

Loss?

Grief?

Crippling guilt?

"Anything real," I finished, twisting the shower off. For a minute I just stood there, shivering in the cold. I knew I needed to get Mom out of there, but I couldn't move.

"Sweetie, I just need to know you're all right. At least if you lived in the house, I'd be able to see for myself … "

Oh. So that's what this was about. "I can't move back in," I said, so softly I didn't think she'd hear me.

But she did. Super-sonic mom hearing, I guess. "You say that, but your father's been talking—"

"He doesn't want me there."

"It's not that. He's just worried—"

"Look, Mom, I really can't do this right now." I threw my towel around my waist, holding tightly to the ends. "I've got a lot of homework to do. And some of the guys are going to call later, to talk about, uh...soccer techniques."

Sure. Because that ever happens.

But she didn't know that. And my comment seemed to have the desired effect. I could hear the smile in her voice when she said, "You're making a lot of friends, aren't you?"

"Yup. Tons," I lied. "I think it's been really good for me to be part of a team."

"That's good. Great. Well, listen, why don't we talk later..."

"Sure," I said, pulling back the curtain. I had this big, fake grin plastered on my face. "But don't worry, okay? I'm feeling a lot better. You don't have to worry about me."

"Good." She exhaled, the lines softening on her face. "Maybe tonight, you can come by—"

"Mom, I really need to get to work." I ushered her out of the bathroom, glancing quickly over at the window.

I saw nothing.

"Those teachers are really working you hard," she said as I stubbed my toe on my desk chair. The pain was sharp and immediate.

Mother f—

I closed my eyes and saw Lora's body, lifeless and bloody, lying on the ground beneath the window.

I closed my eyes and saw Aaron.

Maybe I did need therapy.

"It's the end of the year," I said, shaking as Mom stepped through my door. "Things'll calm down soon."

Now she wouldn't look me in the eye. It was like she was holding something back. But I couldn't worry about it because I was *so close* to being free from her. "Listen," I said, easing the door closed inch by inch. "I really am fine. I promise."

Some lies are necessary.

Mom smiled. I smiled back and shut the door, locking it.

Then I bolted over to the window.

"Please be all right," I whispered. I couldn't yell, because Mom might hear me, but I couldn't bring myself to look down either. If Lora was dead, there was nothing I could do about it.

My eyes started to stray down, without my permission.

But I couldn't do it, wouldn't do it, couldn't do it.

"Lora," I hissed, terrified my mom would come out of the garage and see her clinging to the ledge.

Sure, that's why I'm terrified.

"It's all clear," I said into the empty air, my eyes straying to the base of the garage. I saw cement and the manicured edge of the grass.

No blood.

No bones bent.

A rustling sound caught my attention. I turned to

the left, relief flooding my body as Lora's face appeared around the backside of the garage. She was following the little ledge, impossibly light and fast, like a walker on a tightrope. I wanted to close my eyes until she reached me, but I couldn't afford the possibility of her slipping just as she came into my grasp.

When she finally reached the window, she practically fell into my arms. Or maybe I was reaching for her. Then I was pulling her through the frame, whispering god knows what to who knows what god.

What I know is this: Lora climbed onto the bed just as my mom stepped out of the garage. I closed the heavy blue curtains, blocking us in. Still, long after I'd whispered "Please never do that again," and Lora said "I promise," I knelt there, hands clutching her arms, thankful beyond words that she was alive.

5

ELORA

Once the madness had died down, Taylor spent the afternoon convincing me to stay another night. His argument hinged on the fact that his mother *surely* wouldn't visit again for another few weeks, as was her schedule. He made grand promises about stopping by the house every day, if necessary, to make sure she wasn't tempted, and ended the entire speech by gifting me two cell phones.

Quite convincing.

Still, the thing that swayed me had nothing to do with his bargaining, and everything to do with the way he'd looked at me when I'd climbed back into his room. His hands had been shaking and his eyes were alight with fear. He'd been *terrified*. No human on earth could have faked that level of concern.

So I decided to give him one more chance.

After that, Taylor explained how to operate my cell phones, and together we "surfed the web" for articles on transfer students. It quickly became clear that I would need to provide the high school with some kind of record, regardless of whether I had actually ever been to school. Taylor felt the best course of action was to purchase a fake transcript, but I had a feeling I could create one myself.

"How hard would it be to make these?" I asked.

"It wouldn't be easy. You see how perfect it looks?" He pointed to the place where tiny letters were arranged in lines. "It's not watermarked or anything, but I'd still be nervous trying."

"I bet I could do it."

"Really?" A slow smile spread across his face, born of mischief. "What program would you use?"

"Oh, I don't know. I guess I would ask my friend Taylor for a recommendation." The moment I said it, my heart squeezed. Never in all my life had I considered calling a human a friend. But I wouldn't have said it if I hadn't meant it.

I *couldn't* have.

He stared at me with bright eyes. "Excel," he said after a moment.

"I'll try."

He laughed, taking control of the mouse. "I have a feeling it comes naturally." He clicked twice. "Here. Use this program. The grid will help you line up everything perfectly."

"I will do my best," I said, feeling antsy. Even with the program, I'd have better luck glamouring my own transcript. But to do that, I'd have to get him out of the room.

"Are you hungry?" I asked tentatively. I had heard, somewhere, that humans ate constantly.

"I could eat."

"It's not too much trouble?"

"No, it's not too much trouble to expect to eat." His smile was sheepish. "I should have offered."

"We've been busy."

"I'll go look for something. Any dietary restrictions I should know about?"

"You mean, for instance, my body can't process meat?"

"Sure. Anything like that."

"My body can't process meat."

"Really?"

"Yes. It sounds strange, doesn't it?" Humans tore down rainforests just to make grazing ground for cattle—how could they understand that too much iron was poison in my veins?

But Taylor just smiled, a lopsided grin that made me want to dance a jig. "It's not strange at all. Last summer I worked at a fast food place. Ever since, I haven't been able to eat red meat without feeling sick."

I fought to contain my relief. "Spinach isn't great, either."

"Tell me about it. I'll see what I can find."

The moment he was gone, I set to work glamouring the most realistic high school transcript I could. I had to use the Internet search engine to understand the meaning behind the letter grades, and then I had to exercise restraint in choosing my own. When Taylor returned nearly twenty minutes later, I was reclining in the desk chair and admiring my work.

"I'm so sorry," he said, holding two plates in his hand as he shut the door. "My mom caught me and wanted me to eat dinner with them. We got into this whole big thing—here." He held out a plate. From what I could tell, the plate held potato mash and corn.

"I thought it was customary to dine with one's family," I said.

"Not necessarily." His tone had a defensive edge. "She goes to bed early, because she teaches, and my dad has a lot of late meetings."

"Meetings for what?"

"Oh, right." Taylor tapped his fingers on the desk as if bored. "He's a low-level employee at Benson and Wallowitz. It's the city's leading accounting firm."

"That's interesting."

"Not really. He wanted to be a marine biologist."

"To study the creatures of the sea?"

"Yep."

"Fascinating. What happened?"

"I did." Taylor laughed, picking up the glamoured transcript. "You made this with Excel?"

"I'm a fast learner."

He touched the page gingerly before handing it back to me. "This is really your first time using a computer?"

"I told you it was."

"Amazing. Oh." He reached into his pocket, pulling out something sharp and shiny. "I almost forgot."

Oh, Darkness.

The fork glinted in the light, its tines taunting me. My thoughts began to race. My gloves were on the other side of the room. I couldn't very well use wind to lift the utensil in front of Taylor. And then there was the little issue of putting iron in my mouth.

Then again, many metals used by humans did not contain iron. But was it worth the risk? And the burn?

"Taylor," I said, my voice small and defeated.

"What did I do?" He studied the fork for an answer. "Is it dirty?"

"No, it's fine, it's just... I can't really use certain metals," I explained, searching for words and failing. Would something so small be the thing to expose me? "I'm just—"

"Allergic?"

"Allergic." I repeated the word, hoping he would take it as agreement.

"What about plastic?" He slid the fork back into his pocket. He wasn't mocking me or trying to make me feel foolish.

What game is this?

"That would be lovely," I said. A crow cried outside the window, and I glanced at the cell phones on the bed. "Take your time."

After he left to fetch the new utensil, I tore a corner

off a small piece of paper and wrote the words *Green, begin. Red, end.* I wanted the instructions to be simple, and vague in their origins, in case the phone fell into the wrong hands. That way the interceptor would have no cause to believe it came from a faerie. I slipped the paper and one cell phone into the bag the phones had come in.

Moving to the window, I let out a squawk, calling to the crow who lived in the tree. The bird left her post, gliding down to the windowsill.

I held out the little blue bag.

The crow fluffed her feathers, cawing pleasantly, and I whispered softly in an old fey dialect that animals could understand. "Take this to the marshes below the Dark Forest, to a marsh sprite by the name of Illya. Her wings are green and veined as leaves; her amphibian frame, spotted with black. You will know her by her eyes, cerulean around a golden iris. Unusual among her kind."

The bird dipped her head and took the bag in her beak.

"Thank you, friend." Stroking her feathers with one hand, I dropped a glamour over the bag to help it blend with the approaching dusk. The crow nodded once and, rising from her perch, disappeared into the sky.

6

TAYLOR

I was walking back from the pantry when I saw it. A flash of black streaked across the sky. Without even thinking, I hurried across the living room and peered out through the curtains.

This is what I saw:

On the garage, the window above my bed was open, and Lora was leaning out. Her long hair spilled over the sill, red on white. For a second I thought she was going to climb out again, in spite of the fact that she'd just promised she wouldn't. But then something stranger happened: the flash of black turned out to be a crow, and once it settled onto the windowsill, Lora started talking to it.

Um. What the hell?

I mean, okay, she was raised in the country, so talking to horses wouldn't have been that bad. But crows? That was a little too Demented-Disney-Princess for me. Still, long shadows draped across the windowsill, making it hard to see clearly. I wasn't a hundred percent sure what was happening.

I needed to get a better look.

I ran to the door. If I could get outside without Lora noticing, I could sneak across the yard and hide behind the tree. And yes, I knew I was snooping, and maybe it was an invasion of her privacy, but all of this *was* happening in my room, and it was too weird to ignore.

One. Two. Three. I forced myself to count down as I turned the knob. My chest was aching and I had this terrible feeling that everything was about to change. For a minute, the world was too quiet as I peered out through the opening, and I thought Lora had spotted me. But no one called down from the window. No one looked down.

No one was sitting there.

When I got outside, both Lora and the crow were gone.

7

ELORA

Taylor had been asleep for several hours when my telephone started to vibrate. Luckily, his snoring was loud enough to muffle the sound of me sneaking from the room. The world was quiet as I slipped out the door of the garage, too wary to risk late-night flight, and raced across the grass to the yard's only tree. Halfway up the trunk, I pushed the little green button on the telephone.

I pressed the phone against my ear, worried beyond rationality that my endeavor had failed, and when I heard the voice of my longtime friend I nearly sobbed with joy.

"What happens when the light touches darkness?" Illya whispered.

"The fractured fragments of Faerie become whole." I drew a shroud of mist around my body. Twirling my fingers in the air, I worked to muffle the sound of my voice. Across the yard, the house was dark, but I could not help but watch the curtains for signs of life. There was, of course, the chance that Taylor would awaken and look out his own window, but we would cross that bridge if we came to it.

"It's you!" Illya breathed. In my mind, I could see the marsh sprite struggling to levitate a telephone as big as she was. "I was afraid it would be not you."

"I've hoarded this little gadget like a relic of old," I replied, running my hand over the phone as if I could reach Illya's webbed fingers. "I am happy to see my endeavor was a success."

"It might not have been, if your messenger had not led me to the border of the wasteland. It seems the magic of humans is limited to their world."

"I am sorry for your troubles," I said, a shiver tickling my spine at the thought of mortal magic. "Now, tell me what has befallen the Court since my departure."

"The servants are acting on your orders, behaving as if nothing is amiss. Some of them are better than others," Illya huffed. "But those who remain loyal to the crown are oblivious. They're too busy caring for the Queen."

I narrowed my eyes, planting my feet against a branch. "What ails the Queen?"

"Her only daughter has disappeared from her court," Illya shrieked. "Her beloved heir—"

"*Symbol,*" I corrected. "And I hardly thought she would notice. Is she being terrible to you?"

"You know the Dark Queen. Any dissatisfaction, and she lashes out."

"I am sorry for that."

"Don't be. It has strengthened our resolve to be free. Lady," Illya's voice dropped away, as if she had turned her head to search for spies, "your followers are disquieted by your departure. They fear you have abandoned us."

"I told them I was going on a quest. That should be enough for them."

"You forget your origins—"

"I never forget." I clenched the phone tightly in my hand. "I can never forget."

Illya softened her tone. "It was difficult enough for them to trust the daughter of the Dark Court. The daughter of the Queen. And now, when you have finally gained their allegiance—"

"By working ceaselessly and tirelessly to unite servants from all corners of the Court—"

"You leave us with barely an explanation. How can you expect none to question your loyalties? If they knew you'd even set foot in the wasteland ... "

"They will know what they need to know, and so will you."

"Lady—"

"Peace, sweetness," I said, wary of my regal mannerisms returning. "They've trusted me this long. Can you not convince them to trust me a little longer?"

Illya's breath beat against the phone like wings. "I miss you," she said finally.

"Don't," I replied, a response born of nobility. All that power. No love. "You know how to contact me if anything goes awry."

"It won't," Illya said, and the clarity of her small voice

was surprising. "Everything is going to happen the way you have planned. The Court will fall and we will be free."

"Then you understand why you must do as I ask. No matter what the Queen or her hideous courtiers do, you must not succumb to their cruelty. Be brave, Illya, for all of us."

"I will," she promised, pausing a minute. I knew what she was going to ask before she gave life to the words. "Read me the riddle?"

"It isn't safe. Anyone could be listening."

"Oh, who would be listening there? Even the Seelie fey are forbidden from entering the wasteland. I could help you decipher it."

I sighed. Who could argue with that voice? Scanning the darkness for any possible spies, I pulled the curling leaf from the pouch I'd strung around my neck. The Bright Queen's writing glowed softly against the green:

"Bane of the darkness, perfect for light,
Steal him away in the dead of the night.
Bind him with blood, this young leader of men,
And bring him to Court before Light's hallowed reign."

"*Light's hallowed reign,*" Illya hissed as I curled the leaf back into its hiding place. "But that's—"

"Beltane, I know. Three weeks away."

"It isn't enough time!"

"It has to be." I tucked the pouch into the collar of my nightgown, away from prying mortal eyes. "Now help me with the rest of it. What do you make of *bane of the darkness*?"

Illya was silent a moment. Then, in a low voice, she said, "The worst of humanity. Probably the one with the most power."

"Explain."

"The one with the most power will be the most corrupted."

"That's what I thought," I said, thinking of the two faerie queens. "And the riddle does ask for a *leader of men*. But how can that be *perfect for light*?"

"I am more interested in why the subject is male," Illya mused.

"Perhaps the Bright Queen wants more than a toy … " My gaze traveled to Taylor's window, and lingered.

Illya's gasp brought me back. "Lady! How can you speak of such things? I cannot imagine anything more vile. To think of faeries and mortals … *together*—"

"Forgive me." I tore my eyes away from the window. "Consider it a slip of the tongue."

"I will do my best. Now, tell me your plan to seek out this corrupted mortal."

"I'm not going to seek him out. I'm going to make him come to me."

"How?"

"How do you smoke out a tyrant?" I smiled, returning my gaze to the night. "You threaten his reign."

8

TAYLOR

Monday morning, I was supposed to meet Lora outside the school office at quarter to eight. We'd come up with some ridiculous story about my cell phone falling in a toilet to explain why I needed to use the office phone. But plans like this require more than perfect timing; they require luck, and mine had apparently run out.

First, Lora refused to ride in my car. Something about the metal frame made her feel sick. In the end, we decided she'd walk and I'd drive, to keep up appearances. I didn't want Mom stopping by my bedroom to ask if my car had broken down.

Then my car actually did break down—that is, it stalled twice before I made it out of the driveway.

Needless to say, all of our carefully laid plans went to hell before I even set foot in Unity High. But hey, that didn't stop me from sprinting down the halls (risking the dreaded referral) and almost yanking the office door off its hinges. Doris, the lavender-haired secretary of innumerable years, looked up at me like I'd lost my mind. My arm was aching from pulling the door. But none of that compared to the feeling of my heart dropping like an anvil at the sight of Brad Dickson touching Lora's arm.

You've got to be kidding me.

She smiled up at him.

Please let me be dreaming.

But no, I was fully awake, and Brad was looking at Lora like she was a hot spring he couldn't wait to jump into.

"Hey, buddy," he said to me, taking a piece of paper from Doris's hand. A schedule? "What's up? You wet your pants or something?"

"Yeah, and I was going to borrow a pair from Doris, but then I remembered I don't like purple."

Brad narrowed his eyes. "What?" Under normal circumstances, he'd have jumped at the chance to call me a "fairy," but these weren't normal circumstances, were they? The fact that Lora hadn't socked him yet was proof enough of that.

"I thought I forgot something in here," I mumbled, following them out of the office. Lora flashed me a grin. We'd managed to put together an outfit from my grandma's old '60s jeans and a shirt from my mom's Victorian phase. Lora had been very explicit about wanting to fit in.

She should have looked normal. I guess she would have if I didn't know otherwise. But since I did know, every glance reminded me of the secret we held between us. And that, for the moment, was enough to keep me from hating Brad. Looking at her, I couldn't hate anybody.

I didn't let myself consider what that meant.

"Sorry, man," Brad said in a way that implied he was anything but sorry. "I'm being rude. This is Lora." He said her name like he was running his tongue all over it. "I get to show her around."

"I'm Taylor." I held out a hand to her. It struck me as both odd and funny that I'd never actually shaken her bare hand. Sure, we'd slept in the same room for the past two nights, but still, the handshake felt intimate. It was like we were starting over from a different place.

I liked it.

"Hello, Taylor," Lora said, holding my gaze. For a second, the locker-lined hallway faded. All I could see was a pool of white light surrounding her like a halo.

"Nice to meet you," I said softly, taking a step closer. I wanted to bask in the glow, if only for a minute.

"The pleasure is mine."

"We should get going," an unwelcome voice chimed in. The hallway returned, the lights dimmed, and an arm slipped around Lora's waist.

She turned to Brad with a snarl in her voice. "Excuse me?"

He took his arm back, laughing nervously. "You don't want to be late for Matheson's class. The guy's a dick."

"How nice of you to look out for me." Her gaze softened just a little. She shot me a glance and her lips twitched.

"That's what I'm here for," Brad said. But Lora, thankfully, was no longer listening. Returning her attention to *yours truly*, she touched my arm. "Goodbye, Taylor."

"See you around." I nodded casually, afraid to get sucked back into her eyes. Afraid, and wanting.

"See ya, Tay-tay," Brad said, raising his eyebrows for only me to see. Laughing, he led her down the hall.

I didn't see her again until third period. By then I'd imagined all sorts of ridiculous scenarios: Brad had somehow managed to disarm her bullshit meter and they were making out right now. Brad had tried to grab her ass (his signature move) and she'd clawed his face off. She'd gotten expelled. They'd spent second period in the broom closet. She'd already been outed as a runaway and was on her way to the police station.

The bad possibilities were endless. The good ones? Practically nonexistent. So when I saw her saunter into English, free of any hickies or ankle monitors, I felt like I'd been granted an incredible gift. Like maybe luck was on my side after all.

Then she spoke. "Well, Brad sure is an interesting fellow." She lowered herself into the desk next to mine.

"That's one way to describe him."

"He asked me to accompany him to a movie."

"Of course he did. Did you slap him?"

Say yes, say yes, say yes.

"No." Suddenly she was coy. "I said I would go."

"What?"

She tapped my arm. "I said I would go if he could bring me a flower that shone with the light of the stars."

"You gave him a riddle?"

"He seemed to think so."

"You gave him a riddle he can't solve?"

She giggled. It was adorable. God, my chest hurt.

"Why?" I asked.

"Nobody likes to be told no. And many enjoy a good challenge."

The bell to start class rang, and she gripped the edges of her desk. I had to admit, for a newcomer the bell's shriek would probably be a pain. For the rest of us, following the schedule of the bells was second nature. We were like rats that way.

"You okay?" I glanced around, looking for something appealing that might distract her. All I managed to find were ivory-turned-yellow walls and a spattering of inspirational posters. In spite of the fact that I'd taken no part in decorating the school, I couldn't help but feel embarrassed.

This place is so ugly.

"I think I would rather stand," she said, eyeing the desk's metal poles with suspicion.

"You can't."

"Will they force me to leave?"

"For that? Probably not."

Before I could think of a way to stop her, she'd slid out of her seat. "Then I can, and I will."

People were starting to look over at us.

"I thought you wanted to blend in," I said. "I mean, considering … "

"I very much want to blend in. And from what I have

seen so far, the harder a student tries to mold herself to the standard, the more she is mocked by her peers. Obvious assimilation is seen as weakness."

"You've been here *two hours*."

"I'm perceptive. It is really quite—"

A loud snort came from the front of the classroom.

Ah, crap. Now Teach is involved.

Mrs. Rosencart glared over what could only be described as spectacles. "Miss … Belfry, is it?"

Lora stretched her arms over her head. "You may call me Lora."

"And you may call me Mrs. Rosencart," came the irked reply. "Please take your seat."

Lora scrunched up her nose. I tried not to think about how cute it looked. "Where would you have me take it?"

Mrs. Rosencart pushed her spectacles up her nose. "I don't appreciate a smart mouth in my class, Miss Belfry. You'll learn that very quickly."

"Forgive my confusion, Mrs. Rosencart, but if providing education is the mission of Unity's teaching staff—and I believe it is, I read it on a plaque—I can't understand why you would experience a lack of appreciation for a smart anything." Lora crossed her arms over her chest, as if satisfied that the misunderstanding had been cleared up.

Mrs. Rosencart's pale, wrinkled cheeks flooded with color. "Miss Belfry," she said very slowly. "Sit."

Lora started to laugh. I couldn't believe her nerve.

Still, part of me thought she knew exactly what she was doing, and was goading our teacher for sport.

Can she do that?

"Delightful strangeness," she murmured, touching a hand to her lips. "I saw a man speak to a well-groomed canine the very same way this morning. She didn't obey, and neither can I. This chair restricts my blood and cramps my limbs. I am much more comfortable standing."

Mrs. Rosencart pulled out her infamous pink pad of paper and started scribbling fiercely. I thought the pen would push right through the paper. "Enchanting philosophy, Miss Belfry, but this is not your living room." She finished filling out the referral and tore it from the pad.

Meanwhile, Lora was staring at an oak outside the window like it was the most amazing thing she'd ever seen. For a minute, I thought she might start talking to it.

She doesn't talk to trees. She doesn't talk to crows. You imagined it.

"My living room?" she said. "Well, unless you believe every corporeal thing is in a constant state of decay, it's far from my *dying* room, now isn't it?"

Several people laughed.

Mrs. Rosencart waved the piece of paper in Lora's direction. It took me a minute to realize she was shaking. "I understand many girls your age are anxious to receive attention—"

"Just girls?"

"But I assure you this is not the way." Mrs. Rosencart

pressed her lips together, but she didn't look menacing. She looked like a fish. "Perhaps you'd like to inundate the principal's office with your clever little theories."

Lora stepped up to the desk and took the paper merrily, like she was about to undergo some sacred rite of passage.

"Thank you," she enunciated, then practically skipped toward the door, abandoning the old backpack I'd given her. "I would be happy to visit this office, if you could provide me with the slightest bit of information as to where I might find it."

I jumped from my desk, knocking over my binder in the process. "I'll take her."

———

Lunch period couldn't come soon enough, and by the time it did, I was convinced all the clocks in the school had been switched with trick clocks that moved twice as slowly. I'd come close to falling asleep in fourth-period French, but each time my head dropped, an image of Lora flashed through my mind and a team of goblins started clawing at my insides. Now the pain worsened as I hurried across the grounds, looking for signs of her existence. It took several minutes of panicked searching, but I finally caught sight of her vibrant hair under a maple tree. I wondered if she was alone.

She wasn't. Sitting beside Lora was Kylie Angelini, Queen of the Outcasts at Unity High. Maybe it was because she was the president of the Gay-Straight Alliance. I liked to think it wasn't because of her wheelchair. But I could still remember my first gym class at Unity, when Brad followed her around all period pointing out how *lame* everything was. Lame. Because of her legs.

Soon, other assholes followed suit.

Still, in spite of everything, Kylie managed to be sweeter than the vegan cupcakes she brought to lunch every day. When she saw me, she lifted her lunch pail in welcome—an antique tin box with Tinker Bell on the front—and shouted, "You're late!"

I smiled a little too big. I couldn't get over how different she looked since she'd changed her style over spring break. She'd replaced her tennis shoes with combat boots and started making her own skirts. Her once mousy brown hair was now jet-black and chopped at an angle. When she leaned forward to take a bite of her burrito, the hair swung down, framing her chin in two sharp points. I think she was trying to look tougher.

"Is that cheese?" I asked, staring down at her burrito.

"Vegan cheese." She held the burrito out in offering. That's when I noticed the electric-pink fairy on her sweatshirt, hovering over the words *They Exist*.

"Tastes like plastic?" I teased.

"Cheese-flavored plastic," said a snarky voice. Kylie's evil twin stepped out from behind the tree. Where Kylie was sweet, Keegan was sour. His lumpy body was the antithesis to her wiry frame.

Still, they shared the same warm brown eyes.

"I've got to start making my own lunches," Keegan said, crouching down next to his sister. His blue jeans were faded and wrinkled; his velvet blazer impeccably pressed. Chestnut hair stuck up all over his head in perfect just-rolled-out-of-bed fashion.

I bet it takes him an hour to style it.

Kylie gave him a look. "It's not all about flavor. You have to make sacrifices for the things you believe in. If you don't, what's the point in believing in anything?"

"Kylie: one. Keegan: zero," I said, pulling an obviously meat-filled sandwich out of my bag. "Any wisdom you'd like to share with the class?" I asked Lora.

She stared at me, considering the question. "The history teacher is full of shit."

I choked on my first bite of sandwich.

"Figuratively speaking," she added.

"You're swearing now?"

Lora wiggled in her spot. "I'm having a lot of fun. I find your idioms charming. Everyone speaks so properly where I'm from."

"Where are you from?" Kylie asked.

"Jupiter," said Lora, "according to a boy in my last class. Somebody in choir suggested Yugoslavia. That was pretty cool." She examined the piece of pizza in her hand with mild interest.

"Very cool," I said. I felt a little unnerved that she was assimilating so quickly.

"Countless boys have engaged me in conversation,"

she continued, taking a hesitant bite of her pizza. "No girls, though, except for Kylie."

Kylie rolled her eyes. "Give them time. The boys will all try to pee on you first, and the girls will keep their distance, sniffing to see whose scent you carry." She flashed a mischievous smile. "Speaking of which, how many dates have you lined up so far?"

"Just three," Lora said, very matter-of-factly, and my chest deflated. "But only if they bring me a flower that shines—"

"With the light of the stars. Right!" Kylie laughed, and the air returned to my lungs. "You guys, she has the most hilarious way of getting boys to back off."

"So I've heard."

Kylie rounded on me. "You know about the riddle? Don't tell me she gave—"

"No," both Lora and I said together. Heat flooded my face, and other places too. I wasn't sure, but I thought Lora might be hinting that she *wouldn't* give me the riddle, if I ever asked her out.

"I've seen her in action," I said.

Kylie looked relieved, and I thought she and I should spend more time together. Meanwhile, Lora was studying her pizza.

"What's wrong?" Kylie asked.

Lora poked her finger into a gob of cheese, which was gooey and pockmarked with spots of brown. "How do you acquire dairy in the city?"

"Trust me," Kylie said, opening a container of apple-sauce. "You don't want to know."

"I can't eat this." Lora shook her head, wrapping the pizza in her paper plate. "This is bad for me."

"Billions of dollars spent on food pyramid commercials and this girl figures it out on her own." Keegan watched his sister pass her applesauce to Lora. "Next she'll realize that smoking pot turns you into a serial killer."

I chuckled, glancing at Kylie's brother. Most of the people at school ignored him, or openly mocked his lack of interest in the opposite sex, but he didn't try to befriend them like Kylie did. He walked through the halls as if no one else existed, besides his sister.

I couldn't even imagine what that felt like.

Lora reached into her backpack and pulled out a pink flier, a shade brighter than her referral had been.

"Hey, how was the principal's office?" I asked.

"Oh, wonderful." She was practically beaming. "She's the most interesting adult I've met so far."

"Really."

"Definitely. I will have to make it a point to visit often."

"Not too often," I muttered, wondering when her first detention would be. I pointed to the flier in her hand. "What's that?"

"Nothing." Kylie reached for it.

Lora was too quick for her. She held the flier out for me. "Kylie's the president of the Merry-Straight Alliance."

"Gay," Keegan supplied. "And it's not an alliance. It's a bunch of gay kids pretending the straight kids don't hate them."

I wanted to argue, but it's not like I'd ever gone to any of the meetings. I plucked the flier from Lora's hand.

"I'm going to join," she told me. "Are you a member?"

"Uh, no," I said distractedly, searching for an explanation.

What's the problem?

"Do you want to be?" she asked. "I think we have the opportunity to effect real change here. Maybe even shift the power structure completely." She smiled, but there was a fierceness in her eyes. I wondered why this was so important to her.

"Well, I have soccer practice a lot of the time, and, uh … " I trailed off, unable to finish my thought. Across the lawn, I could just make out the picnic table where Brad sat, surrounded by his usual band of drones. His taunt from Saturday's game circled my head, whispering "fairy," just because I hadn't felt like putting a guy in the hospital.

I turned the flier over in my hands, my eyes blurring over the list of meeting times. "Sure." I folded the paper in half. "Why not?"

9

ELORA

A scream rent the air, high and sharp like the battle cry of a hawk. I lurched from my place of rest, pupils dilating until they had taken over the whites of my eyes. The darkness gave way to strange silhouettes scattered around a small enclosure, and though I scanned my surroundings with nocturnal expertise, it took me nearly a minute to understand where I was.

Yet with this understanding came greater confusion.

Crouching on the floor of Taylor's bedchamber, the edge of the blanket still wrapped around my leg, I knew without glancing toward the window that it was the middle of the night. But I couldn't explain the scent of fear hanging in the air, heavy enough to taste, nor could I identify the cause of the scream. I crawled toward the sleeping mortal on silent hands and knees, hoping the closeness might provide insight.

As I drew near he thrashed to the side, all but flinging himself from his little bed, and moaned regretfully as if his beloved had forsaken him. Ever so gently, I brushed my fingers against his arm.

His eyes popped open.

For a moment we spoke only in breaths, his sharp and ragged, mine hissing and long, as we searched, in our own ways, to bring our hearts relief. I was the first to part my lips, yet he was the first to speak.

"What happened?" His eyes traveled the length of the bedchamber, and I realized that in his dreamy state, he believed I'd come to warn him of some danger.

Nothing, I thought to myself, but the word caught in my throat and shied away from my lips. "You cried out," I said, staring at the strands of hair that clung to his fore-head. "I heard you."

"Sorry," he mumbled, turning away from me.

"Why?" I asked. His back was soaked with sweat, seeping through the fabric of his shirt, and I placed my hand upon it, to cool him.

"For waking you up," he said.

"It seems I have returned the favor. But I require little sleep."

"Okay…" He twisted around to look at me.

I couldn't help but wonder, berating myself all the while, what would happen if I let the glamour slip for a moment. Would he be able to see? It wasn't a terribly disturbing thought. The disingenuous nature of my disguise would cause any faerie unease. Sure, we were tricksters, but playing a human for this duration was a flat-out lie.

And yet my desire to be revealed ran deeper than this. I wanted to show myself to *him*, specifically. It was a desire originating not from my body but from my spirit, and it went ricocheting through me, igniting my heart, my mind, everything.

All my life, I had been warned of faeries who lost their minds in the wasteland. Is that what was happening to me now?

"I didn't mean to wake you," I said. "I know you have trouble falling asleep."

"You've been watching me?"

"No more intently than you watch me." The rogue words defied my guarded lips.

Bad faerie.

"Sorry."

The sincerity in his voice surprised me. So much of what the Dark Court said about humans seemed untrue of this one. Perhaps I was not losing my mind. Perhaps I was simply reacting to him empathetically, the way I did with so many earthly creatures. For a moment I missed my train of ravens, flying around my head like a dark veil. Even my mother's wolves could be sweet, and playful, when the Dark Lady's moods did not make them surly.

"I should be the one who is sorry," I said. "You've done much to help me feel comfortable here. Isn't there some little thing I can do for you?"

Clever girl, limiting the terms of the bargain.

After all, he had been content to offer me room and

board for nothing. I was the one who had promised him his heart's greatest desire. Why had I done that? The words had just slipped past my lips, as if I were possessed.

Or under a spell.

Did humans have a magic all their own?

Taylor was watching me. His hair had fallen into his eyes. I had a sudden vision of him dancing in the moonlight, his body adorned in leaves and vines: the ritual for a faerie child entering into maturity. "Remember what I said to you at the park?" he asked. "About wanting you to be safe?"

"Yes."

"That wasn't the whole story."

My breath caught in my throat. Here, he would divulge his true intentions. Here, I would be proven right about humanity.

But he did not look evil in the darkness. He looked *broken.* "I moved out of my parents' house over a year ago."

"Any particular reason?"

"It's just better this way," he said quickly, hiding his bitterness. Three days and I was already learning his tricks.

"I think I can understand," I said, reminding him that my situation was far from perfect.

The words leant him obvious strength. His back straightened as he spoke. "I like the privacy. I can come and go without bugging anyone. But it's quiet. The sound of my breathing keeps me awake. So I lie in bed at night letting every possible thought come into my head. Sometimes the

thoughts are really stupid. Sometimes they're dangerous..."
His gaze drifted to the books stacked on his desk.

Maybe his glance was inadvertent, but I took the opportunity and ran with it. "Are you asking for something to fill up the silence?" I said. "Perhaps a story?"

"No, I just—never mind." He hid his face in his pillow.

"Not so fast." In Faerie, a well-told story was worth more than gold. If I could choose the right one, I would not feel so indebted to him. "What kind of story?"

"I don't need a *bedtime story*," he snarled. "Just... tell me about yourself."

I froze, staring into the darkness. "Is that what you desire?"

"It is."

I chose my words carefully. "Then I will do as you ask. But my story will start in a curious place, and you will just have to trust me."

"I trust you," he said without missing a beat.

My heart constricted. My entire body was trembling, but I opened my mouth and pushed out the words: "Once upon a time, a planet came into being, spinning through the universe amongst a billion burning stars. The planet, now called Earth, had a body and a spirit, which shared no visible connection but were intrinsically linked. So when the planet's body separated into innumerable forms of life, her spirit separated too, into millions of self-aware entities, and that is the origin of faeries."

"Sorry, Tinker Bell," Taylor said with a laugh.

I smiled at that. "In those early days, the faeries lived only as spirits, nestled inside flowers and stones or dancing across the earth in sunlight and rain. But as more creatures came to life, the faeries began to experiment with matter, manipulating the elements to create physical bodies."

I paused as Taylor shivered. The window above the bed lay open a crack, at my request, and a breeze drifted steadily into the room, carrying the scent of hyacinth. I reached for the blanket Taylor had tossed aside in the throes of sleep and pulled it over him. He turned to me, and a multitude of emotions danced across his face: surprise, embarrassment, gratitude.

My breath quickened as his hand neared mine, accidentally brushing against me as he settled onto his back. I had the sudden desire to take those fingers and clutch them in my own, but I fought it, knowing it to be foolish.

It's in his nature to hurt me.

"You can have some of the blanket," he offered, and my confusion deepened.

"That's okay," I said, thinking of other things that might lend me warmth. I couldn't believe my boldness, even if only in my own mind, and turned away, terrified and entranced at the same time.

Taylor's voice brought me back. "What happened next?"

"Humanity was born," I said softly, "providing the Folk with new features to incorporate into their many forms. Using humanity as their inspiration, they made bodies with human faces and limbs, adding dragonfly wings or shimmering fins. This was a time of glorious discovery for the fey, and they tried on every imaginable ensemble, emerging transformed each time.

"But things began to change. Humans separated themselves from the natural world, studying it from afar as if it were not a part of them. They stopped entering the dark forests and began fashioning their houses from dead trees, afraid that live trees held spirits they couldn't contain. And as the human world grew more controlled, more finite, faeries living in physical forms grew more finite as well, until only the oldest among them could transform at will. For the rest of them, their bodies became like shells, encasing them.

"Fearing the changes brought forth by humanity, the Folk traveled to the places where the connection between body and spirit remained uncompromised: untouched forests, peaks of desolate mountains, and the depths of the sea. They relied on glamour—magical illusion—to keep humans away. But no matter how far they went, one aspect of human life always managed to reach them: iron. Iron-infested air attacked the faeries' lungs. In its purest form, iron could burn the flesh from their bones. And at the height of the Middle Ages, when humans laid iron over their doorways and fashioned it into instruments of death, the faeries found they were losing the ability to reproduce."

"Wait," Taylor broke in. "How does that work? If faeries are spirits who put on physical bodies, how can they reproduce?"

"When faeries fashioned bodies from the elements of the earth, those bodies were as real as the earth herself. As real as you are." There was an edge to my voice that I hadn't intended.

"I didn't mean—it's just fascinating," he said quickly.

I wanted to touch him so badly then, to illustrate the realness of my body. "As fascinating as where human bodies and spirits come from?"

"Okay, okay," he said with a smile. "So the faeries just manipulated elements and formed bodies—"

"From soil and leaves, from air and starlight. Yes. Call it magic, or concentrated will, or focused energy. So if a faerie made a body like a tree, she could self-populate. And if she made a body like an animal, she could give birth like that animal does. The earth is filled with miracles and magic, and faeries are no exception. For many centuries, they were blessed with the ability to have children."

"Until they weren't anymore?"

"Exactly."

He closed his eyes, scooting an inch closer. His smallest finger came to rest upon my arm. I stared down at it, savoring the connection between us in spite of the danger.

"What did they do?" he asked.

"They didn't know what to do." I exhaled slowly. I couldn't believe the tiniest of touches could bring me such joy. I didn't want to believe it. "They knew they had to try to reach humanity and take back what they had lost, but they could not fathom how to do it. Humans no longer listened to them. They believed the faeries were minions of some demonic underlord, if they believed in them at all. It seemed hopeless."

"But it wasn't?" His voice was very soft now, the cooing of a slumbering babe.

"No. For out of the darkness of their despair emerged a leader, whose cruel and cunning tongue promised to bring salvation to faerie kind: the future Unseelie Queen."

Taylor's eyes fluttered and I heard the soft rhythm of his breathing. For a moment I sat perfectly still, before passing the silent words from my lips: "My mother."

10

TAYLOR

"How old were you?" I asked, watching the walls in the stuffy basement room. Maybe if I stared hard enough, a window would appear, *presto!* Cracks lined the ceiling, hinting at a mess of leaky pipes in the wall, and I could hear someone turning on a faucet up above.

"Eleven," Keegan said, his desk squeaking as he nodded to Kylie. "We'd just turned eleven."

"Wow." I leaned forward, resting my elbows on my knees. "Was it hard?"

Keegan shrugged. "They wouldn't let me go back to Sunday school, with all those other boys. I guess they weren't worried about the priests."

Sitting to Keegan's left, Kylie winced. "That's not funny," she said, nervously arranging her skirt. Fat black letters covered the white fabric, spelling out slang words: *sick, weak, bomb, money.*

"It's not funny it happens," Keegan said. "It's funny they could read news story after news story about creepster priests and still think *I'd* be the bad influence."

"Explain to me the metaphor," Lora said from her desk by the wall. Today she was wearing ripped jeans under a black babydoll dress—my mom's "uniform" from college. "I do not understand this *coming out*." Her gaze traveled over each member of the group.

Besides the four of us, three other people had shown up for the weekly meeting of Unity's Gay-Straight Alliance. There were two girls in the back of the room, snuggled together like ferrets, and a boy sitting at the desk closest to the door. With his darting eyes and sweating hands, he gave off the distinct impression that someone had forced him to come to the meeting, though I was pretty sure that wasn't the case.

"It's about not hiding," Kylie explained. "Staying in the closet means hiding who you are."

"And maybe … playing in your mother's pumps," Keegan added.

"You didn't do that." Kylie smirked at him, her face losing its tension for the first time since she'd arrived.

Keegan grinned back. "You did."

"So the closet is a metaphor for keeping oneself hidden," Lora said, a curious intensity in her eyes.

Kylie nodded. "It's safe and warm, but it's dark and nobody can see you."

"So when you come out, you step into the light of the world," Lora finished for her.

Kylie's gaze traveled to the floor, to the dust gathering like tiny tumbleweeds. "And then everybody can see you."

For a minute, everyone was silent.

Keegan repositioned himself in his chair, the desk scraping across the floor. He seemed to enjoy doing it, like maybe he was leaving his mark. "What's really interesting is, once you've revealed your true colors, people start to reveal theirs."

I scanned the room, watching the different reactions. From the back of the room, the two girls nodded. The boy in the front clutched the sides of his desk.

"So when you came out, your parents actually told you to get out?" I tried to envision such a scenario. I couldn't imagine what kind of trouble I'd have to get into before my mother threw me out on the street.

Then again, I was a lot closer to the street than I used to be.

"Yup," Keegan confirmed. "But it was fine. We moved in with our aunt and never looked back." He shot Kylie a glance. "Well, I did, first."

"What about you?" I asked Kylie, whose hands had taken to wringing themselves.

"Oh, she's only half a heathen," Keegan said.

"What does that mean?" Lora asked.

"I'm bi," Kylie explained. "Maybe I could've stayed at home. But after Keegan left, they were really … strict."

"They were always strict," Keegan said.

"They're just … " Kylie searched for the right words. "They're just different."

"I'd say they're pretty normal."

Kylie ignored her brother. "I knew it was only a matter

of time before they asked me if I was…you know. I couldn't lie to them. So I called Auntie Jane and had her come get me."

"At, like, two a.m.," said Keegan.

Kylie lowered her eyes.

"Hey." He reached for her. "I'm just playing with you."

Her voice was soft, a kitten's mew. "I know."

He turned back to me. "Seriously. They're assholes."

A slew of horrific scenarios ran through my mind, complete with dungeon chambers and exorcising priests. Then it hit me, hard as a brick in the face. Parents didn't have to lock their kids in dungeons to make them feel worthless.

I caught Keegan's gaze and held it. "I'm sorry."

He laughed. "I'm not." His eyes were glued to me, but I got the impression he was talking to Kylie. "Bad things happen to everyone. You either care about what other people think or you realize their hang-ups have nothing to do with you."

Kylie sniffed, raising her head to face the group. "People hate you and they haven't even met you. But it's better than the alternative." She ran her hands through her hair, the dark strands shining in the fluorescent lights. "Because when you're hiding, all you do is hate yourself."

———

After the meeting, Kylie caught up with Lora on the school's front lawn. "Come shopping with me," she entreated, glancing at me as she wheeled down the walkway. "Unless you have plans."

"I do not," Lora replied, eyeing me as well. I blinked back at her, unprepared for the sudden onslaught of sunlight. "But I have to tell you," she continued, "I'm developing an aversion to crowds."

Kylie laughed. Keegan snuck up behind her and put his hands over her eyes.

"Don't!" She sped away, nearly running into a pack of Unity's elite. Alexia Mardsen towered above the pack, surrounded by a halo of cigarette smoke.

For a moment Kylie froze. Then, lifting her head, she looked into the eyes of Unity's queen bee and glared.

Alexia took a long, exaggerated drag on her cigarette and exhaled. I couldn't help but watch the movement of her lips. The girl made our cheerleaders look like band geeks. With her pale brown skin and black, wavy hair, it wouldn't have surprised me to learn she'd descended from the Amazons. To date, I'd heard she was part Black, part Puerto Rican, and part Japanese, but I couldn't have said for certain. Anytime someone asked her what she "was," she made up a different answer to toy with them.

The only labels she liked were on her clothing.

"Just passing through?" she said to Kylie, stubbing her cigarette out on a tree.

Kylie held her gaze before moving on. Keegan hissed dramatically.

Alexia just smiled, like they were entertaining her.

"What was all that?" Lora asked when we'd gained a good distance from the pack.

"Party politics," Keegan said. "We have a long-standing rivalry with the Populari."

Kylie giggled, returning her attention to us. "One of the many reasons we don't go shopping in crowded malls." She flashed a mischievous smile. "We have better places to be."

"Siberia?" Keegan offered.

"Thrift store shopping—"

"Spelunking—"

"In Old Town."

"Yes," Keegan said stuffily, "rejected rags from the seventies look just like the fall line from Dolce and Gabbana." He stuck out his hip in a surprisingly good impression of Alexia.

"Ignore the nonbeliever." Kylie linked arms with Lora. "It totally works if you have *imagination*. And if we don't find what we want, we just make it." She ran her fingers over her skirt.

"You made this?" Lora asked.

"She makes everything," Keegan said. "She's a witch! Burn her!"

Kylie laughed. "So you wanna come?"

"I'd love to," Lora said. "Lend me a minute?"

"Sure." Kylie nudged me in the side before leading Keegan away.

"You don't have to ask me," I said, watching the twins race along the walkway. I really didn't want to spend the evening without Lora; I still had the acute fear that she was going to disappear. But I knew I'd reach a new level of psycho if I insisted on tagging along.

"I know," Lora said. "We just haven't discussed—"

"I know."

"And I don't want to overstay."

"You won't."

"You're right."

"I didn't mean it like that." I clenched my jeans in my fists, hating that I could never find the right words. I couldn't tell her she could stay forever. Was that even a promise I could make? But I couldn't put a time limit on her visit either. "What I mean is, you could never over-stay." My gaze traveled to the oak branch arching above her head, curling like a claw toward her hair. "I want you to be safe—"

"It's not your responsibility."

"Lora. You're not inconveniencing me."

It seemed, for once, that I'd said the right thing. She nodded, reaching up and grabbing the branch. It looked like she was shaking hands with the tree. I remembered I used to do that sort of thing, back when I was a kid and the guys wouldn't have mocked the shit out of me for it.

"Have fun," I said, when what I really wanted to do was stay and watch her move like a memory of my former self.

"Thank you." She hesitated, like she was waiting for something. Then she gave a tiny bow of her head and chased Kylie and Keegan across the lawn.

Weird day.

But I had no idea how weird it was about to get, because the minute my friends were gone, Alexia beckoned to me.

Me.

The guy she hadn't noticed in four years. Now she was staring at me with the calculated expression of an owl about to swallow a mouse. And she was alone.

I ambled over.

"Yeah?" I said, looking around for hidden cameras.

"What do you think you're doing?" she demanded. "Is there some new hazing ritual I should know about?"

"Excuse me?" It was, for the moment, the best I could manage.

"Oh please." She rolled her eyes. "Do you have to feign innocence?"

Do you have to talk like you're better than everyone else? I thought, fully empathetic to Kylie's contempt. Being a haughty, self-entitled beauty queen was bad enough. But Alexia wielded her words like a weapon, cutting down anyone who challenged her.

"What do you want?" I asked.

Alexia pulled a gold Zippo from the pocket of her skin-tight jeans. She flicked the flame in my face. "I want to know what your game is," she said, lighting a new cigarette. "One minute you're playing lapdog to Brad Dickson, and the next you're playing civil rights in the basement. Something about that doesn't add up."

"What are you talking about?"

"What's the bet, Taylor? Fifty bucks if you get Keegan to profess his undying love to you?" She pushed me with her palm. "A hundred if you can turn Kylie straight?"

Her voice drilled into my brain. I stumbled back, trying to escape it. "You're kidding, right? You think I'm friends with them because of a bet?"

"I don't think you're *friends* with anyone," she said with a sly little smirk. "You haven't had friends in years."

Gee, Alexia. Tell me what you really think.

She exhaled slowly, smoke circling her head. "You've been moping around since sophomore year, playing the part of the loner, and *suddenly* you decide to join the soccer team? Methinks you've grown tired of eating alone on your little swings."

My guts twisted. I didn't know what was worse: the fact that Alexia knew I'd been eating alone, or the fact that she was right about me. After two years of being totally and completely alone, at school and at home, I *had* wanted to make friends with the guys on the team. I just hadn't realized I'd be risking my soul in the process.

And I wasn't Brad's lapdog.

I'd *never* be Brad's lapdog.

"Look, you can think whatever you want," I said, meeting her gaze. "I joined the soccer team because I'm good at it."

"Yes, you are," Alexia drawled, in a way that implied she wasn't talking about sports. "Once you settled in with the gorillas, I thought I knew what your game was. Then you go and get tangled up with the basement brigade—"

"I *like* them."

"The redhead, maybe. You don't exactly have closet-case written across your forehead. But you're much too smart to go after Kylie and risk the backlash—"

"I wouldn't care," I said, standing at my full height in an attempt to gain back some of my pride. I was furious at her callous dismissal of my friends. "You know why?"

She raised her eyebrows.

"They're cooler than you," I said.

Something flickered across her eyes then, something like fear. She recovered quickly. "Fine. Plead ignorance. But you need to understand something, Little Boy Blue." She stepped closer. "Important things are happening at Unity. You can't keep jumping between the carriage and the Camaro without getting crushed beneath the wheels. My suggestion? Pick a side."

———

When night rolled around, I flopped onto my futon, ready to just listen to Lora's voice. I didn't even care what she talked about. Circus clowns, dragons. Prehistoric tap-dancing lizards. Her voice was so soothing (not to mention *sexy*), it wouldn't matter.

Unfortunately, she didn't appear to be in a talking mood at the moment. She was sitting cross-legged on my bed, staring so hard at her homework that I doubted she was really absorbing anything. Maybe her time with the twins had made her realize I wasn't all that interesting. Or maybe she was just waiting for me to talk to her.

I never could tell, with girls.

I decided to risk it.

"I hate Mr. Gantoni!" I growled, knocking my history book to the floor.

Lora looked over, her lips curling. "Hate seems a bit strong."

"Okay, I don't *hate* him. But why am I taking AP History if it's still going to put me to sleep? These are college level classes. You'd think a course on Medieval History would be interesting."

"And yet..."

"And yet he makes the Middle Ages so *boring*."

"An amazing feat."

"I used to think it was this wonderful era, you know? Like something I'd want to be a part of. Knights fighting honorably. Monarchs looking after their people. Chivalry." I turned onto my side. "It's all bullshit. These fat, disgusting kings gorged themselves to death while the rest of the world starved."

Wait, how is that different from today?

"It was a very dark period of time," Lora agreed, tucking her pages into her binder. "But there were other things."

"What things? The search for the Holy Grail was a bloody crusade. People spent all their time thinking about an afterlife because they were poor and miserable. Tell me one good thing about the Middle Ages."

"Faeries."

Okay, so she did want to talk.

"Faeries?" I repeated, feeling more than a little weird saying it. But it wasn't like I cared about *faeries*. I just liked the sound of her voice.

That's all.

"I thought you were going to tell me about yourself," I teased, looking away so she didn't feel embarrassed.

"I am." She looked up. I could *feel* her eyes on me and I turned, letting her catch me in her gaze. Letting her hold me. "I will," she added.

"When?" I said without missing a beat.

"Possibly tonight."

"Is that a promise?" I pressed.

"Yes." She paused. "Possibly."

I smiled. I couldn't help it. She looked so vulnerable right then; I needed her to know I'd never take advantage of that. "But first ... the Middle Ages!" I announced, like the ringleader of a circus. "And, you know, *faeries*," I said with less enthusiasm.

Lora laughed. "The Middle Ages are teeming with fantastically devilish fables about faerie kind. Poets warned of them, priests scorned them, and for the most part, humanity feared them."

She patted the spot beside her. I couldn't get over there fast enough.

"Let me guess," I said, reclining on my elbows, hoping she'd get comfortable beside me. "The history book got it all wrong and faeries were the heroes of the Middle Ages."

She smiled slyly, lying back on the bed. "Oh, it would be nice to say the faeries were benevolent. Surely, they did not kill babies or dance with a red devil on moonless nights. But they were not innocent, not by the time the green world had been taken over by stone and steel. Maybe they got a little angry watching humanity gnaw away at the fabric of their world. The truth is," she said, pointing a finger at me, "they bit back."

I made a biting sound and she laughed. I wished I could take her finger between my teeth. I'd never wanted to taste someone so badly.

"It started with one faerie," she said, switching off the lamp on the bedside table.

A little mood lighting?

With the moonlight filtering in, and the breeze playing with her sleeve, the room felt romantic. Before I met Lora, I hadn't given much thought to romance. But she made me want to do all the cheesy things guys did in movies: sprinkle rose petals, sweep her off her feet, literally. Now that she was lying so close, my desire to feel her skin was stronger than ever.

"Her name was Virayla, and she lingered on the edges of the human world, studying humanity." Lora touched a strand of my hair.

More. Now. Yes. One touch and I wanted her more than anything. But satisfaction doesn't work that way, does it? We have to wait until we're aching for it.

"Why did she study humanity?" I asked.

"Because humanity had to be dealt with," she said, and smiled wickedly.

My blood rushed down, down, down. "Dealt with?"

"Well, the humans were dealing with them. It was kill or be killed, and the faeries didn't want to die. Would you?" Even in the dim light, her eyes were bright. Her skin looked so soft. I wanted to touch every part of her, and that just made me ache even more.

"I, um … no."

"Neither do I." She lowered her eyes. It was shocking, how she could sound playful one instant and devastated the next. I wanted to hold her, just to show her it was going to be all right.

"Hey," I murmured.

"Neither did they," she continued, and the sadness slipped off of her like rain. But this time, her smile didn't fool me. I knew she was building up walls around her, and I was determined to get inside.

Figuratively speaking.

"She killed the humans, didn't she?" I asked, trying to sound as casual as she did. "Virayla, I mean."

Lora shook her head. "She could not simply take their lives. To do so would have gone against her nature."

"What exactly does that mean?" I wanted to keep her talking, to watch her tongue as it flicked against her lips. I could almost feel that tongue sliding up my neck, lips circling my earlobe, though I'd never actually been kissed that way. She invoked all kinds of fantasies that, one week ago, would have embarrassed me. With Lora it felt safe, like she wouldn't hate me if she knew what I was thinking.

When her lips started to move again, my body stood at attention. I shifted onto my stomach to hide any indecency, but the movement caused her to roll closer to me.

"It means that, because the faeries are spirits of the earth, and the earth is their body, to malevolently harm any of the earth's creatures would be to harm themselves. Therefore, to exact physical violence against humankind would be akin to taking a knife and cutting out a piece of one's heart."

"So, even if humans killed them, they couldn't fight back?"

"Quite literally put, they could not forcibly take unwilling lives. But if a mortal entered into battle willingly..."

"All bets were off."

"Exactly." She grinned, leaning into me. "Though it rarely came to that. For soon Virayla realized something startling: because of the poor quality of the average human life, a great number of them were willing to risk death to experience the ecstasies of Faerie."

"Risk death?"

Keep talking. Keep looking at me like that.

"Happily," she said. "It seems that plummeting to one's death was agreeable to a mortal if preceded by a rapturous kiss from a tree-dwelling nymph. The rocks strewn about the river didn't seem so bad when one was mesmerized by the voice of a singing naiad. When given the opportunity, long-suffering humans tripped all over themselves to get a taste of Faerie. In Faerie, for one lovely night, they could fill themselves with earthly delights.

"One by one, the faeries joined Virayla's cause. Wood nymphs, beguiled by the promises of mortal knights but horrified by their inclinations toward violence, began luring them away from their homes and into the forest to revel in one joyous night. And these ensorcelled knights, sick with the memory of their faerie lovers, forgot their families, forgot their kings. They withered away."

I know the feeling, I thought. And maybe she knew, because she caught my eye when she said, "Kelpies and naiads rose from rivers and lakes, appearing to fishermen and sailors under the deceptive cover of the waning moon. They came draped in sea plants, their skin glistening green and blue, and led the men who dared intrude upon their homes into watery graves."

"What about Virayla?" I asked, turning onto my side again. One quick movement and her leg would be hooked through mine. And we wouldn't even have to do anything; we could just lie like that. Linked. Close.

"Oh, Virayla was the worst of them," she said, and her gaze traveled down. For a second, I thought she'd figured out what I was thinking. Then I realized she was avoiding me.

"Lora?"

"She'd lure them with music," she said. "Make them dance until their limbs were broken and bloodied. She'd craft furniture from their bones and invite their families to a tea party in the woods. It wasn't until the party was over that they would realize they'd been sitting upon the remnants of their loved ones' bodies, drinking blood from little cups. She called it Tea Party Justice."

"Good God." I slapped my hand over my mouth, not sure if I should laugh or throw up. "That's … demented."

"Indeed. But you have to understand: the more humans she killed, the more likely she was to survive. And, for a time, it seemed she might succeed."

"But she didn't?"

"No, she did not. You see, another group of faeries was rising, a group determined to thwart Virayla's plans."

"Why?" I was hanging on her every word. Hell, I was hanging on her every movement.

"They thought she was wrong. You see, all faeries believe the earth has to be protected. The earth is their body; without it, they would cease to be. But while the faeries of the burgeoning Dark Court believed humans should be eradicated because they were destroying the earth, the soon-to-be Bright Court believed that, because humans were *part of* the earth, they had to be protected."

"Complicated."

"Wars always are."

Her words had turned bitter, and I couldn't help but wonder at her attachment to this story. Was it sentimentality, or was she trying to tell me something? Maybe the story was her religion. That could explain the whole talking-to-animals thing. Wait—did she think the crow was a faerie?

"So they went to war?" I asked, my mind spinning with possibilities. But my body was heavy, and it was trying to pull me down into sleep.

"Oh yes," she said, her voice soft and soothing. "For many years, the Dark Court battled with the Bright. But as the Middle Ages came to a close, something happened that changed the course of faerie history forever. Deep in the mountains of Greenland, a faerie baby had been born. Immediately, both courts pulled back, traveling alongside one another to visit the child they thought might be the last faerie ever born. But while the rest of the Folk fawned over the babe, Virayla befriended his mother, hoping to gain her favor."

My eyes drooped as I said, "She wanted the baby?"

"She did. Virayla believed the child would serve as a symbol of the Dark Court, a reminder of all that was at stake for the fey. And the baby's mother, both terrified of humanity and eager to help the Folk survive, offered the child willingly. And so the boy was whisked down the mountain, cradled happily in Virayla's arms, to be raised as an honorary prince of her court. His name was Naeve, and he had black hair and golden eyes."

11

ELORA

During my first week at Unity High, Brad Dickson made six spirited attempts to bring me flowers that shone with the light of the stars. By the following Monday, he appeared less hopeful, and he left ingenuity behind.

"Take your pick," he said, cornering me outside my history class. He held out a bouquet of white flowers: daisies and roses mingled with lilies and baby's breath. "I got every kind they had. Plus some I found in the grass." He pointed to the daisies proudly. "I know I got it this time."

I touched a daisy's petal, smiling in amusement. "They're very pretty. Though ... uprooted unnecessarily, I'm afraid."

Brad's face hardened. "Look." He dropped the bouquet to his side. "I'm going to do you a favor since you're new here, and so obviously choice."

Choice? I thought back to the previous Saturday, when Taylor had led me from the electric jungle of the grocery outlet to the springtime Farmers Market. One memory stood out among the rest: the piles of animal flesh laid out in a bin, stamped with phrases like *New York Sirloin* and *Choice FDA Beef*. Had Brad just likened me to a slab of cow meat?

He continued to watch me, yet I had the distinct feeling he was not seeing me at all. "A girl like you can have it all." He tilted his chin with practiced knowing. "But you've got to stop hanging out with rejects. It's going to kill your rep."

"Let me see if I understand you correctly." I spoke in the voice often used by Mrs. Rosencart, drawing out my words for maximum comprehension. "Within my physical frame, I contain the ability to rise to great power, but if I continue to spend my days in the company of those I deem most worthy, my reputation shall suffer an untimely death?"

"Uh, right." Brad crossed his arms over his chest. "And maybe tone down that intellectual crap. Guys aren't into that."

"Really?"

Brad nodded.

I brought my fingers to my lips. "Oh dear."

"More than anything"—he touched my shoulder—"get the hell out of that gay club. I know you just feel sorry for them, but don't, because they bring it on themselves."

"But Brad," I pleaded, giving the impression that I wanted his permission, "I've already inspired them to change the name."

"To what, Fags R Us?"

"The Merry-Straight Alliance." My stoic expression slipped, revealing a hint of a smile. "Cute, isn't it?"

He gripped my shoulder. I imagined the ease with which I could tear his fingers off his hand. "What do you even do in there?" he snarled, leaning closer, his breath carrying the scent of fowl. "Do you guys, like, make out?"

For a moment I just stared, pulling him into the oceans of my eyes. Allowing him to drown. "We learn things," I said finally.

"Like . . ."

Like human distinctions of sexuality don't exist in Faerie, but if they did, I would probably identify as polysexual.

But I didn't tell him that. The fluidity of faerie sexuality was not his business, and besides, this meeting had a purpose. "I learned that, because Kylie refrains from eating the flesh of animals, she has to find clever ways to keep iron in her blood."

"That's what you talk about?"

"Oh, we talk about all manner of things," I said slowly, to make it sound enticing. "But don't you find it fascinating, iron and blood and all that?"

Pay attention, now. This is important.

He shrugged. "I guess, if you're into that goth shit."

"Everything's a label with you." I plucked the blossoms from his hand. "Thank you for the flowers."

Brad frowned at the bouquet. "These are the brightest ones I could find. I figured . . . " He let his voice trail away, his eyes still draping over my body, as if all it would take to seduce me was an empty stare and suggestive silence.

"Not to worry," I said. "I have faith in you."

Very little faith. But faith nonetheless.

I turned and walked away. The conversation was over, and the seed had been planted. Still, I thought about him all day.

12

TAYLOR

We'd been recruiting members to the Merry-Straight Alliance for less than a week when Brad launched his first strike. It happened on a Tuesday. I was heading out of gym class when Coach pulled me aside to "talk about a delicate matter." Whatever the hell that meant. I was pretty sure I'd been wearing my cup properly all these years, and frankly, if I hadn't, I had bigger things to worry about.

So I wandered into his office in kind of a daze, trying to figure out which of my life problems fell under the jurisdiction of a high school gym teacher/soccer coach. It didn't help that he wouldn't look at me. I watched the clock ticking above his head. Time slowed down, then stopped, and I had to say something to break the silence.

"Is this about next week's game? Look, I know I missed practice, but this is the first time it's ever happened, so—"

"You won't be playing in the game Saturday."

"Because of one practice? You can't be serious."

He sighed, and I couldn't help but wonder why he was looking at me this way. His eyes flicked up from beneath his baseball cap, narrowed into slits. It was like he didn't want to look at me but couldn't help it. Like I had green and purple spots all over my face.

What was his deal?

"I'm very serious," said the man who'd been totally useless all season. "You're lucky to be getting off this easy."

"Am I missing something?"

Coach finally held my gaze, and I wished he hadn't. He looked sick with himself, like he couldn't wait to get out of the room. "Come on, Alder. It's just you and me here. You don't have to pretend. I know about your involvement in that club, and frankly, I'm not thrilled about it. Of course, there are laws..."

Okay, it was official. He'd lost his mind. The guy was clearly rambling, making no sense at all—

"But the minute you touch one of my players, the game changes."

The game changes? God, did he have to use sports metaphors even now? And since when had I ever touched one of "his" players? Sure, I'd wanted to pop Brad in the jaw on occasion, but I knew better than to stoop to his level.

Most of the time.

But guess what? He wasn't finished talking yet. He'd taken a break, to gather his (completely insane) thoughts, but now he was back at it again. "I know it's different for you, with your... condition..."

What am I, leprous? And nobody told me?

"But I have to hold your kind to the same standard as

everyone else." He held his chin in his hand, fingers spreading over his lips. Maybe to protect himself from my "condition."

"Wait," I said. "Did you say 'my kind'?"

He snorted, liked I'd asked him for a kidney. "Forgive me if I don't know the correct terminology."

Hmmm. Your words say "forgive me," but your voice says "fuck you kindly."

That's when it hit me.

It probably should've dawned on me sooner, but I'd never been referred to as a "kind" with a "condition," so it took me a minute to figure things out. He was calling me gay. He'd heard I'd joined the Alliance and he thought it meant I was gay. Because anyone who didn't think gay kids should be treated like garbage had to be gay.

"Wait." My chair screeched as I backed up, prepared to walk out on this entire conversation. "You think I touched someone? Like, *touched*?"

Coach folded his arms over his chest, peering at me from under the bill of his hat again. I wanted to give him a big fat hug, just to freak him out, but then he'd accuse me of harassment.

God, this was infuriating.

"Don't try to deny it, Alder. I have multiple testimonies."

"Multiple—"

"I can't be looking behind my back every second."

Behind his back? Was that supposed to be funny?

"And when I'm not in the locker room, I expect you to behave in a responsible way. So when I hear reports of you grabbing the guys in inappropriate places, as an educator, I have to step in. Now, if these accusations had come from a female, I might think twice, but—"

"What? *Why?*"

"You know how young girls can be. They like attention."

From who? From him? After all, wasn't this the man who'd spent the entire season close enough for the cheerleaders to trip on him?

"I think it would be best for everyone if you simply resigned from the team," he finished up, unaware of how badly I wanted to throttle him. "Nothing messy. No parents need to get involved."

Part of me wanted to tell him to ring up my parents right then. It's not like my dad could have felt *more* disappointed in me. But I didn't want him looking at me the way Coach was looking at me. Like I was a different species.

"Look, Coach. I didn't do anything—"

"I don't expect you to understand. It's in your nature—"

"Listen to what you're saying! You're talking to me like I'm a different person. I'm not a different person."

Coach stood up, towering over me. "Now, you listen to me. You can resign or we can let the principal deal with it. That could result in suspension, if you're not expelled. You're not about to get special rights here."

Just like that, my indignation gave way to fury. He actually believed that gay people wanted special rights. He believed that girls who'd been hurt were just trying to get attention. In reality, the Brads of the world were the ones getting special rights. Brad was the one doing the lying, and the bullying, and the *groping* at any party where there weren't parents around, and people like Coach chose to believe him because it didn't mess with their view of the world. Might continued to equal right.

We'd learned that as children.

So I was stuck. But I wasn't powerless. I stood, flattening my palms on his desk. Now he'd have to either stand his ground or move back.

He moved back.

Coward.

"Fine. I'll resign from the team. But you know they can't win without me." I leaned in. "So if they do win, I'll know they cheated, and that you looked the other way like you always do. I bet the School Board would love to hear about that."

His face scrunched up until it was one big wrinkle. "Don't you threaten me."

"It's not a threat. It's an opportunity to play with honor. What you do with it is up to you."

Who's the educator now?

"Oh, and Coach?" I looked him dead in the eye, showing him that a real man doesn't back down. "Don't bother watching your back around me. I'm pretty sure you're not anyone's type."

———

As I drove home from school, all I wanted to do was crawl into bed and listen to Lora's story. I wasn't even afraid to admit it anymore. At first I'd thought there was something wrong with me—I mean, a seventeen-year-old guy getting into a fairy tale? Didn't that make me a "queer" or a "pussy" or a "fairy"?

Now I knew that's what people wanted me to believe. But if I liked something, that was good enough. I didn't need to defend myself to the doubtful voices in my head, because those voices had been put there by guys like Brad and Coach Hunter and my dad—guys who lived in fear of what other guys thought of them and conformed accordingly. Where was the bravery in that?

Where was the strength?

If I knew I was strong, it didn't matter what they thought of me.

Because of this realization, it was a little pathetic how much I panicked when I saw my mom heading for my car. I'd just pulled into the driveway, and I was *this close* to reaching the sanctuary of my room. But there she was, knocking on the window.

What if Coach gave her a call?

Having confidence was one thing. But watching Mom

struggle through a chat about "teenage sexuality" would be too much to handle.

"How's it going?" I asked, stepping out of the car. I was Mister Casual, too cool for school. Surely she'd see that and leave me alone with my bad self.

"Hi, sweetie," Mom said, her voice shaking a little. That was a bad sign, but I couldn't just bolt. She was juggling bags of groceries.

"Let me do that." I reached out, and she handed over the bags reluctantly, a surprised look on her face. I didn't know why she always acted like I'd get mad whenever she needed my help.

I wasn't my dad.

"Thanks, honey," she said.

"No problem." I gestured for her to walk in front of me. The last thing I needed was to stand outside waiting for Lora "I refuse to ride in cars" Belfry to get home.

When we reached the kitchen, I couldn't help but laugh. Bags already covered the countertop, brimming with groceries. Mom shopped like she was preparing for the apocalypse.

"Impressive," I said.

Her face relaxed into a smile as she lifted boxes of pasta from the bags. On the stove, a pot of water was already boiling. *Multi-tasking, as usual.*

"I've unearthed a recipe for a yellow squash casserole," she said, dumping pasta into the water. I watched the noodles sink to the bottom of the pot. "Yellow squash! Do you like yellow squash?"

"I could grow some yellow squash," I said, glancing through the window at the garden.

"That would be wonderful. Yellow squash, zucchini. Anything you want."

"Sure," I said, making mental notes.

"I'm making too much food." She smiled sheepishly, brushing a hair from her face; a strand had fallen from her bird's nest bun. When I didn't respond, she added, "Why don't you stay for dinner tonight, help us eat all of this?"

I stirred the pasta, searching for a decent excuse. The last thing I wanted was to watch Dad inhale his food while Mom poked sullenly at her masterpiece. I couldn't deal with it right now. I needed to be alone.

With Lora.

"I have this project," I began, which wasn't a total lie. Helping Lora was definitely a project of some kind. "How about sometime this weekend?"

"This weekend," Mom mumbled, like I'd suggested we get together ten years from now. "Why not this week?"

"I have plans."

She drizzled olive oil across a pan and placed it on the stove beside the pot of pasta. "With who?"

I bit my cheek, folding up the empty grocery bags. Did she have to act surprised that I might actually be hanging out with somebody? "A friend," I said, tucking the bags under the sink. "And I can't bail on her."

Her, get it? A girl.

"Of course not," Mom said. Her tone was casual, but she was probably offended that I was choosing a stranger over my family. Except Lora wasn't a stranger.

I already felt closer to her than anyone else.

The smell of garlic rose as Mom dropped cloves into the pan, sautéing them in the oil. A memory flashed through my head. Aaron and I were kids, running like demons through the kitchen, as Mom hummed happily at the stove. We'd pulled everything we could reach from the refrigerator, holding them up for her to add to our impromptu feast. Light was coming through the window and I felt so warm. Happy. Loved. I don't know where my father was.

"Honey, you don't have to avoid me," said Mom, bringing me back to the present. "I'm on your side."

"I know." She was always on my side—when I was the only one in the room.

"We have something important to discuss," she said, and just like that, I knew I was going to lose this battle. Her back was turned to me and she'd flipped on the fan above the stove, making it hard to hear. "I told your father I wanted to check with you…"

As I stepped closer, I saw something weird just beyond the doorway to the dining room. A roll of wallpaper was propped against the wall.

"What's that?" I asked, perspiration dotting my nose. I

liked to think I was warm because I was standing so close to the steam. "Are you guys redecorating? The, uh ... "

I didn't have to finish my thought. There was only one room she'd have to "discuss" redecorating. Aaron's room.

Mine and Aaron's.

"Your father thinks it's best ... " Mom stepped away from the stove, wiping her face. "Would you strain the noodles, please?"

I lifted the pot, not bothering to use potholders to protect my hands. The searing heat helped distract me from the pain in my chest. I didn't know how Mom expected me to react to this news. I wasn't even sure how the conversation made me feel. Part of me had believed the room would always stay the way it was, but another part of me felt it would be the best possible thing for it to be redone.

Emptied of memories.

"Please don't get upset," Mom said, tiptoeing over eggshells I couldn't see. "Nothing is official yet. That's why I need you at dinner." She scraped the spoon on the bottom of the saucepan. "You know how your father can get."

"You mean he'll pry himself away from the idiot box long enough to have a conversation?"

I shouldn't have said that. I knew it would only embarrass her. But I was sick of her defending him: *You know how your father can get.* Give me a break. The man didn't *get* a certain way. He was more consistent than any of us.

"He's been watching these programs about missing children," Mom said, jumping right into her defense mode. "The kind where you call in if you recognize the perpetrator? I think it's his way of coping..."

What could I say to that? For every bad mood my dad had, she had an explanation. I ran cold water over the pasta, trying not to think of the horrible dinner I'd now been sucked into.

Then an idea came to me, a way to make the experience more bearable. What if I could bring a guest to dinner? Dad couldn't really explode in front of company. And Lora would take it all in stride, the way she did with everything else.

"I really do have plans this week," I said. "But maybe my friend would be willing to come over here for dinner."

Mom considered the proposition in silence. She stood very still, frowning into the pan of sauce. For a second I wondered if she was afraid of losing her baby boy to this stranger, this mysterious temptress. Then I realized the flaw in my logic—I wasn't her baby boy. Her baby boy was decaying under six feet of dirt at the Whittleton Cemetery.

Then, wiping her hands on a towel, Mom smiled. "That sounds lovely. We'll plan for Friday."

She glanced out the window. Pink and gold streaked the sky. The sun was starting to set, which could only mean one thing in her mind. "You'd better go work on your project. Your father will be home soon."

I left the house in a hurry.

———

"Are you all right?" Lora's voice filtered over from across the room. It was late. She'd been sprawled across the bed doing homework for the past hour, and I'd been staring at the ceiling. Pretty soon my eyes would glaze over completely. Maybe I'd even sink into the furniture.

In Futonland, your only problem is being folded in half.

I could live with that.

"Taylor?" she said, closing her math book. "What's wrong?"

What could I say?

Coach acted like I was a terrible person just because I joined a school club.

Or maybe:

My parents are redoing the bedroom I used to share with my brother. My kid brother. The one who was supposed to outlive me.

I shrugged. "Rough day."

"Would you like to talk about it?"

"Absolutely not."

"Would you like to talk about something else?"

I turned to look at her. "Would you?"

Hint.

"I would, actually." She smiled, all teeth, and it looked dangerous. "I would like to talk about Brad Dickson. You two are friends, yes?"

"Are you kidding?" I glanced at the bed, waiting for her to invite me over. Like maybe I was a vampire, and I needed permission. "Brad and I are the opposite of friends. He's the bane of my existence."

"The *bane*?" She laughed, and then did the most wonderful thing. She patted the spot beside her.

"He's the literal worst," I said, crawling onto the bed. I kept my distance, arms at my sides, just looking at her. Sometimes being the perfect gentleman sucked. But it was better than the alternative.

"Tell me something, Mr. Alder," she said, tucking a strand of hair behind her ear. "Do you think the world would be better off without people like Brad?"

"Are you offering to bump him off?"

She didn't laugh. She didn't even smile. "Consider me curious."

My body prickled with heat. I didn't know if it was because I wanted to be close to her or because of what she was saying. "I think the *school* would be better off without him," I said after a minute. "You know he's getting me kicked off the soccer team? All because I joined the Merry-Straight Alliance—"

"Oh, Taylor. I'm sorry." She reached out, like she was going to touch my hand. But she didn't, and it was so much worse than if she hadn't even tried. "I should have warned you that this might happen."

"What do you mean? You *knew*—"

"Not about the team," she said. "But all social change meets resistance."

"The club doesn't have anything to do with Brad."

"It has everything to do with him. We're challenging his reign."

"By supporting a *club*?"

"You can't have rulers *and* equality, Taylor. It doesn't work like that. Just ask Naeve."

"I—who?"

"The last faerie baby, remember?" she said. "At least, at the time when he was born … "

"Do you want to tell me about it?" I leaned in, showing that I was interested.

She didn't move away. "That depends. Have you grown tired of my little story?"

"You can tell me any story you want." A story about magic and warring faerie courts. A story about a runaway who falls in love with the boy who comes to her aid.

Oh, sure. That's not a fairy tale.

Lora nodded and settled into the pillow behind her. "Young Naeve grew up under the watchful gaze of the Dark Lady, as pampered as any babe could be. When he'd grown into maturity, she took him as one of her many consorts."

"Whoa. Really?"

What I meant was: *That's fucked up.*

"When life is never-ending, such things are not unheard of."

"I guess not."

She didn't seem to catch my sarcasm, but that was okay. Her lips were moving again, and her eyes lit up when she talked. "For a time, the war between the courts calmed. No one wanted to risk harming the faerie that could be the last of their kind. And after much deliberation, an arrangement was made: the dark faeries would not attack humanity if the bright faeries would not seduce, befriend, or protect them in any way. The cost was high for both courts, but they were willing to make these sacrifices for peace."

"But something happened," I said before Lora had the chance to go on.

She grinned. "How did you know?"

I shrugged. "If things don't keep happening, the story ends." *Hint. Hint. Hint.*

She inhaled, and her arm pressed against mine. In that second, all my stupid problems went on vacation.

How does she do that?

"Something did happen," she said, taking her arm away. She stared at it, like maybe it had touched me without her permission. "Several centuries after their agreement was made, Virayla made a startling discovery. She was pregnant."

"That, I did not expect."

She laughed. I couldn't stop looking at the arm that had just been touching me. I wanted to slide my fingertips from her wrist to her shoulder, trailing every inch.

Then I wanted to do the same with my lips.

"How did the faeries react?" I asked. "Did it make them work harder for peace?"

"Unfortunately, no. You see, their agreement had not

really solved their problems; it had only masked them. And when the bright faeries learned the Dark Lady would soon have both Naeve *and* a child of her own, they weren't exactly pleased. They began to whisper of war again—a war that would settle things once and for all."

"A battle to the death," I said.

"Yes. So when the daughter of the Dark Lady was born, she was born into a world on the brink of total devastation." Lora paused, looking away. "And she was born into a family where one of the members wanted her dead."

"Who?" I touched her arm, just brushing the elbow.

She turned back suddenly. I wondered if maybe I'd shocked her with my touch. But she always responded that way, I realized when I thought about it. As if the touch of my fingers brought her pain.

When she spoke, it was almost a whisper. "Naeve," she said. "You see, Naeve was supposed to be the last faerie ever born. But when the princess was born, all that glory and attention was transferred to her. By no fault of her own, she stole both his identity and the attention of his surrogate mother. And, like any spoiled child robbed of his birthright, Naeve took out all his anger on her."

"Sibling rivalry. With magic." I whistled. "Sounds dangerous."

"Naeve certainly wanted it to be. He did his best to harm the princess, but his efforts were never as effective as he would have liked. When he led her to the edge of a precarious cliff, she flew for the first time. When he lured her into the sea, she created a whirlpool that sucked him to the bottom. He tried many times to turn the beasts of the forest against her, but she had a way of connecting with them that he could not match. She slept amongst the wolves, swam beside sharks, and even borrowed venom from poisonous spiders and snakes, a skill she often used to keep Naeve at bay."

"Was he still ... " I paused when her head tipped to the side, almost resting on my shoulder. It felt so good I couldn't believe it. It felt *right.*

Did she feel it too?

"What happened between Naeve and the Dark Lady?" I asked, whispering so that maybe she'd lean closer.

She inched nearer and I turned, inhaling her scent.

"After the princess was conceived, Virayla never touched Naeve again," she said.

"Why?" I asked, lips close to her forehead.

"His love seemed to sicken her. She had seen the birth and death of all living things, had seen lovers live and die, for centuries. I believe it was too much for her to see the eternal nature of things. Behind love lies inevitable loss, and she could not afford the devastation."

"What about the princess? She must've loved her own daughter."

"No," Lora said softly. "I don't believe she did."

I don't know why, but I could've sworn she was talking about herself.

"That's terrible," I said.

She shrugged, lifting her head.

Wait! Come back!

"The princess knew not what she was missing," Lora said in a low voice, like she was controlling it. "But Naeve did, and as the years went by, the traps he set for her grew more dangerous."

"But he couldn't kill her flat out, right?"

"Oh no, he had to be clever. He used Virayla's own trick against her daughter. He tried to lure her to her death."

"In order to get the Queen all to himself? Didn't he think she'd be a little pissed that he'd gotten her daughter killed?"

She didn't answer. Her breath was sharp and shallow, almost like she was crying.

I slid my hand over the top of hers, my fingers slipping into the spaces between her fingers. I wanted her to know that she was safe with me. No matter what had happened to her before, I wouldn't be like the people she'd run away from. The people I'd run away from.

I would never hurt her.

"The mind of a broken thing is easily corrupted," she said finally. She hadn't taken her hand away. She even opened her fingers a little, to let me in. "Perhaps Naeve thought he could convince the Queen her daughter's death had been an accident."

"And then she'd turn to the *messenger* for comfort?" I squeezed her hand, the tiniest bit. "Seriously?"

"He was not thinking. He was feeling, and with a broken heart. The princess had to find a way to escape him, to escape the life she'd been born into."

"What did she do?"

Lora sighed softly, like she was getting ready to sleep. I didn't mind. I hadn't really expected anything to happen between us tonight. But if she'd let me, I'd stay close to her while she slept, in case she needed me. I'd had plenty of practice in dealing with bad dreams.

"The princess came up with a plan to solve both of her problems at once," she said, turning her hand around and lacing her fingers through mine. Warmth spread through my chest. "A plan that would strip Naeve of his power and restore peace to faeriekind."

13

ELORA

Midweek, I was lingering in the girls' locker room, searching in vain for a way to escape the inane ritual of gym class, when I heard a noise. First, the strangled cry of an animal caught in a trap. Then, muffled sobbing. Creeping on the tips of my toes, I sought out the source of the sound.

I found myself in the girls' bathroom, standing before the end stall and straining my ears. The sound had tapered off the moment I'd entered the room. Still, I heard intermittent sniffling.

Crouching down, I peered beneath the stall, just enough to see the wheelchair resting behind thick black boots.

I took a step back. "Kylie?"

"I'm fine," came the high-pitched reply.

"Are you certain?" I leaned against a sink, creating space Kylie could not see. "Are you hurt?"

"No, I'm, uh—" Kylie pushed out a laugh. "I'll be out in a second."

I waited patiently. Several minutes passed.

Kylie flushed the toilet and came out of the stall, covering her face with her hand. Feigning indifference to my presence, she shot glances at the mirror through her fingers. Then, as if she'd come to some conclusion, she turned on the faucet and splashed water on her face.

It dribbled down to her shirt.

"Damn it."

I ripped a paper towel from the dispenser and held it out. "Here."

Kylie's hand shook as she took the towel. "Thanks."

"Are you sure you're all right?"

Kylie stared at me in determined silence, her lips set in a firm line. She glanced through the doorway at the empty locker room. "Uh huh." The words caught in her throat.

One unexplained phenomenon of the human world: some humans are more comfortable lying than others.

"Kylie," I prompted, in a voice used to coax timid animals. "I am your friend."

"Yeah." She nodded. "I know. I just...I did something stupid this weekend."

"I find that hard to believe."

"Keep listening." But she didn't continue. Instead she traveled back and forth, pacing, while outside the bathroom our gym class was beginning.

"Tell me something," she said. "If you got asked out by someone you knew was a horrible person, would you go? I mean, would anyone go? Anyone with half a brain would have known he was bluffing—"

"Just stop." I didn't tell her that she had more brains than most people I'd met in my life—she wouldn't have believed such a compliment. Human teenagers had a knack for ignoring their positive attributes. So instead I said, "This is about Brad, isn't it?"

"You got that from 'horrible person,' huh?"

"He's very respected here."

It was an odd thing for me to say, and she frowned, playing with a cuticle.

"One might even call him the leader of the school," I continued. "But those who command with fear are rarely kindhearted..."

"I didn't go to his house because I was afraid of him. I went because I thought...it's stupid."

"Please stop saying that."

"I thought if he got to know me, things would be different."

"If he had half a brain, that would be true," I told her.

"Therein lies the problem." A hint of a smile played on her lips. "I guess a part of me knew, going in, that it was a trick. But I still thought maybe I could change things. Maybe I could get him to see our side." She shook her head.

I placed a hand on her arm when she fell silent. "What happened?"

"He asked what I wanted to drink. I said soda. He acted all put out, like I was being a loser for not wanting to get wasted. But I wouldn't back down. He had to meet me part way, you know? So he brought me the soda and even watched me drink it. I thought he was being attentive. Trying to make up for being a jerk at first."

I waited for her to continue.

"I started to feel sick," she said, turning on the faucet again but making no move to use the water. For a moment, I was reminded of my first night in Taylor's room, the way he'd used the flowing water to center himself. I almost smiled.

Kylie glanced over. "I told him I wanted to go home," she said. "But he started to freak out, like I was going to throw up in his car. He told me to wait it out. So I just closed my eyes. I guess I fell asleep." Tears welled up in her eyes and she clenched her jaw to stop them. Still, they fell.

"Kylie?"

She swallowed, pressing her hands to her face. "I woke up and he was yelling at me to get up, even though I couldn't move. Lora, I was in his room. I felt all heavy…"

I frowned, my blood boiling in an instant. For the better part of Kylie's story, I hadn't really understood. Now I understood too well. "What did he do?"

"Nothing," she said in a rush. "His parents had come home. That's why he was yelling. The movie they were supposed to see was sold out, so he snuck me out through the back door. My aunt thought I was drunk. I've never even *had* a drink in my entire life."

I waited a beat. "You didn't tell her—"

"I'm not telling anybody. People would just laugh at me. They're already laughing at me."

"What do you mean?"

Kylie swallowed, finally turning away from the mirror. When her gaze settled on me, I got chills. "It's not what you think. He wasn't going to—" She started combing her hair with her fingers, moving so jerkily it must have caused her more pain than comfort. "He just wanted to take a picture of me."

"Why?"

"There's this rumor going around. People say I have both boy and girl parts. You know, because I like both? This morning, in English, I heard people saying he was going to take off my clothes and take a picture … to prove … " She crumpled against the sink, covering her face. "Why would he do that to me? What did I do to deserve this?"

"You didn't do anything." I knelt beside her. "It doesn't have anything to do with you, trust me."

"Of course it does! All my life, people have wanted to hurt me."

Cruelty seeks to conquer sweetness. Always. It is the way of things.

But I didn't tell her that. I touched her hair softly, whispering, "It's okay. You're okay now."

The words, meant to soothe, only made her cry harder.

"All right," I said, my veins filling with cold possibilities. "Maybe you're not. But you will be."

———

"Damn it." Taylor slammed his fist against the doorframe. "Damn it, damn it."

"Taylor." I reached for his hand.

He stepped out of my reach. "This is my fault," he said, rubbing his knuckles. Trying not to wince.

"How is it your fault?" I asked.

"I knew Brad had access to drugs—his mom's a professional pill popper." Taylor slumped down on the edge of his bed. "I can't believe he'd do this. We have to tell someone."

"And betray Kylie's confidence?"

His head snapped up. "You just told me."

"I knew you would keep it a secret. Won't you?"

Taylor sighed. "Of course. But I can't just let him get away with it. What about next time, when his parents don't come home early? Who knows what else he's done to ... *fuck*."

I sat beside him, placing my hand on his knee. I did it to comfort him, maybe to bend him to my will. There was absolutely no reason to touch him other than that. And as my fingers spread over his knee, a rush of warmth most certainly did not shoot through my gut and go traveling down to the depths of me.

"There are other ways of dealing with such things," I said, taking my hand away. Still, that spreading warmth remained.

"What do you mean?" His gaze had traveled to the place where my hand had been, as if willing it to return.

I denied him. "I've begun to formulate a plan. A rough plan, which needs some smoothing out."

"What is it?" he asked, turning his green eyes on me. Green like emeralds. Green like glistening leaves.

Green like the Seelie Queen's.

I'd seen her only once, but I remembered.

"The basic idea is to lure Brad on a date—"

"You're going to actually go out with him?" he snapped.

"I'm going to give him a taste of his own medicine."

"What, drug him? And … strip him?"

My lips curled at the idea. "I'm going to scare him."

"No. No way. It's too dangerous."

"I was raised amongst danger. This is nothing, compared to—"

"No." Taylor shook his head. "He could hurt you."

"I could hurt him."

For a moment he just looked at me. He did not appear surprised. "Are you going to hurt him?"

"I might." Already I could taste vengeance on my lips. Better to focus on tasting vengeance than tasting the boy in front of me …

Elora!

"Does that bother you?" I asked, swallowing my inappropriate thoughts. Burying them deep inside of me.

"Yes. No." Taylor shook his head, lying back on the bed. "I want to hurt him, too. But—"

"You would rather I not dirty my hands."

He closed his eyes. "Yes."

I leaned over him, my shadow swallowing his light. "My hands are not as clean as you think. I am not some pure, bright angel."

"Good." He rose on his elbows to meet me. His eyes were close, and his lips. I felt the greatest thrill when he said, "Neither am I."

———

That night, I made a mistake. I thought Taylor was sleeping when he wasn't. And carefully, ever so quietly, under the covers, I sent a text message to Brad Dickson.

"Are you up?" my message asked.

"In more ways than one," Brad replied.

I rolled my eyes. But I sent another message: *"Look out the window. Don't you love meteor showers? I've heard it said that iron was brought to earth by crashing meteors."*

Brad's reply, *"WTF?",* did not faze me. I had a task to complete. And no matter what happened, I would complete it.

I climbed onto my knees. Outside, the world was beautiful and dark. It almost seemed a shame to light up the sky. But I focused my attention on a patch above the city, and after several seconds, dozens of bright, glittering stars streaked the sky.

At least, they appeared to.

"What are you doing?"

I gasped, and froze. *If I remain very still . . .*

"Lora? Are you taking off? Because the stairs would probably be the better way to go." Taylor's tone was light, but I heard the fear beneath it, the joke that was not really a joke.

"I was ... looking," I said, slinking back onto the bed. Every inch of my body was tensed. I told myself he couldn't have seen my illusion.

"Was that lightning?" he asked.

"Could have been. Let's get some sleep." I didn't mean it. I wanted to stay up all night telling stories. Either that or plotting our revenge.

My head had just touched the pillow when he said, "Lora?"

"Yes?"

"Where was the Dark Court, physically?"

"What do you mean?"

"Well, your story seems like it takes place in the real world. But in the real world, where could it be?"

I had to be careful with my answer. I couldn't lie—of course I couldn't. But there was a danger in making the story too real.

I treaded carefully. "It is not as simple as that. The human and the faerie worlds ... they are touching, but they are not the same. In essence, Faerie is the place where the physical and the spiritual worlds meet. One cannot simply walk there, unless one knows the way."

"But if one did know the way," Taylor asked, mimicking my speech patterns, "where would one walk?"

I laughed, unable to resist his persistence. "One might seek out an entrance in the parts of the earth that are prone to periods of extended darkness."

"Any reason you're being so vague?"

"It allows the story to maintain a sense of mystery. Besides..." I searched his face in the darkness. "If I tell you its exact location, are you going to go looking for it?"

"If you want me to." He kept his voice casual, but there was something behind it I couldn't place. Hunger, maybe.

Or desire.

He doesn't know.

"Would you want me to go looking for it?" he asked.

He can't know.

"It wouldn't be very safe," I said.

"Because of the courts' rivalry?"

Now that the conversation was approaching reality, I couldn't say too much. If he understood a hint of the truth behind the story, I'd have to stop telling it completely.

But I promised it to him.

"Are you looking for a fight, Taylor?"

"Not with you."

"That isn't what I meant."

"I know." He was looking at me with those piercing eyes, asking silent permission to join me on the bed.

I lowered my gaze.

"I'm just trying to understand the courts," he said after a minute. "Why would they go to war if they didn't have to?"

"Why does anybody?" I asked. I felt a dull ache in my abdomen, born of the fear that I would not be sleeping next to him tonight.

"Well, here in the real world, we have leaders who send us off to fight. Generally when they want some commodity."

"The real world," I said softly. I could show him things about the real world that would make his heart want to crawl out of his chest.

"If you really think about it, not much has changed since the Middle Ages. We're just pawns," he added, still watching me.

"As were the faeries." I tried to lower my gaze again, but I couldn't. "Taylor..."

"Yes?" Just like that, he was crawling toward me.

"I..." The words died on my lips as he rose to his knees, hovering at the edge of the bed. Our faces had rarely been so close.

"You sick of me?" he asked.

He was testing me. Perhaps the entire universe was testing me. All I had to do was say yes and I would pass the test.

"Not a bit," I said.

"Do you want me to go away?" His voice was soft. I could almost feel his breath.

"I want you to stay."

I made room for him and he climbed up beside me. This time, we lay face to face. In spite of the danger, our hands found their way to each other, and I did not fight it.

I'm the one that did it.

"What now?" he said, his face mere inches from mine. We were sharing the same pillow. His thumb slid over my fingers, sending currents of heat shooting through me. My heart felt safe, as if cradled.

"Do you want to know more about the courts?" I asked.

His eyes bore into me when he said, "Whatever you want."

"I want to fulfill my promise to you."

"Then do it."

"All right," I said, trying to keep the tremble from my voice. If I just stuck to my story, I would not have to speak of impossible things. Of desire I could not have imagined before.

Of longing.

"The faeries of both courts were like pawns, as I said. The queens were the ones who so desperately wanted to go to war. But those queens employed different tactics to keep their followers loyal."

"What does that mean?"

"Well, the Bright Queen wore the guise of the nurturer. She was already known as the greatest healer in Faerie. She would not use force to govern her people, not if she didn't have to. Instead she used distraction, keeping them constantly entertained. She held festivals for the full moon, rituals for the new moon, dances for autumn and spring, galas for summer and winter. They drank berry wine, oak-aged wine, grape wine, petal wine, and they ate

until their bellies stretched the bindings of their elaborate garb. They were much too drunk, dizzy, and filled up
with inconsequential things to realize they were merely the
Queen's puppets on strings."

Taylor made a soft sound when I untangled my fingers from his, but I did not take the hand away. Instead, I
trailed my fingers over his, returning the favor. I thought
it might calm me down to be in control of the movement.

It didn't.

"The Dark Lady, on the other hand, controlled her
court by keeping her followers fighting amongst themselves. She separated them into courtiers and servants,
and encouraged her courtiers to treat each group of servants differently, to instill jealousy between them. Thus
the satyrs fought with the nymphs, the pixies distrusted
the sprites, and each servant was so busy fighting another,
they didn't realize the Queen was abusing them all."

"And that worked?" Taylor asked, studying my face. It
was funny, the subtle differences between us. The intensity of
his touch forced my eyes to close, but his gaze never left me.

"It always works, for a time," I said, drawing my hand
away. Trying to calm the storm raging inside me. But he
chased after me, tickling my fingers. "Look at your own
history," I said. "I mean, human history."

"I've been doing that a lot lately."

"Then you know what follows tyranny."

"Revolution."

"Clever boy," I said, leaning into him. "As time passed,

and war loomed on the horizon, the servants of the Dark Court began to question the mutual hatred. They would look across the mountain at their neighbors and wonder how the feud had begun. Even the Queen's daughter, who was granted any luxury she might desire, longed for the warmth of friendship and connection. Perched in one of her favorite trees, or wandering along the rocky mountainside, she watched the servants brawling, their misery apparent in their eyes. Her heart ached for them, and for the life all the faeries might know if they could overcome this segregation."

"Hmmm," Taylor said softly, closing his eyes. The clock on his desk read two thirty-five, and I knew we should sleep. But I would finish this part of my story, and if I fell asleep by his side, well … it couldn't be helped.

Exhaustion was setting in.

I rested my head on his shoulder. "Then it became clear: if the inhabitants of the Dark Court were to survive throughout the ages, and save the planet they depended on for their lives, all members of the Court would have to reunite. And in order to do this, in order to bring together the broken fragments of Faerie without sacrificing innumerable lives, these disillusioned creatures needed a leader who could take down the Unseelie Court from the inside."

Me.

14

TAYLOR

I sat alone in the basement classroom, obsessing over Lora's story. I couldn't get it out of my head. At first I'd thought she was just an amazing storyteller, drawing on childhood fables to help me sleep. Then I'd started to suspect the story was her religion. Now I understood it was an allegory for her life. She was the princess in the story. Her mother, represented by Virayla, was the leader of the cult she'd left behind. And Naeve was someone her mother had seduced. Maybe molested. My skin crawled at the possibilities.

Worse still was the thought of what Naeve had done to Lora throughout her life. The torment of the princess was clearly symbolic of things too terrible to say. How could I live with myself, knowing that people like Naeve were out there? How could I pass Brad in the hallway without ripping out his throat?

I had to do something. I had to . . .

Kylie burst into the room, followed by Keegan and Lora. "I don't believe this," she howled, punching a desk. "Ow!"

I jumped up, ready for a fight. "What happened? Are you okay?"

"Careful," Lora warned, as more people arrived for the meeting.

The Merry-Straight Alliance was slowly growing. I noticed two girls I hadn't seen before. One had flame-red hair, almost the exact shade of Lora's. The other's hair was strawberry blond. I could tell by their matching blue eyes that they were sisters. The younger of the two, probably a freshman, caught my eye as she passed. She smiled.

Part of Lora's fan club, I thought as the sisters sat down. I was pretty certain the school had more redheads now than it had two weeks ago. Still, no one could quite match Lora's shade. She was one of a kind.

"Let me see your hand." Lora was kneeling in front of Kylie, her black lace dress brushing the ground. Kylie held out her hand for inspection. The pocket of her sweatshirt opened, revealing something small and gold.

A lighter?

I narrowed my eyes.

Lora clasped Kylie's fingers and closed her eyes. For a minute, it looked like she was drawing out Kylie's pain. I wished I had that kind of power. I wanted to pull Lora into my arms and take all of her pain into me. But this desire had complications. What if the closeness reminded her of bad things?

"What happened?" she asked Kylie, smiling briefly at me.

"They're trying to ban same-sex couples from prom." Kylie pulled her fingers from Lora's grasp. "This is so unfair!"

"What's fair?" Keegan sat on top of a desk. "They shove us in this dungeon and keep us out of the public eye. Big surprise."

"It isn't right," Kylie insisted. From the look on her face, it was clear she was contemplating sacrificing the knuckles on her other hand.

"Why do they even care?" I drew a frowning face on my desk and then erased it, wary the graffiti might somehow be tracked back to me. Then, irritated with myself for being so paranoid, I drew it again, darker this time. "Shouldn't they focus on more important things?"

"Like pregnant fourteen-year-olds?" Kylie suggested.

The redheads giggled.

"Oh, *no*." Keegan scoffed, holding a hand over his mouth. "Two boys dancing is *way* more horrifying than dumpster babies."

Kylie shook her head. "Three girls dropped out of school *this year* after getting pregnant, but me taking a girl to the freaking prom is the problem. I can't stand this."

"Wait a second," I said, the wheels already turning in my head. I couldn't imagine someone wanting to punish Kylie for taking a date to the prom. She was, hands down, the nicest person I knew. "Who made this decision? Unity or the School Board?"

"Unity," Kylie replied without hesitation. "Straight

from Principal Jade's mouth. She's trying to keep it quiet because she's up for review next year."

"Inside job." Keegan frowned. "Wait—how do you know this?"

"I...heard," she said, keeping her eyes on me.

"So why don't we tell the School Board?" I asked.

"Then we'd be royally fucked," Keegan answered. "Look at what happened in Tennessee."

"And Ohio," Kylie added.

"Mississippi," said one of the redheads.

"All right." I held up my hands. "We take it up with Jade. What's happened so far?"

"Nothing official," Kylie said. "But a group of parents called in to make sure prom is for *traditional* couples only."

"Big deal," I said. "They can't make the decision for everybody."

"It is a big deal," Kylie countered. "The parents who complained were alumni. People who've given money to the school." She lowered her gaze. In that moment, I was certain she was thinking of Alan Dickson. Of all the people who'd offered Unity monetary support in the past four years, Brad's father was at the top of the list.

"Brad strikes again," I muttered.

I hadn't meant for it to be heard, but Lora turned to me, her eyes wide. "His dad's loaded," I explained quickly. "But so what? He can't ask for his money back."

Kylie smiled, barely.

I stretched out my legs. I wished we could move these meetings to a room with a window, but according to the principal, upstairs rooms were reserved for larger clubs. "All we have to do is get more parents to call in, on our behalf."

Keegan raised his eyebrows. "Yours or mine?"

I drew another face on my desk, hiding my embarrassment. "We're not the only people in the school with parents."

"Right," Keegan agreed. He opened his notebook and started scribbling an equation. "So take the student body and subtract the parents of hetero students. Then subtract the parents of the closeted kids. Then subtract the parents who kicked the crap out of their kids for coming out."

"And minus the parents who think they can scare their kids straight," said a girl named Alyssa, who sat in the back. Her partner from the previous meeting was nowhere to be seen, but the quiet boy in the front (*what was his name again?*) continued to show up, sweating and wheezing and never saying a word.

Keegan nodded at Alyssa. "Right. Minus the parents who actually support their kids, so long as their friends don't find out. And you have…"

Kylie snapped her fingers. "Sally Striker."

Keegan laughed. "Her mom's living in the sixties—anything goes!" He turned to me. "You see the problem."

"But you admit," Kylie said, pointing a finger at

Keegan's nose, "that there *are* parents who don't make Cinderella's stepmother look like a saint?"

"I've heard *stories*," he drawled, grabbing at her finger. "But the fact is, most people, however decent, will go out of their way to avoid confrontation. I think Jade's banking on that."

"Well then," Lora said, rising to her feet. "That leaves us with two options." I had the feeling she'd been waiting for this moment to speak, to lead us. "We either create a prom of our own, make it more decadent than their prom ever could be, and exclude them—"

"That would be awesome," Kylie broke in.

"And expensive," said Keegan.

"And impossible," Alyssa added. "If they won't let us bring dates to this prom, why would they let us have our own?"

"We do it all ourselves," Lora said. "We secure the location, invite those we want to invite, and advise them to come to our prom on the same night of the other prom. No need to involve Unity at all."

"I like it," I said, imagining a ballroom filled with rebels and outcasts. If Lora were in charge of things, she'd probably host an elaborate masquerade ball.

An anti-prom for the ages.

"Still expensive, and still probably impossible." Keegan shook his head. "And we could get kicked out of school for something like that."

"You said there were two things we could do," said the

girl with the fiery hair, looking dotingly at Lora. "What's the other thing?"

"Show up anyway," I suggested.

"Yeah, right." The girl laughed. "And get denied at the door."

"Actually," Lora said, fixing her gaze on me, "I *was* going to say that."

"Really," Kylie and Keegan said together.

Lora waited for me to explain.

Better make this good, Alder.

"Well," I began, "it's easy to tell you no from behind closed doors. But when you're there in person, all dressed up with a ticket in your hand, what are they going to do?"

"Throw a sheet over you and push you to the side." Keegan crossed his arms. "There aren't enough of us."

"There are *hundreds* of us," Lora countered. "There are far more outcasts in this school than anyone else. The outcasts are actually the norm."

Keegan shrugged. "That's true of any totalitarian regime."

"And how are such regimes overthrown?" she asked, tapping his nose with her finger.

"Revolution," I broke in. "If all the outcasts in our class show up at the prom, they can't turn us away to please the few."

"Wait a second," said Kylie. "It's taken us weeks to double our members. How are we supposed to gather all the outcasts in the school before prom?"

"Easy," said Lora, a blush creeping over her cheeks. "First, we invite them to a very exclusive event."

———

The meeting had been over for ten minutes, but I was still trapped in the confines of Unity's basement. I stood outside the girls' bathroom while Keegan paced the lockers nearby, kicking a fast food bag across the floor.

"Do the janitors even come down here?" he asked, kicking the bag into a row of lockers. It split down the side, spilling fries.

"Would you?"

"If I were a janitor, I'd walk with a limp and invent weird facial tics." He stooped low, dragging one leg behind him. "Damn spoiled kids."

I smiled nervously, glancing at the bathroom. Keegan's mood was cheerful; it didn't take a genius to guess that Kylie hadn't told him about her evening with Brad. "What are they *doing* in there?" I asked.

"Toilet diving. All the best drugs get flushed down the basement toilets."

"The Great Toilet Capers. Why didn't I think of that?"

His face broke into a grin. "They're up to something."

"Right."

"No, seriously." Keegan crept up to the bathroom. "They're always huddling together, whispering about shit." He beckoned for me to come closer.

I leaned in. "That's what girls do. Hell, that's what *we're* doing."

He pressed his ear against the door. Then, quick as a fox, he hurried down the hallway. "You coming?"

I followed reluctantly.

"Kylie sneaks out at night," Keegan said when we reached the bottom of the stairs. "I hear her going out the back door."

"Seriously?" My emotions shifted, too quickly to examine them. "Maybe she smokes."

Keegan shook his head. "Our parents were super anti-drug, so … she's retained some of that."

"Maybe she's getting some fresh air," I said, not mentioning the object I'd seen sticking out of her sweatshirt. It might not have been a lighter. But I was pretty sure it was.

"Sometimes she tells my aunt she's going away with her theater group for the weekend," he said. "Except they don't really have weekend—"

"Okay, I get it. She's meeting someone." I stared at the bathroom door like it was a mirage that might disappear. Maybe it would all disappear: my friends, my chance at happiness. My ability to sleep at night. "That doesn't mean she's meeting Lora."

"Maybe she's not," Keegan agreed. "I mean, I'm pretty sure you'd notice if Lora was sneaking out too."

"I'd think so," I said, trying to ignore the mocking voices in my head. I had a distinct memory of waking up disoriented the night I'd brought Lora home, staring through the darkness at an empty room. But exhaustion had pulled me back to my pillow, and later I'd told myself it was a dream. Of course she hadn't snuck away in the middle of the night. Of course she wasn't meeting Kylie.

"Hey." I narrowed my eyes. "How the hell would I know where Lora goes at night? Why would you even—"

"Save it," Keegan said. "Kylie told me she's staying with you."

He might as well have kicked me in the gut. I felt like the broken bag on the floor. How could Lora have told Kylie our secret? If any adult found out, it would jeopardize our entire arrangement.

I stepped back, trying to distance myself from the situation.

"Interesting," Keegan said. "I guess she doesn't tell you everything." He held out his phone. "Give me your number."

"What?" I had the weirdest feeling of being led, blindfolded, by a guide who knew exactly where we were going. It didn't calm me in the least. "Why?"

"Relax," he said as I programmed my number into his phone. "I won't tell the other boys I have it."

"I'm not—" I forced a laugh. "I don't care about that."

"Good." He took the phone back.

"I don't. I officially stopped caring when I found out I was banned from the soccer team."

"What?"

I smirked bitterly. "Apparently, I'm not allowed to be on a team with other boys if I can't keep my hands to myself."

"You can't be serious."

"Afraid so."

He shook his head. "Brad did this."

"Not just Brad. A bunch of his cronies backed him up. Apparently I've groped a few."

Keegan leaned against a locker. "And so far from football season."

I glared.

"Sorry," he said. "It's just … if I hadn't learned to laugh at everything I probably would've quit society a long time ago." He pushed off from the lockers. "We have to do something about this."

"It's already done." I saw the girls emerge from the bathroom, but the action barely registered to me. I was trapped in the memory of Coach's discomfort at just being *near* me.

"They're not going to make it to State," Keegan said. "You're their best offensive player."

I smiled a half-smile. Lora sidled up to me, but for the first time I didn't melt in her presence. Too many emotions battled inside me, tearing me this way and that.

"Can you give us a sec?" I asked her, barely keeping my voice steady.

Kylie raised her eyebrows as she pulled Lora toward the elevator, shooting glances back as she went.

"If we can pull off this prom thing, I won't even care," I said when the elevator doors closed. "If we can pull this off, it'll be better than anything." I chuckled to myself.

"What's funny?" Keegan asked.

"I don't even care about sports."

"Could've fooled me."

"No, I love playing. But I don't want to go pro or center my life around it. I just love being out there, running across the field—"

"Grabbing guys' asses, apparently."

I ignored him. "When I'm out there and nobody can touch me, it's the one time I actually feel free. Like I'm flying."

Kylie's voice filtered down from the top of the stairwell. "What are you guys *doing* down there? We have to make, like, two hundred invitations!"

"We'll get there when we get there," Keegan yelled.

"Yeah, yeah, yeah."

"Patient, ain't she?" He ambled up the steps. When we reached the middle of the staircase he held up his phone, speaking so only I could hear. "Next time she sneaks out, I'm calling you to see if Lora's gone too. So be ready."

———

I was dreaming of glitter and paint, and the most elaborately decorated invitations Unity had ever seen. They started out simple enough, just like they had in real life: Slogans like *Reclaim the Prom* or *Take Back the School* (along with Keegan's one addition: *Destroy the Norms!*) sat in bold letters against the blood-red paper. Beneath these slogans, invitees were advised to go to Unity High at midnight this

Saturday, and to dress all in black. ("If you do not own black, black will be provided for you.") But as the dream progressed, the slogans morphed into something dark and dangerous. The glittered letters took on a life of their own, growing claws and wings, threatening the lives of anyone who didn't RSVP. In the background, I could hear the sound of clattering chains and the faint buzzing of an electrotherapy machine.

My eyes popped open. My cell was vibrating. Lurching forward, I toppled to the floor, searching with my hands. My fingers made contact with the phone. I pushed the silencer repeatedly, still drowning in the swamps of my subconscious. The number flashing on the screen was unfamiliar. I dropped the phone on the floor, wondering vaguely why there seemed to be footsteps in the garage below. Then I sat up.

Lora was gone.

I jumped to my feet.

Lora was *gone*. She was gone, someone was leaving the garage, and the number on my phone had to be Keegan's.

I darted across the room, searching the empty bed for clues. From the floor, I heard a single beep as I received a text. I dove for it. My elbows screamed as I slid over the rug, reading the sentence Keegan had sent: "*Was I right?*"

I cursed and pulled on my clothes. I was out of the room in two minutes.

Racing through the garage, I didn't bother to turn on the light. The sky was black as I stepped onto the lawn. I pulled my phone from my pocket, checking the screen to see if I'd received any calls, and rounded the garage to the driveway. Keegan hadn't called again.

Now I was faced with a dilemma. Should I walk or should I drive? I glanced at the phone, irrationally hoping for some guidance while my mind fought to wake up completely. Walk, drive? Walk, drive? And *to where*?

Then I saw her. She wore a nightgown, the long black number I'd stolen from my mom's Goodwill box, with buttons going up the back. She was walking down the sidewalk in bare feet. I started after her, keeping to the hedges that lined the neighbor's yard.

Lora neared the end of the shadowed street, looked left and right, and literally *disappeared* into the night.

I shook with fear, along with a healthy dose of denial. My phone dropped to the sidewalk and I tripped over a very visible skateboard. By the time I'd retrieved my phone and reached the end of the street, hitting the callback button with my thumb, I had a cut on my knee the size of a silver dollar.

"I lost her," I hissed into the phone when Keegan answered. "She disappeared into thin air. I lost her." I gasped for breath, for reprieve from this horrible suffocating feeling, as I waited for Keegan to speak.

"Relax."

"What?" I wheezed, scanning the block. The word made no sense, was utterly incomprehensible. I had *lost* a person in the middle of the night.

"Relax," he said again, his voice muffled. I had a vision of him walking down the street covered in a blanket. "You know the park on Langley and Evanstead?"

"With that weird play structure shaped like a face?" I searched for signs of life in the darkness. "Yeah."

"I followed my sister there. She's heading across the grass toward the merry-go-round. Can you get here fast?"

I glanced in the direction of my car. One block felt like a galaxy away. But walking to the park would take too long. "Yeah. I'll be there in a minute."

I took my time as I walked toward the car, allowing myself to catch my breath. Even if I was forced to drive a little out of the way, to avoid being spotted, I knew I could get to the park before Lora did. Still, I didn't waste time or call Keegan for further instructions. I started the car, minus the lights, and drove down the street.

The park was dark, unlit by moon or lamplight, as I strode across the grass toward the merry-go-round. Tall spruces dotted the grounds, spaced almost mathematically, and I darted between them like a cartoon cat. I was nearing the play structure, the giant yellow face with a wavy-tongue slide, when I spotted a hooded figure up ahead.

Kylie.

Her back was turned to me. I sprinted toward the closest tree. With my hands placed on the bark, my body hidden behind the trunk, I inched my face to the right until I could see what was happening.

For the moment, nothing was happening. Kylie continued to stare into the distance, fidgeting occasionally with the sleeves of her sweatshirt. I started to wonder if anyone was going to show up. Maybe Keegan was wrong after all and Lora was just going for a walk. She was used to life outside the city, after all. Walking around at night was probably normal for her.

Then I saw it. The figure was tall, almost as tall as I was, and walking with purpose across the grounds. I held my breath. I couldn't make out the figure's clothing. Darkness was doing its best to confuse my eyes, and no matter how I squinted, the shadows moved and twisted to keep me guessing. In spite of this, I could tell that the figure was female and would reach Kylie within seconds, and then, anything could happen . . .

The figure reached the merry-go-round, knelt down in front of Kylie, and kissed her on the lips.

15

ELORA

"No way," said a voice below me.

I turned, peering down through the branches of my hiding spot. "Taylor?"

He looked up, into my tree. "Lora?" His hair was sticking up in every direction, the way it had the first night I'd slept in his room. I couldn't tell for certain, but I thought his shirt was on backward.

Kylie rounded on us then. "Taylor?" she said, as her companion turned to face us.

"Alexia?" Taylor gasped.

"Keegan!" Keegan shot out of the smiling play structure and tumbled down the slide. He picked himself up by his collar. "Sorry. I just wanted to be a part of things."

Alexia looked from Keegan to Kylie to the tree where I was hiding. She took a step back. "What the hell is going on?"

Kylie appeared to be shrinking in on herself.

"Did *you* do this?" Alexia stared at Kylie. "Why would you do this?"

"I didn't invite *them*," Kylie said as Taylor and Keegan approached. Her voice sounded pinched. "I only invited Lora."

"Why?" Alexia scrunched up her face. I got the impression she was not used to showing such vulnerability.

"I've got a better question," Keegan said, wagging his finger between Kylie and Alexia. "How long has this been going on?"

Kylie lowered her head, and Alexia glared at her before speaking. "Almost two years."

"What?" Taylor crowed.

Keegan patted his shoulder as if sympathetic to his shock. "And you've kept it a secret because ... "

Alexia scoffed, startling us. It had taken her a moment to gather her wits, but now she appeared to be back in control. "You really need to ask that question? Look at your life, Keegan."

"Oh." He stepped forward. "You're a coward."

"I'm ambitious."

"So? I'm ambitious too."

Alexia curled her lip. "Oh yeah. I heard you applied to Harvard. I got a full scholarship."

"Screw you," Keegan spat. "It's always the rich kids who get everything paid for."

"How ironic," Alexia replied. "But why did I get a full scholarship?"

"Gee, I don't know. I guess you're better than me."

Alexia laughed. "I'm Student Body President. Soon I'll be elected Queen of the Prom—"

"Wait." I slid out of my arboreal seat, approaching slowly. "How does one get *elected* queen?"

"You're kidding, right? She's kidding?" Alexia snapped.

"She's home-schooled," Taylor explained.

"That really isn't an excuse."

Kylie turned, frowning at her girlfriend. To me, she said, "Next week, the senior class will nominate five girls and five boys to the Prom Court. Then, on prom night, we'll choose one king and queen."

"One king," I murmured, fighting back a smile. "And these victors are the most respected in the school?"

"That's one way of looking at it," Keegan scoffed. "Really, it's a popularity contest—"

"Exactly," Alexia said, to Keegan's surprise. His eyes widened and he stepped back. "Every election in this school is based on popularity. And I win them—"

"By sleeping with the faculty?"

"By being a rich, beautiful, heterosexual bitch."

I stared at her. "But you aren't."

"No." Alexia shook her head. "I'm not even a bitch, really. I just play one on TV." She flipped her hair with a wink. "Face it, Keeg. I'd never win these pointless little contests if everyone labeled me a big old bull dyke."

Keegan covered his mouth.

"You laugh, but you know it's true," she said. "They don't see complexity in the gay community. They don't see personality. They see Dyke or Fag tattooed across your forehead and they act accordingly. But I'm going to be something amazing. I'm going to graduate at the top of my class, and I'm going to Harvard, yes, on a free ride, and you know why? Do you know the difference between you and me?"

"I'm open about who I am and you're a closet freak?"

"I'm a leader," Alexia replied. "You're not. They look at your transcript and see that no one in this school even knows your name, so they pass you by. They look at my transcript and see that I command the respect, or at least the fear, of over half the school. That's leader material. I was born to lead and I'm going to lead, and I'm sure as hell not going to let some small-minded stereotype keep me from achieving my goals."

"Whatever you have to tell yourself."

"Judge me," she challenged, closing in on him. "Prove me right." She turned to Kylie, who had taken to pushing the merry-go-round in circles. "Going somewhere?"

"No," Kylie said, removing her hand. "I'm not running, and I'm not hiding."

"That's why you did this?" Alexia was beside her in an instant. "Is this because I'm not taking you to the prom? Honey, I told you it's a formality. We'll sneak out early and go to my mother's beach house—"

"That's not why I did this." Kylie frowned. "I said I didn't invite *those two*, and I meant it."

"Then it's just a coincidence they're in this park in the

middle of the night? Out for a lovers' stroll, boys?" Alexia raised her eyebrows.

Taylor looked at me before meeting Alexia's stare. "We followed them."

"Why?" I heard Kylie's voice, but my eyes were trained on Taylor. Cold liquid was spreading through my guts.

"Duh, you were sneaking around in the middle of the night." Keegan smirked at his sister.

"You followed me?" I said quietly to Taylor.

"I tried to," he confessed. "Sorry."

"What do you mean, you tried to?" I couldn't keep the nervousness from my voice. What had he seen?

"I saw you, down the street from my house, but then you turned the corner and I couldn't catch up to you." He narrowed his eyes, like he hadn't quite gotten that right. And he hadn't, because I'd let the darkness swallow me. I'd *summoned* it.

"You shouldn't have done that," I murmured.

"I just wanted you to be safe."

"That's not your responsibility."

Alexia was watching us with interest, as if our discord was a small consolation for Kylie's betrayal. But as silence fell over the grounds, she trained her gaze on her girlfriend. "Well?"

Kylie hugged herself. "I needed Lora's support."

"For what?"

"Something happened," I said when Kylie didn't answer. "Brad did something."

"What did he do?" Alexia snarled, unaware that Taylor and Keegan were nearing the merry-go-round. "Tell me." Her face wore the oddest look, as if all the contents of her world had been dropped on the ground.

"He didn't. He just tried to … " Kylie looked to me for help. "It's not what it sounds like."

Alexia knelt, sliding an arm around Kylie's shoulders. The movement appeared instinctual, as if she was barely aware of her own actions. Her gaze settled on me. "Somebody better tell me what the hell is going on."

I inhaled, glancing at Kylie. She nodded, and I stepped up to her side. Quickly and quietly, I recounted her experience with Brad.

When I was finished, Alexia just stared. Fury flashed in her eyes. "That worthless piece of—"

Keegan stormed past her, back toward the street.

"Keeg!" Kylie called after him. "Keegan!"

"I'm fine," he replied, not stopping.

Taylor jogged over to him and touched his arm. "Where are you going?"

"I'm going to take care of it," Keegan said, his voice flat and emotionless.

"Just wait a minute," Taylor said.

"I think enough time has been wasted," came Keegan's reply. Again, he began to walk toward the street.

"Oh, please be a hero," drawled Alexia.

Keegan stopped and rounded on her, showing the first hint of anger in his eyes.

"Please do something stupid and end up in prison," Alexia said. "Please cause your sister more pain."

Keegan's face crumpled at her words. "This is your fault."

"Excuse me?"

"Why was she there?" he yelled. "What's the one reason she would go to that asshole's house?"

"Oh, God." Alexia turned to Kylie.

Kylie looked up. "I just thought, if he liked me, maybe things would be different for us. You wouldn't have to hide—"

"Oh, sweetie." For a moment, I thought Alexia might cry. "You're right," she said to Keegan, blinking her eyes. "I should have stopped him when I had the chance."

"How would you have stopped him?" I asked. When we'd made our plans to meet here tonight, Kylie had hinted that Alexia had her own personal vendetta against Brad, but she wouldn't give me details.

Alexia sighed. "The truth is, I've been watching Brad for a while. He has quite the little business selling sedatives to the underclassmen."

"So you knew he did things like this?" Keegan asked.

"I knew he sold drugs to immature children who'd take anything to get high. Calm down, baby," she said, steadying Kylie's shaking hands. "Some freshman almost died last year from an overdose, and no one said a word. They're afraid of him. Well, the students are. See, when I said I commanded the respect of half the school, I wasn't just talking about the students. I'm friends with the principal. I'm also friends with security. In fact, you could say security and I have gotten pretty close, as much as friends can."

"You've been flirting with Janky Jim?" said Taylor.

Alexia smirked at the security guard's nickname. "I've been talking to him, which is more than any other woman will do, so I suppose he might consider it flirting."

"But why would you do that?" Taylor asked. "Wouldn't that distract him from Brad's dealings?"

"Exactly." Alexia kissed Kylie's forehead, brushing the hair from her face. "I wanted Brad to believe that security was severely lacking. I wanted him to think he could deal whatever he wanted, anywhere, any time."

Taylor wrinkled his brow. "What am I missing?"

"I wanted him to get sloppy. That way, when I suddenly blew Mr. Jenkins off—an act that would undoubtedly make him feel abandoned and angry—he would devote all of his time to busting wayward students. And when he did, his disappointment at my sudden lack of interest would cause him to come down on Brad twice as hard. He's usually pretty lenient, you know?"

"Last year he caught me skipping," Taylor said, nodding in agreement. "I talked him out of telling Ms. Bates."

Alexia nodded. "He's a big believer in giving second chances. I couldn't risk him going soft on Brad. I needed him to come down with the full hammer of justice."

"Holy shit," Keegan breathed. "You're trying to get Brad expelled."

"My plan was to get him kicked out right before the prom."

"You think he'll care about the *prom?*"

Alexia rolled her eyes. "I think Brad's the type of boy who slacks off the entire year and then preys on his teachers' sympathies to get extra credit at the end. If he got kicked out a month before graduation, he'd have no chance to catch up at another school."

Keegan's eyes widened. "You mean … "

"He'd flunk senior year. It seemed a decent plan at the time. But now I see I let myself get greedy. I'll set this plan in motion right away."

"No. You can't!" Everyone turned to look at Kylie.

Alexia narrowed her eyes. "You *don't* want him kicked out of school?"

"We do," I said, stepping into a pool of moonlight. "But we want to send him off in style."

———

The excitement should have ended there, but it didn't. My phone started buzzing just as I was falling asleep. There was a short moment of panicking, when I thought I was in danger, and then I felt foolish for forgetting the obvious.

I'm always in danger.

I glanced across the room. Taylor was mumbling, so I knew he was asleep. I should have taken the call elsewhere. But I didn't, because in spite of everything, being close to him made me feel safe.

I pushed the green button.

"Danger hovers on the horizon," hissed the voice on the other end.

"What happened?" I whispered.

"The Queen has organized a search party."

"Headed up by the Traveling Trolls, or the Brigade of Backless Ladies?"

"You know who she appointed to lead it. You must know."

"I have a pretty good idea. But has Naeve risen to the occasion?"

"All too well. He's interrogating each of us before he leaves."

"Interrogating," I repeated, allowing the euphemism. Closing my eyes, I watched a scene unfold behind my lids: Naeve stood by in his regal armor while his favored courtier, Olorian, broke mountain trolls piece by piece. Beside them hovered the Lady Claremondes, my mother's lady-in-perpetual-waiting, who was hanging pixies from her noose.

"Has he come for you yet?" I asked.

"He'll have to catch me first." Illya laughed, a sound born of fear rather than amusement. "He suspects I know something. And he will stop at nothing to bring you back to Court safely."

"Safer dead than alive, I imagine."

"The Queen would not allow it."

"She may not be able to stop it this time." I paused,

pushing away my bitterness. My fear. "I am sorry to make you endure this treachery."

"It is not all suffering. The servants continue to bond. Even the centaurs and the naiads have put away their feud."

"The courtiers created the feud," I confessed, awed by the way my time in the human world had loosened my tongue. "They always create a feud when the servants become too friendly."

"The courtiers killed that naiad? But I thought—"

"You believed what you were meant to believe," I said. "One decade ago, the centaur and naiad servants planned an uprising against their masters. Unfortunately for them, the Lady Claremondes learned of their secret while lurking in the waters of the Selyphin."

"Slithery little snake."

"Indeed. It was she who dragged that naiad's corpse into the centaurs' forest quarters."

"But the girl had clearly been trampled."

"The girl was already dead when the Lady Claremondes found her. Poisoned by polluted waters, I'm afraid."

"But the trampling…"

"An effect the Lady Claremondes created by a rock-slide and simple glamour." I closed my eyes, unable to escape the memory of the girl, the way one bruise blended into the next, purple and yellow and black.

"But everyone believed it," Illya breathed, her voice laced with despair. "The centaurs became exiles among the servants."

"Until the naiads retaliated by leading that foal into waters too deep, inciting discord that spanned years."

"Why didn't you tell me? I could have warned them. I could have saved lives."

"Anyone who spoke of it was silenced."

"But Lady—"

"I was a coward, Illya."

"You were afraid," she said, excusing my transgressions. "We all were."

"I am still afraid. But I no longer let it stop me from doing what is right."

"Then you've completed your task? You know who the *bane of the darkness* is?"

"I have my suspicions." I peered out from under my blankets. Taylor had turned onto his stomach and was snoring into his pillow. "But suspicions are not enough to ... spirit someone away from his home. And his family. I need evidence."

"How will you get *evidence*?" Illya asked.

I thought it must not have sunk in yet, that I was walking among humans, engaging with them. *Touching them.*

"That, my darling, is the greatest part of all. In a little over a week, the local students are hosting a ball, where one boy will be crowned king of the school. After that ... " I closed my eyes, blocking out the sight of the sleeping mortal. "I'll be seeing you shortly."

16

TAYLOR

Friday came, and then I was trapped. Trapped in my least favorite room of the house. Trapped in one of a million forced, awkward meals.

In short, I was having dinner with my parents.

Lora sat beside me, a multicolored tapestry compared to the black-and-white photo that was my family. Teal eyes, blue veins, red lips. But it was her hair, crawling like fire toward the yellowed tablecloth, that had the power to burn away the façade of a happy home and reveal the house for what it was. A skeleton stuffed with forgotten artifacts, emitting an unnameable stench.

A carcass.

I knew she could sense my nervousness. My hands were so sweaty I'd dropped the ketchup twice. I couldn't stop bouncing my foot.

She poked me with her plastic fork.

That made me smile. She'd carried the utensil to every meal since her first dinner in my bedroom; and though an allergy to silverware wasn't something I'd ever heard of, stranger things had happened since her arrival. Like every time we touched, I felt the electric charge of a thunderstorm. And tonight she was wearing a mysteriously acquired dress, an emerald vintage cocktail dress that made her hair crackle and pop.

My eyes traveled from her dress, where they'd lingered without her permission, to the place settings laid out before us. The table was designed to seat six, so the four of us could have been arranged one on each side. But Mom had put Lora next to me, leaving one side of the table unoccupied.

No one was allowed to sit in Aaron's place.

"Well, this is nice." Mom sat across from us, disappearing into her hideous floral dress. She was shrinking, the way people did when they aged, but that was nothing compared to Dad's khaki shirt and pants. He looked like he was going to sink into the wallpaper.

Maybe he'll fall into the family room.

Then he'd be with his real family: the people who lived in the TV.

"It *is* nice," I said to Mom, wondering if lies were the glue that kept all families together.

"Thank you for inviting me," Lora chimed in.

Mom squinted, like she was seeing her for the first time. "You're welcome," she said. Then, silence. It seemed like she was searching for the right words to say: an *I've heard so much about you*, or a *Taylor tells me you two have caused quite a stir at Unity.* But she knew nothing, not even a whisper of Lora's influence in my life.

"I made your favorite," she said finally, smiling at the sloppy mess on her plate.

My favorite when I was in kindergarten, I thought, nodding anyway. Did all parents view their children this way, as if trapped in time? Could I return home covered in scars, a warrior, a junkie, and still be seen as the snowy-headed toddler who hated Brussels sprouts and wanted a squirrel for a pet?

"Thanks, Mom," I said.

I couldn't help but feel the tiniest hint of pleasure as I bit into my bun. The Sloppy Joe was Mom's personal recipe, with one small adjustment: the ground beef had been switched with vegan soy crumbles, to suit Lora's dietary restrictions. Only my father was unaware of the switch.

"My pleasure, sweetie." She glanced to the right, to the roll of wallpaper propped up against the wall.

Now? I thought, my eyes widening.

Mom nodded.

"Looks like you're redecorating," I squeaked. *Smooth. That didn't sound rehearsed at all.* I cleared my throat. "Dad?"

His eyes narrowed. I guessed it was difficult to focus on something that didn't feature a scrolling eight-hundred number. "You didn't fill him in?" he said to Mom, scowling.

Apparently, he couldn't see me at all.

Mom swallowed audibly. "We started talking about it. But—"

Dad threw his napkin onto the table. Unfortunately for him, it was a *napkin*, so it didn't make too much of an impact. "Damn it, Amelia. Every time, I have to—" He stopped when he glanced at Lora.

I shouldn't have brought her here.

Still, I felt grateful for her presence. She exuded a calmness that fell over everything. It muffled the anger, the unease. The pain.

"The matter is settled," Dad said in a softer tone, like he was a kindly grandpa and we'd all asked to hear about life in the Olden Days.

Spare me.

Mom kept looking at me, like, *Now's your cue.* But she hadn't briefed me on my lines, and she'd be sorry for it. I couldn't stand this ambiguity anymore.

My heart couldn't.

"Actually, I think it's time," I said, resisting the urge to push my hand against my chest. My heart felt like it was going to burst through my skin. I couldn't believe how badly it was hurting. "It's not like you couldn't put the room back if you had to, and in the meantime, it'll clear up space for you—"

"Put the room back?" Dad said. "How could we put the room back?"

"I'm not saying you would." I glanced at Mom, my

eyes saying, *Help me. Help me!* "I'm just saying, redecorating doesn't have to be permanent. It could just be—"

"We're not redecorating for fun. Jesus, Amelia." Dad shook his head. "We're selling the house."

My fork clattered to my plate. Really, I wanted to stab it into my chest. That would calm this throbbing pain, right? "*What?*"

Finally, Dad looked me in the eye. "We can't afford it. We can't justify keeping a house this size, now that—"

"We wanted to wait until you turned eighteen," Mom broke in. "But we just can't. As it is, your father won't be able to retire until … " She trailed off.

I couldn't believe it. I couldn't *process* it. They were selling the house. My house. My home. So what if I hadn't been living within its walls? I'd always believed I could come back if I wanted to.

In that moment, I realized the story I'd been telling myself about a happy family reunion was just that. A story.

A lie.

"Isn't there any other way?" I asked. Beneath the table, Lora's hand slid over mine. It should've made me feel safe, but it just made me angry. Why had I brought her here? How could I have been that stupid?

Dad's eyes shifted from me to Lora. I could tell he'd seen the movement of her arm by the way he frowned. I could tell, too, that he hated me for bringing her here.

For bringing both of us.

"Are you going to take me with you?" I managed. I

could hardly form proper sentences, but what did it matter? I was going to lose everything.

"Of course you'll be coming with us." Mom said it firmly, like maybe she was trying to convince herself. "You're seventeen," she added.

Oh, so that's why. You have a legal obligation to keep me. But I'll only be seventeen for a few more months.

I couldn't focus on her face. I kept watching Dad, studying his reaction to what I was saying. He was ignoring me, still staring at Lora. That told me all I needed to know.

He wanted to leave me behind.

Why wouldn't he?

It might've made sense to keep the house when Aaron and I were living in it. But now, with just the two of them ... They were all that remained of our family.

I was nothing.

"Where will you go?" I asked. It made no sense to say "we." Why prolong the inevitable?

"Not far," Mom said, because Dad was busy looking at Lora. His focus on her was getting creepy. "We just want something smaller. More practical. Don't worry about the details."

"Why would he worry?" Dad said. "When does he ever worry about anything?"

That was about all I could take.

"I get it." I stood up, pushing my chair against the wall. Lora made no move to follow. She seemed mesmerized, watching my father watch her. "Sell the house. I'll take care of myself. Everyone will be perfectly happy." I shoved the chair out of my way. "No one will worry about anyone else."

"Taylor," Mom said. Not *Of course we worry about you.* Not *I care about you enough to keep you.* Just my name. Just *Taylor.*

"Let him go, Amelia," said Dad.

"He's our son."

"He's made absolutely no effort to be a part of this family!"

I closed my eyes. How could he hurt me like this? No matter what I did, it was wrong.

Finally, Lora stood. At least she worried about me.

But she's leaving too.

"It appears," she said in a soft, low voice, "that dysfunction comes in many shapes and sizes. It was foolish to think myself unique."

Both my parents were staring at her now. She stared back, unafraid. "Since you have shared such insight with me, I will return the favor in kind," she said, leaning in. My dad actually jerked away. It was beautiful. "Love is a living entity. If you forsake it, it will leave you."

She turned away.

But Dad grabbed her arm. He looked possessed. "I know you," he said. "How do I know you?"

I stepped forward, prepared to knock him out if I had to. But Lora pulled herself out of his grip with no trouble at all. "You must have mistaken me for someone else."

———

I spread out a blanket beneath Unity's fattest oak and gestured for Lora to join me. She did, sitting beside me and gazing up at the sky. Fifteen minutes ago, I'd ushered her out of my parents' house, creating the façade that I was walking her home. After the weirdness at dinner, I wasn't taking any chances with my parents figuring out our little scheme. But once we'd reached the end of the street, I'd known I wouldn't be ready to go back there for a while.

Maybe ever.

I sat in silence, fraying the cuticles on my hand. I didn't want to talk about my family. I didn't really want to talk about anything, but I felt something needed to be said.

"Sorry," I mumbled, turning away.

"Don't be." Lora touched my back. "If you met my family, you wouldn't feel so strange." Her breath was warm on my neck. "What you see as imperfection draws me to you. People grow languorous from their joy. They derive strength from their pain."

It was a weird thing to say. I didn't think my pain gave way to anything but more pain. Lying down on my back, I guided her along so that she lay next to me. The sky framed her face, and I was suddenly filled with the clarity that whatever she was, she was not an angel. She hadn't come to save me. Maybe she'd come to destroy me.

Still, I wanted her.

"Tell me what you want." The words were out of my mouth before I could stop them. Now all I could do was wait and hope that something besides her breath filled the air.

She appeared to consider the request. "Sometimes the hardest thing is finding the right question to ask."

"I thought that was a pretty good one."

She liked that. Laughing, she draped her upper body across my chest. Her thigh pressed into my leg. I could feel its heat, could feel how close it was to sliding over me, and I wanted to pull her on top of me. My anger at my parents hadn't subsided, and it made me feel brave, but beneath that was the overwhelming fear that she could crush me if she rejected me tonight.

I waited.

Above our heads, leaves twirled and waved. I watched them move in the air, marveling at the passage of time since Lora had arrived. The days used to pass slowly. Now I could barely keep track of the weeks as they flew by. Prom was only a week away. Then finals and graduation.

I didn't want to think about what would happen after that.

Lora's lips were close now, pulling my attention away from the trees. All of her was close, and I tried to convince myself that it meant she liked me. She wouldn't be lying here, so close, if she didn't. Would she? She wouldn't keep crawling toward me, the way I literally fell toward her, unless she felt something too. If I could just kiss her— God, if she would only kiss me—I could finally be sure.

"Dangerous game, beautiful boy," she said when I touched her hair.

"I'm not afraid."

Our lips inched closer, as if pulled by invisible strands in the air. I struggled with my conflicting thoughts. What if she was waiting for me to make a move? What if she already knew it would never happen? Would I waste away in misery, never knowing the taste of her lips?

"Come here," I said, my hand on her face.

She kissed my palm. "You're angry," she said, moving her mouth over my fingers. It felt so good, I thought I might die right then. "You're in pain," she murmured. "And you seek to replace that pain with other things. But it is not what you need from me now."

"How would you know?" I was devastated by the weight of her words.

"Because I know you, Taylor Alder. Haven't you figured that out?"

I sighed, not knowing how to feel. "You don't," I said. "I haven't let you."

"Then let me."

Unpleasant warmth spread through my chest. "I want to." I swallowed, pushing back the confession that was trying to spill out of me. "But I think you'll hate me."

"If you think I could hate you, then I'm the one who has kept myself hidden."

I sat very still, feeling brave and fearful and reckless. *Don't say it. Don't say it. Whatever you do, do not say it.* "I killed my brother."

I couldn't read her face, and it terrified me.

Finally, she said, "Tell me."

"I got my first set of paints when I was eleven," I said, feeling my mind separate from my body. I needed it this way. When I spoke, it was as if a stranger inhabited my body while the real me sat off to the side, listening. "By the time I was in high school, they were calling me a prodigy. I could look at anything and paint it perfectly. But I could never do it in my head. All these local artists were looking at my stuff and raving, but instead of enjoying it, I kept beating myself up because I couldn't draw from memory." I turned onto my side, away from her.

Lora brushed my arm with her fingertips. I couldn't believe she would still touch me after what I'd said. But it gave me courage, in the midst of feeling utterly disgusted with myself.

"I got obsessed with it. I'd stare at something for hours and then try to draw it from memory, but it never worked. Then my dad started in on me about it. He loves giving me shit."

"Why?"

He hates me.

"I don't know." I shrugged. "Maybe he thinks it'll make me try harder. But it just made me think I wasn't good enough."

More like useless.

"Aaron was so good about the whole thing. Most kids would've been jealous, but he wanted to help me. He got it into his head that we just had to create the right image, something exciting enough for my mind to remember."

I laughed, closing my eyes. "He'd tear the kitchen apart, using ketchup and oatmeal to make himself look like a monster. He'd burrow into the flowerbeds. One time he got caught in the attic crawl space, even though I told him I wouldn't be able to see up there. But there was one place I wouldn't let him go."

I waited, in case she wanted to stop me. Go back in time. Forget.

But she didn't.

"You know that pine tree in our yard?" I said. "In the winter, when everything else is bare, that tree stays perfectly green. Aaron used to say if he could just get to the top, right after it snowed, he'd be able to create the perfect image. But—"

"You wouldn't let him?"

"It was too dangerous. Then, there was this day." I covered my face with my arm. "This awful, stupid day two years ago, when this *asshole* at school snuck that stuff into my food, you know, that shit that makes you throw up? Just to mess with me."

"Brad?"

"Actually his older brother, Buddy. I basically puked all over my clothes and completely freaked out. Our washing machine had been broken all week, and Mom was afraid to call someone to fix it because Dad was always stressed about money. I came home from school and I was so pissed. The first thing I heard was Aaron crying, which meant Mom had been crying. Which meant Dad had threatened to leave again. And I just … I messed up."

"You let Aaron climb the tree?"

"I thought it would make him happy. But the second he ran out of the house, I went after him, yelling that I was kidding." I dropped my head into my hands. "It wasn't enough."

"He made it to the top before you reached him?"

"No." Part of me wished he had. Part of me wished I hadn't seen the whole thing. "He'd made it halfway up when I came out the front door. He actually turned and smiled at me; he was so happy. And I was screaming like a crazy person, demanding he come down."

"But he didn't?"

"No."

"And he fell?"

I waited a beat before answering. "He was almost to the top when the branch snapped. He fell to the ground like a rock. It happened so fast, there was no way I could've caught him." I blinked, horrified at the thought of crying in front of Lora. "I just stood there, staring at him. He looked like he was sleeping. I kept telling myself, maybe he is sleeping."

Tears spilled over, pain stinging me in my deepest places. I felt like I'd been split open, my insides pouring out onto the ground. Now she could see me. Now she knew. Now she could hurt me, break me, hate me. Now I needed her even more.

"I still visit him every Sunday," I said, curling in on myself. "I've gone early, while you're sleeping. And every time, it reminds me I shouldn't be staying with them."

"Why?"

"Seeing me just reminds them of what happened. It's the reason I moved into the garage, you know? To give them a break. But it wasn't enough."

"Taylor."

"If I'd left, maybe they could've moved on. They wouldn't have stayed in a house they didn't need. They wouldn't be in debt."

"*Taylor.*"

"He's right to blame me. He knew how much it would cost to have kids. It's why he never wanted us in the first place."

"Taylor, you're seventeen years old!"

"So?"

"So, they are the adults. They are the ones who made those decisions."

"It's not like that in my family. They need me—"

"They need you to be a teenager. They need you to have a childhood. It is their job to take care of you, like it was their job to take care of him."

"It doesn't work like that."

"It should. It can. They were supposed to take care of you," she said again, and it felt wonderful, just the idea of it. But it hurt, too, because they hadn't taken care of me. Not in the way I'd needed.

"They don't want to," I said.

"Then let me. It's not your job to take care of the house, Taylor. It was not your job to raise Aaron."

"But—"

"I'm not saying it was their fault, what happened. But I am saying it wasn't yours. Taylor, look at me."

I turned to face her, though it scared me. The look she gave me was not pity. Somewhere in there, she recognized my pain as if she'd experienced it herself. Maybe our shared pain could bond us. I had a vision, strange and startling, of the two of us wrapped together in seaweed. But as I moved toward her, aching to be that close, to let her sew up the parts of me that I'd opened for her, she slipped from my grasp like a mermaid.

"Trust that I will be whatever it is you need of me," she said, "so long as it doesn't compromise my being. But I cannot deny the feeling that what you need now is a friend."

"I have friends," I said, trying to turn again.

She took my hands in hers, holding them against her heart. "Not like this."

———

That night the story was my obsession. I needed Lora to confide in me the way I'd confided in her. If I could just learn a little more about the place she'd left behind, I might find a way to change her mind about leaving me.

Or maybe I could change her mind about going back alone.

She was sitting on the bed, her back against the wall, and my head was in her lap. She hadn't even asked me to join her. I'd just crawled there, unashamed. Something had shifted between us, but I wasn't ready to put it into words. I didn't want to scare it away.

"The princess followed in her mother's footsteps," she murmured, stroking my hair, "gathering the desperate creatures of Faerie like cracked and broken shells. The symmetry of their rebellions was not lost on her, and she wondered if, in the beginning, Virayla had believed her efforts to be just as noble. Would the princess someday look back at the movement she'd inspired and feel horrified at the monstrosity it had become? Was there a way to avoid corruption, or was every noble revolution destined to mutate into bloody, senseless warfare? Doubts plagued her mind but she plodded on, pushing them aside as she searched for allies."

As Lora spoke, she casually lifted my hand to her stomach. I slid my fingers under her shirt, over her navel. It was the first time I'd touched any part of her that was hidden by clothing. She didn't stop me, but she didn't encourage me to go further, either. There was a part of me that felt she couldn't, even if she wanted to. There was a genuine barrier between us, something I didn't quite understand. Had her family taught her to fear anyone outside their cult? Had they taught her to fear being touched?

I held my hand still for a minute, resting it on her stomach. Her skin was so soft, it killed me not to be constantly feeling it. But I was closer than I'd ever been, and I wasn't going to fuck it up if I could help it. I needed her too badly.

"At first the oppressed servants of the Unseelie Court looked on her with suspicion and scorn. She was the daughter of the Queen. Surely her words were being twisted to fool them. But as time went by, tensions ever escalating between the courts, they began to listen. It had been so long since they'd allowed a glimmer of hope to enter their hearts, so long since they'd even had the luxury to dream, that the moment hope returned, they could not ignore it. It consumed them."

She drew in a shaky breath as I slid my hand up, taking her shirt with it. "So it began, quiet and slithering like a snake beneath a stone. All that could be heard of their plans was the pitter-pattering of feet across the leaf-strewn forest, or the whispering of muted voices in hollows and caves. They met in places the nobles refused to go: murky marshes, dank tunnels beneath the earth, and patches of land surrounded by the sea, casting intricate spells to tie the tongues of those who might betray their secrets."

Tongues. The word hovered in my brain. Quickly, as smooth as I could possibly be, I brushed my lips across her stomach, tasting the tiniest bit.

She let out a sigh that was pure deliciousness. Her

hands went into my hair, either to bring me closer or hold me back. Again, I waited for a signal.

"What happens next?" I asked. We both knew I wasn't talking about the story.

But she ignored the hint. "Their first task was to relearn each others' cultures. Each group took their turn telling stories of their rites and rituals, and how their lives had been cruelly altered by the Court. In this way, they learned to appreciate their differences, and to acknowledge their common hardships. And they celebrated, as more and more of them came together and danced in the way that only immortals in physical bodies can. Centaurs stepped from the depth of the forest to dance beside nymphs in the light of the moon. Elves carried gnomes and dwarves to the highest branches, while sprites danced with pixies in the glowing sapphire sky.

"Then, without prompting, these servants realized what the princess had suspected for some time: the Unseelie Court was an abomination to the natural world, and to freedom, and to life. It had to be disbanded, so that all could learn to live together in harmony. The nobles had to be removed from power."

Hmmm. Removed.

I wondered if I could turn that into a sign. I imagined I could, but probably not one that Lora was trying to send. My fingers grazed the bottom of her bra. She exhaled again and said "Mmm," in this way that made me want to rip off her clothes. And mine. But with this intense desire came frustration. Would it always be this way? Would I always be forced to push at her limits, never knowing if she wanted the things I wanted? Was she really not interested, or did she think it was wrong to be with me?

I wanted her so badly my entire body was buzzing.

Just then, she said, "These possibilities buzzed within each of them, drifting through the land until even the most desolate found hope."

I slid my arm under her and pulled her closer. She didn't pull away, just continued her story, dipping her head down to speak in my ear. "There were thousands upon thousands of them, meeting in different places so as never to be caught. As they stared across the crowds, they realized they could win this battle based on numbers alone."

I closed my eyes, listening. Touching. My fingers slid down.

"This is the trick to revolution," she said, and her breathing quickened. For a second, I thought she nipped at my ear. But it happened so fast, I could've imagined it. "Yes, leaders play their parts, as do meetings and strategies. But the truth of it is, the corrupt and the truly evil will always be smaller in number. They will use cleverness to tame and lies to separate, but once people realize their commonality, their shared pain and their shared desires, they are, quite literally, unstoppable."

Unstoppable, I thought, sliding my hand beneath the hem of her jeans.

That's when she stopped me.

17

ELORA

Night cast her cloak over the land, but there were those who refused to sleep. We gathered in secret beneath the waning moon. Clad in the purest black, we attempted to creep across the grass toward the school. Unfortunately, Unity had experienced three unexpected days of showers, and the field was a muddy mess.

Terrible inconvenience for the soccer team, I thought with a smile.

It had been nearly impossible for them to practice in all that water. They'd slipped and fallen, muddying themselves like hogs, and thus had been utterly unprepared for a very important game. The field would dry, the grass would emerge once more, but the team had lost their chance to go to State.

Pity.

It was nice to know I could manipulate the elements in the human world as easily as in Faerie.

My foot made a sucking sound as I pulled it from a carnivorous puddle. Kylie hurried along beside me, following the cement path. Taylor and Keegan were farther off, darting from tree to tree. The rest of the students wouldn't be arriving for an hour.

I could hardly wait.

Kylie's voice broke into my thoughts. "I can't believe you got the keys to the school."

"I pretty much have a standing appointment on Fridays with Principal Jade. Yesterday, she went to get us some coffee, and … " I let Kylie figure out the rest. It wasn't as if I could tell her the truth.

Who needs keys when you can open doors with magic?

Kylie stopped by the ramp at the back of the school, waiting for the boys to tire of their game. "I'm just glad I didn't have to ask Alexia to steal the keys from Janky Jim."

I sat down on the stairs. "Would that have been a problem?"

"Not really. She owes me a favor, but I want to save it for something good."

"Why does she owe you a favor?"

Kylie looked up at the sky. "I don't hold it against her that she keeps us a secret. I don't. But she acts like prom only matters to her." Purple clouds drifted in front of the moon. The reprieve from light seemed to lend her courage. "It's my prom too. I know it's meaningless, but … "

"There's nothing wrong with caring about something, regardless of what it means to other people."

Kylie nodded, momentarily distracted by the movement out on the field. Keegan had darted across the grass and was hiding behind the tree nearest to the school. Taylor was nowhere to be seen. But I could feel him watching; his eyes burned into me.

"I don't want to care," Kylie said. "But I do. I mean, I want to show up in this killer outfit and dance, and complain about how crappy it is even though I'm having a good time. So much has happened this year..." She paused, staring off into the trees. "I just wish she'd support me. Support us, you know? None of those other people matter."

"Would you feel better if she weren't crowned queen? I bet we could entice the crowd to vote differently."

At the very least, I could alter the results with glamour.

"No." Kylie shook her head. "I don't want to hurt her. I *want* her to win. Maybe that's sick, but it's really important to her. She needs to be loved. Her parents ignore her, you know?" She pulled a small gold object from her pocket. "She started smoking just to see if anyone would care." Kylie flicked her thumb and a flame jumped forth.

I took the lighter for a moment. "Did anyone care?" I asked, enthralled by humanity's ability to harness the power of fire.

"Just me. I keep stealing these from her, but it doesn't matter. She's addicted now." Kylie looked up, making sure Keegan was a good distance away before continuing. "One time she accidentally took too many sleeping pills and her mom didn't even notice. The *maid* found her in her room."

I wasn't given the chance to respond. As if sensing

the secrecy of the conversation, Keegan appeared before us. He bowed low, tipping an imaginary hat. "Perimeter is secure, ma'am."

"Very good." I nodded respectfully as Taylor arrived on the steps. "Everybody ready?"

"As ready as I will be," Keegan said. "Are you sure this is the best place to have this meeting? We spend too much time here as it is."

"It's the perfect place." I stepped in front of the double doors so they couldn't see what I was doing. Holding my left hand over the door, I unlocked it with the slightest bit of magic, while making a twisting movement with my right. Even with real magic, it often came down to sleight of hand. "We're trying to convince them they can take back the school. What better way to boost their confidence than to literally take over the school in a way that none of their social betters have been able to do?"

"Fair enough," Keegan agreed. "One more question."

"Yes?"

"Why are you doing this?"

Because I'm trying to smoke out a tyrant, I thought, but that wasn't really true anymore. Ever since my first day at Unity, I'd had a sneaking suspicion of who the school's biggest tyrant was. And by prom night, I'd have proof. So why *was* I still doing this?

"Because it's the right thing to do," I said, and felt a little thrill at the fact that I *could* say it.

"Be serious," Keegan said.

"I am serious. Equality doesn't work if it's only for some people."

"I'm going to make a bumper sticker out of that."

"If one group of people isn't free, none of us are." I opened the door for my companions. "It took me too long to see that. Come on."

Together we lifted the hoods of our sweatshirts and slipped inside the building, keeping to the left side of the wall. We had just slunk past the glass trophy cases, and were making our way across the hall when a sharp beeping sounded at our backs.

I spun around. "What was that?"

"Oh, God," Kylie said. She followed the sound to a little white rectangle tucked away in a corner, between the left-hand door and the trophy case. Hidden.

"What is that?" I asked.

"Oh, God."

"Kylie?"

"It's a security system. An *alarm*. Oh, crap."

"What's a security system?" The wall beeped again, twice this time.

"A security system requires a security code that you have to type in or it goes off." Taylor's voice was pinched.

"But we're the only ones who will hear it."

Three pairs of eyes landed on me. It was clear that this time my lack of technological knowledge would not be deemed "cute."

"It sends a signal to the cops," Taylor explained. "I think

it does. I'm not sure, exactly. I didn't think schools had them."

"Neither did I," I said sadly. "What do we do?" I placed my hand over the rectangle, trying to stifle the beeps, but I had no idea how it worked. The rectangle began to scream.

"We get the hell out of here," said Keegan, touching his sister's arm.

"No," I protested, but the three of them were halfway through the doors. "Wait. People are going to arrive. They're all going to—"

"Be arrested," said Taylor. He stepped back through the doors.

"We can't let that happen to them. They'll never trust us again. We invited them here."

"Lora." His voice was soft. I didn't remember him coming so close, but he was right there, his hand on my arm. "I don't know what else we can do."

"Wait," I said, allowing him to lead me outside. "Wait."

When we reached the steps, I stopped, staring back into the school. "That's a security system. Unity has a security guard. Maybe he's the one who gets the signal." I held out my hands, exasperated. "Isn't that possible?"

"Maybe," said Keegan. "But what difference does it make? We can't stop him any more than the cops."

"Maybe we can." I smiled at Kylie. "Hey, I hear Alexia owes you a favor."

———

Alexia must not have kicked her sleeping pill habit. She was incredibly difficult to rouse. When she finally awoke, after the fourth desperate phone call, she did not react well to Kylie's inquiries.

"Why the hell do you need to know who responds to the security system?"

Kylie looked at me. We were sharing the phone between us, huddled in the corner of the park, while the boys scanned the lot for signs of police. For a moment I expected Kylie to create some elaborate story.

I was surprised to hear her forgo creativity.

"Because we set it off, and now we need to know if we're going to be arrested."

"What?" Alexia's voice was loud and fierce. It sounded like she knocked something over.

"I know it sounds crazy," Kylie said, "but we need to know if the signal goes to the police or Mr. Jenkins, and we need to know soon. Can you please just help me and yell at me later?"

Alexia did not respond immediately. "How much time has passed since you set off the alarm?"

"Five minutes. An hour. I don't know!"

"Kylie."

"Okay. Like, six minutes. Does it even matter?"

"It would have mattered if you'd turned the thing off in time."

"We can't turn it off. We don't know the code."

"Four four four two."

"Are you kidding me?"

"I went to lunch with Jim the week it was installed."

"So it was installed by him. Wait, you went to lunch—"

"Not only was the system installed by Mr. Jenkins," Alexia broke in, "but it was installed without permission."

"What?" Kylie and I said together. The sound of Kylie's shriek masked the sound of my whisper.

"He's gotten it into his head that he deserves more responsibility. That the school takes him for granted. He told them they needed a security system—you know, in case someone has a hankering for wall-ball in the middle of the night—but they basically told him to screw off. Security is expensive."

"Baby," Kylie hissed, "I don't need the details. I just need the general idea."

Silence.

"Please?"

Alexia sighed loudly. "The details are important. The administrators may well have been wise to deny Mr. Jenkins more responsibility, but he is incredibly gifted when it comes to wiring. His family had a security business for years before some conglomerate forced them out of business."

"That's terrible," Kylie said without enthusiasm.

"It *is* terrible. He went from being his own boss to making, like, eight cents an hour babysitting assholes."

"Tragic," Kylie agreed.

"He's had a bit of a renegade in him since all that happened, and he's been looking for a way to get back in the game. So when the School Board shut down his idea, it was the last straw. He installed his own system in the middle of the night and hid it so no one would see. I think his plan is to intercept some bandit on the run from the law and receive the key to the city. The man watches too much TV."

"That's a heart-wrenching story," said Kylie, "but now he's on his way to bust *us* and get half the senior class expelled."

"Well." Alexia huffed into the phone. "And here I thought I had the most interesting story of the night."

"Okay," Kylie said, almost dropping the phone in her exasperation, "I'll tell you everything. I'll do anything you ask. I just need you to come down here and intercept Janky Jim and get rid of him."

"Oh, is that all?"

"I know it's a lot to ask—"

"More *crazy* than anything else."

"But it's really important to me, and if you give me a chance to explain—"

"Kylie. I'm, like, two minutes away."

"What?"

"All gussied up and ready to win that Oscar."

"How did you—we've been on the phone the whole time. Do you *sleep* in your clothes?"

"Sweet pea, I'm the Student Body President and Homecoming Queen. I can get dressed while I'm driving."

"But how did you know?" Kylie asked, her breath coming out in little puffs.

Alexia made a popping sound with her lips. "I always know when you need me. Go turn off the alarm."

———

Mr. Jim Jenkins had only just turned off his pickup when Alexia came running across the field from the other side of the school. Her heels squished as they dug into the wet grass. Mud sloshed over her designer jeans. But she didn't falter until she reached the stone steps and sat down.

The school was dark. More clouds had settled in front of the moon, and the four of us took refuge behind a voluptuous oak. We could hear Alexia tapping her shoe on the cement, but we could not see her through the trunk of the tree.

A moment later, Mr. Jenkins trudged across the grass.

Alexia immediately began to cry. I did not know whether tears actually streamed down her face, but the sobs escaping her lips were metered to perfection.

She's done this before.

Climbing up the trunk, I peered through the thick foliage and watched Mr. Jenkins sit down. The pants of his dung-brown uniform inched up, revealing mismatched socks.

"Miss Mardsen?" he asked tentatively. His hand lingered a moment above her knee before he placed it in his lap. Tufts of silver hair stuck out from under his cap.

"I'm sorry," Alexia said, erupting in fresh sobs. "I'm so sorry. I didn't know what else to do."

"I'm not sure I understand what you did," Mr. Jenkins said after a moment. "You don't mean to say…" He glanced at the school doors.

"I set off the alarm. I needed someone to talk to and…you're the only one I have."

"Oh my." Mr. Jenkins leaned back, distancing himself from the situation. "Miss Mardsen, that was a very unwise thing to do."

"I told you, you can call me Alexia."

His face softened. "Alexia. What happened?"

"Remember that asshole boyfriend I was telling you about? The one that's a *total loser*?"

"I seem to recall something, yes."

"I just found out he's been sleeping with my *best friend*. I mean, can you think of anything more horrifying?"

Mr. Jenkins struggled for words. "That's terrible. I'm very sorry."

"*I'm* sorry. I can't believe I wasted four months of my life on that—that creep!" She hid behind her hands.

"But I don't understand, Miss…Alexia. You came to the school because—"

"I wanted to reach you," she said between muffled sobs. "I knew you'd come if you heard the alarm. I know it was selfish. I just felt so lost and I wanted to talk to somebody."

"Well, that's—well, I wouldn't call it selfish. But it

wasn't entirely wise. I didn't give you a key to the school with this in mind."

"I know," Alexia exclaimed. "You were just helping me get that book I forgot before midterms. And when I think about the trouble this might get you into, all because of my stupid problems, I just feel so awful." She buried her face in her knees, howling in anguish.

"Now, now, don't do that." He patted her back timidly. "It's okay. Nobody heard but me, and it all worked out just fine. Listen. Would you like to go get a soda and talk all this out?"

Alexia lifted her head. "That would be nice."

Mr. Jenkins rose and locked the doors of the school before he and Alexia walked to their cars. Behind the tree, we waited in silence. When the cars disappeared down the darkened street, we emerged. Twenty minutes later, the first of the invitees arrived.

We let them in through the window.

———

The crowd was a ruffled bunch as I led them down the hall. I was pleased to see that they had, for the most part, dressed in black. When we reached the auditorium doors, Kylie held the door open so they could pass through. Taylor ushered them to their seats and Keegan stood by, doing an impromptu dance.

"What's with the dress code, anyway?" Kylie asked when the students were seated. She gestured to her black sweatshirt and tiered-lace skirt, the latter of which she wore over jeans.

"Stealth," I said with a perfectly straight face.

"You did it for your own amusement," said Keegan. He smoothed his black tracksuit.

I smiled. I got the feeling that he, like myself, viewed clothing as costume. "Possibly," I said. "But the most important reason is to promote a feeling of unity. We are divided from one another by the false idea that we have nothing in common. Dressing in the same color, though a small detail, creates the feeling that we do in fact share commonality."

"Tricksy," Keegan replied.

Beside him, his sister fretted. "I hope Alexia's all right."

"I hope she keeps Jim away long enough." Taylor tossed a glance my way.

I caught it and held on for a moment. "He'd have to walk around the entire school and peer into these windows, which, if you haven't noticed, have curtains covering them at night."

"Oh, he'd do it," Taylor said.

"He's shifty," Keegan agreed.

"This is quite a turn-out." I tallied the crowd for the third time. "Ready to take your places?"

"Yes, sir." Keegan gave a dramatic salute.

"Good. Scatter yourselves amongst them."

Keegan and Kylie entered the auditorium through the main doors. Taylor followed me down the hall, toward the auditorium's back entrance. "This is crazy," he said.

"All the more reason we should be doing it. Will the lighting be easy?"

"Piece of cake. I did tech last year on *Singing in the Rain*."

I just nodded. I sensed that he had more to say.

"I actually considered trying out," he said after a minute. "But I figured I'd suck, so I offered to do lights instead." He shrugged the memory away. "I'll frame you in soft light."

"So I appear to them as a dream." I opened the back-door to the auditorium.

Taylor stepped halfway through the door, stopping in front of me. "You appeared to me that way." He slid his fingers down a strand of my hair, revealing a leaf hiding there.

"The moonlight suits me." I tucked the leaf behind his ear.

"Do you want me to raise the curtain?"

"I can do it."

"It'll take me a minute to get to the lighting booth."

"That's all right."

Taylor paused, glancing at my lips like he wanted to kiss me. Nowadays, I got that impression from him most of the time. More startling still was the feeling that I wanted to kiss him too. Of course, I couldn't act on it.

Why are you doing this? Keegan's voice asked in my mind.

"I'll see you soon," I said to Taylor, looking away.

He slipped past me, heading to the balcony. I went in the opposite direction. I was almost to the stage when the curtain began to lift of its own accord—at least, it appeared that way. I was confident that Taylor had not yet reached his post and would not see it happening. I wanted the curtain to rise in one swift movement, fast enough to startle the onlookers. I couldn't trust hands to do this.

Even my own.

Now every eye was on the stage, trying to spy me in the shadows. Lights were lit about the room, but none upon the stage just yet. Then it all changed. The lights in the room went out and Taylor turned a soft pink spotlight on me. I felt a fluttering in my stomach.

Relax. You've done this before.

But never for humans.

I stepped to the front of the stage, welcoming the visitors into my dream. "Hello friends, strangers … everything in between." I spoke in a clear voice, letting the sound resonate throughout the room. "Some of you know me as Lora. Some of you may have heard other names for me." I curled my lip, watching them glance at one another, whispering. "Perhaps I have heard names for you as well. It seems, at times, the sole purpose of Unity's elite is to brand us with identities that could define us for the rest of our lives. To be perfectly honest, that doesn't sit well with me."

Another pause, carefully crafted, as the invitees raised their eyebrows and shifted in their seats.

"Now, let's face it. Identity itself cannot be ignored. Identity determines who we are. Yet in this world of a million possibilities, we are led to believe that every choice we make is a reflection of our identity. Each time we choose a brand of carbonated sugar water, we are judged for it. Each time we patronize a franchise at the mall, someone else gives us a name. But identity is not the summation of our tiniest choices. It is a combination of our most basic beliefs, our actions, and our dreams. It is formed and reformed every day." I leaned in, as if sharing a delicious secret. "Identity is the reason we are here."

The whispering stopped.

"This elusive concept, which should be treated as an ongoing process of discovery, is used by a small minority to make us feel we are not deserving of the most basic human rights: love, acceptance, self-worth. Identity is used by the beloved to separate themselves from the rest, using rules that they themselves create. Who can give me an example of an identity deemed unacceptable by the elite?"

"Gay!" Keegan offered gleefully from the back of the room.

A couple of people laughed. Several others tittered. But the majority of the crowd remained silent, shifting uncomfortably in their seats.

He tried again. "Fat!" He patted his belly and plodded on before the laughter lost its momentum. "Or chubby. Chunky. Hefty." He grinned sheepishly. "I've heard 'em all. Husky."

"Poor," Taylor yelled from his place in the balcony. Several people turned in his direction.

While their heads were turned, a girl in the back

found her voice. "Dorky," she called out, and immediately tried to duck behind her voluminous glasses.

Someone across the way stood up, adding, "Ditzy."

And just like that, the girls took over the room. One yelled "Slutty," while another offered "Prude." The din grew louder as more joined in, and just when the clamor grew too great to distinguish any words, I brought them back.

"Exactly," I said, my voice booming over the crowd. "The longer we are given to think on it, the longer the list will be. In the created social order of high school, we are required to project very specific identities in order to be accepted. Now, I don't know about you, but I'm *sick* of trying to fit in."

I paused, letting the gravity of the words sink in. Half the crowd had risen to their feet, and these enthusiasts were nodding.

"I'm sick of trying to mold myself into someone else's definition of acceptable, beautiful, valuable. I know I'm valuable. Why must I spend every day of my life proving it to other people? And at night, as I lie in bed, I think about the efforts I made that day to fit into an impossibly narrow standard, and I feel like *I'm living a lie*."

Living a lie as a human. Living a lie as a princess. After all, what is royalty but a social invention? An imaginary title? It only has power because people believe in it.

"But now I'm done. I'm taking back my life and I'm taking back this school. And I need your help."

"What can we do?" The voice was so soft I barely heard

it. When I located its source, I sincerely questioned my perception. Gordon Grayson, the small boy from the Merry-Straight Alliance, who'd never so much as uttered a word in any of our meetings (who had, in fact, ignored my greetings each morning when I passed him on the way to math class), had spoken from his place in the front row. His pointy chin was tilted upward, an arrow aimed at my face, and he pressed his arms firmly into his armrests as he waited for my reply.

"We can do anything we want."

Gordon sniffed, turning his head away.

"Well, answer me this," I said. "When you received your invitation, did you think anyone would show up?"

He looked at me in silence.

I tried again. "Did you think there was any chance we would actually get into the school tonight, or did you think we were being overly optimistic? Foolhardy?"

Gordon clutched the sides of his chair, his knuckles whitening under the strain. "I thought . . ." He cleared his throat. "I thought it was probably a scheme to get us in trouble."

I smiled for him alone. "An elaborate scheme to punish you for believing in the possibility of change?"

His face reddened.

"Not surprising," I said quickly. "It is easier to believe we are being misled than to believe in our own power, isn't it? But we did it. We broke into the school without breaking a window or a lock."

"You did it," Gordon said.

"And you came." I turned to the people next to him.

"And you came, and you came. If it was this easy to come together, think of what we can accomplish with the slightest bit of effort. Tonight, all you had to do was show up to learn that so many people feel the way you feel and want to make a change. Think of what you can do tomorrow, next week, next month. Think of the power our numbers have if we put them toward a cause that benefits us all."

"Like the prom?" Taylor called out.

"The prom," I said with practiced indignation, "is just another chance for them to put us in our place. Or is it?" I grinned. "As someone who has only been in public school for a short while, it is easy for me to see the ridiculousness of such a ritual. We dress up in elaborate ensembles, are forced to pair off into perfect units of two, and prance about like peacocks—all of it, it seems, in preparation for a party that never comes. But perhaps we can gain more from this experience. Perhaps we can use it as an example of the way we will access our collective power for the rest of our lives.

"The principal has taken it upon herself to keep people with certain identities from attending the prom. Just as in the past, it has been decided for us which identities are appropriate and which are not. But you have the chance to stand up to these prejudices, to make it known that you won't tolerate injustices based upon real or invented identities. You have the chance to tell Unity that regardless of someone else's perception, you deserve the same rights as your peers. And to accomplish this great feat..." I looked out at their hopeful faces. "All you have to do is show up."

18

TAYLOR

The week before prom, both Brad and Lora were elected to the Prom Court. That Friday, Brad caught up to us at lunch. He swaggered across the grass and leaned against our tree, hands in his pockets. James Dean style, I guess. And he looked down at Lora like she was the only one there, giving her that patented sleaze-ball grin.

"Hey babe."

Oh, God. Did he really just say that?

"Hello, Brad." Lora's eyes sparkled the way they did when she was excited. Before her, I never thought anyone's eyes could actually glisten. "What can I do for you?" she asked.

For a minute, they played out this old-timey movie scene where two lovers meet for the first time. Coy glances. Little smirks. I thought I was going to be sick.

"I figured it out," Brad said.

"You did?"

"Okay, not at first. But after that meteor shower, I started thinking about the stuff you said. About iron, and … " He stuck out his hand. A ragged dandelion drooped over his fist, still dangling its roots. Smeared across the petals...

"Is that blood?" Kylie's eyes stretched to their limit.

Brad glared at her before turning back to Lora. "Blood has iron in it. Iron comes from stars." He beamed. "A flower that shines with the light of the stars."

What an idiot. Does he really think she'll fall for that?

"You did it," Lora said, climbing to her feet.

Um. What?

"I did it," Brad repeated dumbly. Everything about him was stupid. God, I hated him and his stupid dumb face.

"So now you have to go out with me," he said.

"I have to," Lora agreed, taking the blood-speckled weed. She slid it into the pouch she wore around her neck. "Well done."

"So I'll see you tomorrow." Brad grinned.

"Tomorrow it is."

No. She can't be serious.

Kylie gasped. "But that's—"

"Prom," I finished for her.

"You have to," Brad said again. "I mean, you agreed."

"Oh, yes," Lora said, clasping her hands. "I think I will find that quite enjoyable."

She's messing with him. She has to be messing with him.

"But there is a complication," she added.

"Complication?" Brad repeated.

"Too many syllables?" Keegan asked.

"The thing is," Lora broke in, "I must officially enter the prom with Kylie. It's political. You wouldn't understand." She waved her hand. "But once the party is underway, I see no reason why you cannot be my secret date. That is," she stepped forward, trailing a finger beneath his chin, "if you don't mind being my dirty little secret."

Brad nodded like one of those bobbleheaded dolls.

"We might even have an after party... *if* you're elected King," she added with a wink. "One has to be mindful of her status. You taught me that." She was still touching him. I wanted to pull her hand away. Scratch that—I wanted to rip off his ugly face. How could she do this? Had she ever cared about me at all?

I should've been happy when Brad ambled away, but it barely registered. My heart had ached a million times since Lora's arrival, but now the pain in my chest was something I couldn't even name. It was all consuming.

"Holy crap," Kylie said when Brad was out of earshot. "You're a scary good actress."

Lora shrugged in that careless way of hers, settling in beside me. "Are you all right?"

Sure. I just can't look at you.

"Perhaps I should have told you that I was entering the prom with Kylie," she said. "But I must set an example for the group. You understand that, don't you?"

"Yep," I replied. "I understand everything."

She'll go to prom with Kylie. She'll go to prom with Brad. She'll go to prom with anyone except me.

She narrowed her eyes. "What does that mean?"

"You baited him! You got him to give you his *blood.*" I turned away. There was nothing she could say to make this better. I'd finally seen who she was.

A scary good actress. A fake.

She touched me, and I hated how good it felt.

She doesn't mean it. She doesn't mean it. She doesn't mean it.

"Haven't we been plotting our revenge against Brad?" she asked softly.

"Yeah. We're all supposed to do it together, on a regular night—"

"We'll all be together at the prom. And he already thinks I'm his date—"

"Secret date." Keegan snorted.

Anger flared inside of me. "Don't you guys get it? She's going to get herself really hurt."

"I sincerely doubt that," Lora said.

"What if we get separated? What if he leads you away, and we can't get to you in time ... "

"I will be fine."

It killed me, how nonchalant she was being. Did I really mean so little to her?

Does she really mean so little to herself?

"You're not invincible," I said.

"No. But I'm much more creative than Mr. Dickson."

"There are certain circumstances where that's not going to save you." *And who is going to save her, then? Is it, by any chance, you?* a taunting little voice said. "What exactly are you planning?" I asked.

Lora didn't answer right away. It looked like she was pondering the question. But after that little show she'd put on for Brad, I figured she was playing me.

"We could strip him down and take his picture," she said finally.

Keegan rubbed his hands together. "Let's take his picture in a prom dress."

"Hold on," I said. "Doesn't that perpetuate the idea that it's wrong for a guy to wear a dress?"

All eyes turned on me.

"What? I listen."

"Apparently," said Keegan. "But we're not making a political statement. We just want to humiliate him. You know, an eye for an eye."

"I don't know." Kylie chewed her lip. "I think Taylor's right."

"I think Taylor's skirting the issue," said Lora with a sly smile. She was trying to win me over, but I wasn't falling for it. I knew those eyes didn't sparkle just for me.

Possessive much?

I took a deep breath, trying to center myself. It didn't work. "Why don't you put him in a baby's bonnet while you're at it?" I said sarcastically.

Kylie giggled into her hand. "Wouldn't that be the greatest? Mister Big Man as a baby?"

"We'd never pull it off," I said quickly. The last thing I wanted was to get Kylie on board.

"Maybe we wouldn't have to dress him up. Maybe we'd just have to create the illusion that he was dressed up," said Lora. "They'd only have to see a hint of fabric to believe something was amiss."

"Let me guess," I said. "You'll get the fabric?"

"I can get the fabric," offered Kylie.

"See? Everything's falling into place." Lora grinned. "Besides, if all goes well, we won't have to sink to his level and use drugs. From what I hear, Brad drinks himself into a stupor at every social event. So when he passes out—"

"We slip into his hotel room," said Keegan.

"Hotel room?" I repeated.

"Everyone's renting one," Lora said.

"We'll take a few pictures," Keegan went on, but my mind had taken a trip to other places.

Hotel room.

"We wouldn't even have to undress him," Kylie added.

Are we renting a hotel room?

"We'd hardly have to touch him," Lora said. "With all the rumors going around, we'd just have to show a bit of something—"

"And people would believe it!" Kylie clapped her hands. "But is this okay? Is this right?"

"It's just a little prank," Keegan said. "If Brad passes out on his own, there's virtually no danger. And we won't separate under any circumstances."

He looked at me. In fact, everyone was looking at me, and all I could do was tear out clumps of grass. "Sounds like you guys have made up your minds," I said.

"So you'll help?" Kylie asked. She looked so hopeful I didn't know what to say.

So I shrugged. "If that'll make you happy," I said finally. But I wasn't talking to her and we all knew it.

———

When the school day ended, I couldn't wait to get out of there. The thought of sitting next to Lora was almost too much to bear. I felt so betrayed by her. Betrayed and hurt and angry. But I waited for her outside of class like a gentleman, and I offered to give her a ride, because I still cared.

I cared way too much.

Big surprise, she declined. I peeled out of the parking lot in a pathetic display of frustration. But as I raced down the streets, just fast enough to piss off the cops that *really* needed to meet their quotas, it occurred to me that it wasn't even Lora I was mad at. I knew she didn't like Brad. I *knew* it, in that deep part of me beneath the sinew and marrow. I knew it in my soul, if I had a soul.

She makes me feel like I have a soul.

I was mad at Brad and I was mad at my father. Most of all I was mad at myself for letting the people I cared about get into situations where others could take advantage of them. What kind of a man was I if I couldn't defend the people I loved? Was I really that much better than the assholes of the world?

I'd had enough.

Pulling up to my parents' house, I slammed my car door hard enough to rattle the hinges. On one side of the lawn, like a beacon of light, stood the door to the garage and my sanctuary. On the other side, my parents' house rose up before me, tall and foreboding. Possibly surrounded in flames. I knew where I had to go if I wanted to be able to look myself in the face for the rest of my life. I knew, too, what it was going to cost me.

I plodded toward it. Across the swamps of soggy grass, and up the steps that multiplied as I walked. My heart felt heavy—my entire body felt heavy—but I couldn't let it hold me back. What else could I do? Lie down in the grass and wait for death to take me? I had no choice but to start living.

"Where are you?" I called, trailing mud through the hallway. I'd clean it up later, for Mom's sake. For now I needed the fire and the fury. I knew Mom was in her usual afternoon spot, grading finger-paintings or whatever the kids had done that day.

It struck me, like a blade in the heart, how devastating it must've been for her to work with kids so close to Aaron's age. To see them, so full of life, crawling into their parents' arms at the end of the day. What greater torture could there be for her? Why did she stay?

They need the money.

I never should have let them stay in this house. I should have been giving her money, any money I could make, but it was too late now to let the guilt crush me. I had to move forward, to focus on the things I could change. As the family room moved toward me, or I toward it, my legs picked up speed, and I pushed into the room without time to think.

"Of course," I said. "What was I thinking? You're right where you always are, glued to the couch."

My father turned around, aghast at my intrusion. He didn't know the half of it. I could've said much worse things. Deep inside, all the pain he'd caused me was bubbling up, but I wouldn't use it against him.

We were different in that way.

He recovered, emotions shifting before his face returned to neutral. "Well, well. It's the prodigal son," he said. "To what do I owe this performance?"

"You've been watching too much TV." My gaze flicked to the black, soul-sucking box. The faces of missing teens were flashing across the screen. Black-haired, red-haired, brown-haired, blond. So many faces. I started to feel dizzy.

"I need to talk to you," I said. "Man to man."

He turned back to the TV. "Hope you brought a friend."

"What is your deal? Why do you fucking—" I stopped, reined myself in. But it was too late to take back the cardinal sin. I'd shown my emotions. Now he could gut me and not feel bad about it.

"Very nice," Dad said, not bothering to look at me. "A real man wouldn't lose control like that."

"A real man takes care of his family." I walked around to the side of the couch. Even with his eyes glued to the TV, he'd have to glimpse me in the periphery. "A real man doesn't treat his wife like she's an insect buzzing around his arm." That got his attention. "And a real man looks out for his kids instead of throwing them to the wolves to die!"

I didn't mean it like that. Really, I was going for a metaphor. But the words had already left my mouth, and now I couldn't stop. I'd wanted to say these things for years. I'd only needed Lora to validate them so I knew I wasn't completely insane.

"You are the parent." I stepped forward, boxing him in. "You are the adult. You put it on me, but it wasn't my responsibility to raise your son, and it wasn't my responsibility to save your house! You needed to make those decisions. You and Mom both. How could you put that on me? How could you let me move into the garage and hate myself and think the whole thing was my fault? You made me wish I was the one who was dead."

God, it felt good to say it. Relief rushed through me. I knew my words would hurt him, but I had to say them, this one time. I had to let him know what he'd put on me and how it had hurt. I had to be free of it. Because even if Mom insisted they bring me along to their new home, I wasn't going to come.

I didn't belong with them anymore.

My eyes flickered to the screen as my dad stood up, preparing to tell me what a worthless piece of shit I was. A picture of a sullen-eyed blonde was replaced with that of a pretty brunette. I tore my gaze away from the screen, understanding in that moment how mesmerizing these shows could be. Who wouldn't want to find that missing child and bring her home to her parents? Who wouldn't want to find all of them?

I started to have a fantasy—a coping mechanism, probably—about finding the little brown-haired girl and bringing her to the doorstep of her family. I felt my eyes glaze over a little, like they do when I'm daydreaming. I think a part of me was expecting my father to hit me. But he didn't lash out in any way. His hand was cradling his face. He wasn't angry.

He was crying.

"Dad."

He stepped back as I moved closer, shaking his head. The girl on the screen was replaced with a dark-haired boy with the largest eyes I'd ever seen.

"Dad, I'm sorry. I didn't mean—"

He mumbled something, the words garbled with mucous and pain.

I stepped closer, but again, he evaded me.

He sputtered, "I've been horrible—" The words dissolved into a sob.

I had no idea what to do. Even after Aaron's accident, I hadn't seen him cry like this.

"You haven't been horrible," I lied.

"You kidding me?" He lowered his hand just a bit and I could see the redness in his eyes. "I never knew how to be with you boys. I never knew how to do this."

I never wanted to be a father.

Those words floated, unspoken, between us. I'd known them for a long time. Mom had me when she was nineteen. All their plans for the future had disappeared because of me.

"I'm sorry," I said, though I knew it wasn't my doing. They hadn't asked for me, but I hadn't asked to be born. It was nobody's fault, really. It was just life.

As much as we tried to control it, it got the best of us.

Still, it was almost too ridiculous to watch a thirty-six-year-old man lament his stolen youth. He had to know he'd done the same thing to me.

I took his childhood, so he'd taken mine.

"I know things didn't go the way you planned," I said stupidly. Of course they didn't go the way he'd planned. His youngest was buried in the dirt. But that wasn't what I meant, and I think he knew that.

"I never meant to ... take it out on you," Dad said, wiping at his face. "I thought that if I kept my distance, I could protect you from it."

"From what?"

"From me."

"I didn't want to be protected from you. I wanted you to be my dad. Why did you—" But I couldn't ask the question. I couldn't bring Aaron into things. The longer I stood here, the more obvious it became that he blamed himself for Aaron's accident as much as he blamed me. How would it feel to lose the child you knew you never wanted? How could you not take on most of the blame?

It must've been easier to push it onto me. That was the only way to keep from believing he'd caused it to happen.

Suddenly I wanted to hug him, to tell him it was okay. Already I'd reverted to being the adult in the family. But I couldn't get near him, and not only because he wouldn't let me. I couldn't cross that bridge to make contact. Hell, Lora had been living in my room for almost three weeks and I hadn't even gathered the courage to kiss her, let alone any of the other things I'd have done if she wanted me to.

I'd never learned how to make contact.

Just as I thought of Lora, her face flickered across the TV screen. My heart almost leapt out of my chest. I looked again, hoping I was delirious, but there she was, plain as day.

Laura Belfry—her name splayed beneath her face.

Missing person.

I couldn't breathe. I couldn't think. No, scratch that. I was thinking too much, too fast. All along, I'd known Lora was a runaway. I'd known she had parents. A family. But seeing her there, listed as a missing person, forced my heart into my knees.

"Taylor?"

Oh no. I'd stared at the TV for too long. If Dad followed my eyes to the screen, he'd recognize Lora, and then it was only a matter of time before he'd check my room. I'd lose her.

I'd lose everything.

I threw my arms around him. I gripped him tight, keeping my head between the TV and his line of vision. I might've felt bad about the manipulation if I hadn't already wanted to hug him so badly. Looking back on my life, I don't think he'd ever hugged me. Not even when I was a baby.

"It's okay, Dad, I'm not mad. I love you and Mom, I really do." The number to call with information about Laura flashed across the screen. "I just need to feel like you're my parents for a while. That's not a bad thing." The low volume on the TV taunted me. On the one hand, it kept Dad from hearing about the girl I'd been hiding, illegally, in my bedroom. On the other hand, it kept me from learning everything I wanted to know about her.

Dad tried to pull away. Clearly, this kind of contact made him uncomfortable, no matter how much we needed it.

Real men don't do these things, blah, blah, blah.

I stepped between him and the TV.

"I won't hold it against you if you move on without me," I said, though my brain was screaming: *Don't say it!* I swallowed, stopping up the tears before they spilled out of me. "You can ask me to come if you want," I added, "But it's your decision to make."

Dad was pulling himself together. Except for his red-rimmed eyes, there was no hint he'd cried. He straightened out his sweater-vest and looked at me. "I respect your coming to me, son."

I nodded. I hadn't expected him to tell me he loved me or thank me for setting him straight. But I also hadn't expected him to turn back to the TV like none of this had happened.

"Dad!"

"I can't believe it," he said. I followed his gaze. A picture of a four-year-old stared back at me, a little boy. A stranger. I picked up the remote.

"So young," he murmured. "How can they—"

"Come on, Dad." I turned off the TV. "Why don't you go for a walk? I'll even go with you if you want."

Oh sure. That wouldn't be the most awkward silence of my life.

But I had to offer. Anything to get him away from the TV's evil spell.

He nodded, looking at me like we'd just met. He was halfway to the door when he turned back, shaking his head. "Looks like rain."

19

ELORA

I cut my arm on a branch of Unity's tallest pine. That's what I got for being out of practice. I held my sleeve over the cut as I watched students walk from the box of the school to the boxes of their cars, from which they'd drive to the boxes of their homes or the box of the mall. *Caged little animals.* Today, I couldn't do it. I needed open space and rain on my face. I needed the cool breath of twilight as it descended over the park.

I needed to feel.

For a moment I allowed myself to miss the comforts of home. Over the past few weeks I'd thought of them little, afraid the memories would distract me from my goal. Now they flooded over me, cool, dark, and sweet.

Just as I felt myself surrounded by cold, whispering stones, and stars one can never see in the city, something happened that yanked me out of the Dark Court and back to reality.

My phone was buzzing.

Digging into my pocket, I stilled the rain around me and waited for the caller to speak.

"Tell me you've left the wasteland." The little voice, strained with fear, sent chills through parts of me untouched by the rain.

"Illya? What has happened?"

"Please, Lady. Tell me you're on your way."

"Soon, my friend. But what ails you?"

"He is coming for you."

"Naeve?"

There came no response.

"Illya, tell me what's happened. Surely, he can't—"

"I didn't mean to tell him!"

Oh, Darkness.

"What did you do?" I asked, lungs struggling for a satisfying breath.

"Oh, Lady. Forgive me."

"Illya. What did you do? Did you tell him where I am?"

"I told him the opposite of that! I meant to defend you. It was a mistake."

"What did you say, exactly?"

"I told him he could search all of Faerie and he'd never find you. I only meant to mock him—"

"Oh, Illya."

How could this have happened? It could expose my plans to the Dark Lady. Worse, Naeve could find me.

He could find Taylor.

I had to get out of here.

"Where is Naeve now?" I demanded.

"Hovering on the border of the wasteland. It seems, for the moment, he dares not cross."

"He's reached the border?" I gasped. "Why did you not warn me?"

"I dared not believe it until now. He never spoke of his intentions. I followed him." Illya paused. "I've been stealthy."

I smiled in spite of the fact that my heart was breaking. All this time, I'd known I had to leave. But a part of me had searched for a way to stay.

To be with the boy I could never have.

The boy I should not want.

"You have done your duty to me," I told her, fighting to keep from breaking down. I had to return to my old life and my old ways. No one could see my emotions. "Return to the Dark Court—"

"I will not return until I know that you are safe from him."

"I will be fine," I said. "I've solved the riddle. I know why the cruelest kind of human is *perfect for light*."

"Why?"

"Because the Bright Queen actually *cares* for humanity, and she'd only feel justified stealing someone humanity wouldn't miss. Someone whose absence would *help* the human world."

"Oh, Lady, it's brilliant," Illya breathed, and I wanted to smile. But I couldn't. There was something about my conclusion that bothered me, some little voice whispering in the back of my mind. Telling me I'd missed something.

I pushed it away. "I will return tomorrow night—"

"He could find you by then! Let me follow him until…"

Silence.

"Illya? Are you there?"

"He comes for me."

"What? How—"

"If I should fall, do not forget me."

"Don't speak of it! Please—" The word stuck in my throat. On the other side of the line, I heard scrambling. Then, a cry that was quick to die out.

I bit my knuckle to silence my scream.

Illya. Say something.

But only silence greeted me. I pressed the phone against my ear.

Still nothing.

The line went dead. When the telephone slipped from my hand, I did not try to catch it.

———

Rain poured over me, plastering my hair to my shoulders like a blood-drenched cape. I grasped my thighs with my hands, losing myself in the cold viciousness, the feeling of the shaking tree. Night fell faster than rain, the sky darkening to blue, then fluid indigo, then black.

The stars were slow to arrive.

Lightning flashed, exposing the belly of the sky. The air felt charged. Still I waited, eyes closed, shaking in the center of it all.

A voice bellowed from below, fighting against the roar of the rain. "Come down!"

Taylor's face appeared at the bottom of the tree. The rain flung itself callously into his eyes and nose, trying to choke and to blind, but he refused to lower his gaze. His voice was laced with despair. "Please come down."

He reached for the lowest branch and faltered. "Please don't fall." Lightning illuminated the terrified look on his face.

"Hold on." Dropping easily to the next branch, I guided myself down. I had to be careful not to open the cut on my arm. But when I reached the tree's midpoint, I stopped. Staring down at the ground, at the mortal bending down to pick up a small black object, I wondered if I really wasn't safer in the tree.

"I think I broke my phone," I called, opening my hands as if to say *Sorry*. I would not let him see the anguish that surged inside of me. What good would it do, to let him closer to me?

"You're so weird," he yelled back.

I climbed down the trunk a few feet. "Thank you."

"I mean it." He wiped his face with his sleeve. "You do the weirdest things all the time, and then you say something so freakishly normal. I don't know what to think of you." He put the phone in his pocket as I stepped onto a lower branch.

"So don't think of me."

"I have to." He lifted his arms as if to catch me.

I let myself hang from the last branch. "Please."

Standing on his toes, Taylor wrapped his arms around my waist. I slid into his embrace.

"I have to," he said again. "Don't you understand that?"

"I do." I ran my hands up his arms, feeling the tiny hairs rising. I wanted to sink into him, desperately. To let him comfort me.

I took a step away.

He pulled me back. "I don't even care," he said, lips close to my neck, "what we do. Or don't do. I just need to know if this is real, or if…"

"What?"

"It's just a game, like with Brad."

The words cut into me like thorns. "Do you think it's a game?"

"I don't know." He turned away. "All I know is that you were scary today."

"I was just fooling around. How could that scare you?"

"Because you've looked at me that way! And I believed it. God—" He took his hair in his hands. I placed my hands over them, pulling them down to a safer place.

"I am not playing you," I said. "I might have thought of it when we first met, but I learned quickly I did not need to. You're a good person, Taylor. I only hide around those who would hurt me."

He waited a beat. "Then you feel the way I do?"

"I can't... say."

"Why not?"

"You would not understand." I tried to evade his hand, but it found my cheek anyway. Sliding it down, he cupped my neck, holding me close. "Taylor, please."

"Explain it to me." His lips brushed my cheek, his eyes never leaving mine.

"All my life, I have been taught that *this*"—I gestured between us—"is wrong. That it goes against my nature. And now, after years and years of this belief, I come face to face with this supposed abomination, only to find it the most beautiful, joyful... *natural* thing in the world."

He looked at me, unblinking, as rain fell from his lashes.

I lifted my fingers to his cheek. "Now I must choose between two conclusions. Either my mind has been corrupted by this world I've entered into, or else, all this time, this thing I believed to be true is in fact a lie."

"Would that be so terrible?" His voice was soft as he moved his hands to my hips.

I followed his movements with my eyes, disbelieving the joy his fingers brought. I wanted to feel them everywhere, all over me, now. It scared me how much I wanted him.

"I have left so many of my beliefs behind," I said, giving

him the best explanation I could. "I don't know how much more I can leave."

After all, it had been difficult enough to accept that the forces governing Faerie did not have my best interests in mind. To believe I could be with a human would rip apart the very bindings of my existence. It would jeopardize my belief in everything: my life, my people.

Myself.

Taylor waited a minute before speaking. "I won't ask you to leave anything else behind. But if you need me..." He trailed off, his hands playing with the hem of my shirt.

I leaned in, wanting his fingers to slip beneath the fabric. "I need you."

"You have me."

"But not for long."

His eyes closed, hands gripping at my hips. Pulling me into him without even trying. "You can't leave."

"I have to, Taylor. I have to."

"Not yet."

"Why?"

When he looked at me, I was startled by the clarity in his eyes. "You haven't told me the ending of the story."

———

Taylor curled beside me like a wolf snuggling with his pack. A fluffy blanket came up to our waists. His hair was starting to dry, though mine still hung tangled and wet, and he adjusted the towel on my pillow.

Just like that, he was leaning over me. "What happened to your arm?"

"My arm? Oh." I looked down, my gaze drawn to the place where the tree had tugged at my skin. Immediately, I regretted changing into his oversized T-shirt. It left my arms exposed, and now he could see me.

In spite of everything, I still feared showing vulnerability in front of him.

"The Lady vs. the Tree," I said, trying to pretend that everything was fine. Trying to pretend my world wasn't turning on its head. "The tree won."

"Can I see?"

"All right." I shifted stiffly. I wasn't sure what he would do once I presented him with my arm. The cut was mostly clean; the rain had taken care of that. Now only a thin red line remained.

"Mmm," he said, holding the arm delicately. "It's not too bad. Does it sting?"

I shook my head, waiting for him to give the arm back. But he did something quite curious instead. Lifting the arm to his lips, he pressed a light, solemn kiss upon my skin. My breath fluttered in my chest. There was a holiness to the movement. A ritual aspect. He was using kindness to heal me.

Maybe, even love.

"Thank you," I whispered, barely able to speak.

He nodded, looking away in that shy way of his. "We could bandage it," he said after a long moment.

"That shouldn't be necessary. I tend to heal quickly."

More quickly than you would think.

He nodded again, settling into his pillow.

"Would you like to hear the next part of my story?"

Taylor trailed his nose along my cheek. He must have known, by now, the things we were forbidden to do. But he knew, too, that if he didn't push too hard, I wouldn't push him away.

"Every part of it," he said.

I smiled at that. "The trap was set. The Dark Lady and her courtiers were being waited on by creatures who couldn't wait to wring their necks. All the princess had to do was say the word. But she didn't say anything, not then, for she feared they had neglected an important aspect of their rebellion."

"What was it?" Taylor asked, his breath warm on my skin.

I turned to face him, to center myself, but the look in his eyes did nothing to calm me. "The Dark Lady was more powerful than any of them," I said. "Oh, it pained the princess to admit it. She wished, more than anything, that she could stand against her mother and win. But even the most powerful young thing would be a fool to take on a thousand-year-old being, let alone one who had lived for millennia. On the best of days, the Dark Lady could lay waste to a third of the rebels before they defeated her. The princess wouldn't stand for it."

"What other choice did she have?" Taylor asked,

watching me so intently it made my heart sit up and beg. "The members of their army knew what they were getting into, didn't they?"

"They did. But the princess could not stand the thought of losing so many lives. She needed to find something else, or someone else, who could stand against the Dark Lady and win. She needed—"

"The Seelie Queen."

"Clever boy." I tapped his nose and he bit the air in front of it. "Beautiful, kind Taylor, why do you put up with me? I come here in a whirlwind, offer you nary but a story, and turn your life on its head."

"I would do it again," he said, apparently unfazed by the shift in conversation. "I would do it a thousand times." He scooted closer and I linked my leg through his, pulling it over me. Then we were intertwined, though still not touching with lips or hands. Such things had to be given with permission, and he knew it.

"I shouldn't have brought you into any of this," I said, my words working in opposition to my hands. They went to his head, twining in his hair. "I should have done everything to protect you, the way you have done for me."

I should be leaving, right now, this minute. But I couldn't break away from him. I needed him.

"I don't need protection," he said. "I need adventure."

I shook my head. "You have no idea the trouble it brings."

"I want it," he said, and then he was over me. His head dipped to meet me, hovering just over my lips. Noses touching. Tasting each other's breath. I could feel his body responding to me. I needn't have ever been intimate to recognize the way it felt, and I parted my legs to wrap around him.

It was wrong. Unnatural. Wrong. But I couldn't stop it. My hands dug into his hair, pulling him down, down, closer to my face, and then he nipped at my lips with his own. I nipped back.

Nothing serious, I told myself. *Nothing dangerous.*

But oh, the taste of his lips! And the smell of him. I wanted to feel his breath pushing into my mouth, all of him, pushing into me. I arched my back.

"Please don't go," he whispered, lips dipping to find mine.

I turned my head. "Now, or otherwise?"

He trailed his lips across my cheek, following me. "Ever," he said, and a shudder ripped through me. "Please don't go, ever. Please don't leave me."

"I have to go."

"Then take me with you."

It was the wrong thing to say. Up until then, I could almost have pretended this was a game. But now I sat up, pushing him off me, just enough.

"Why not?" he said, though I hadn't told him *no* with words.

"You can't—" My stomach tightened, forcing out a laugh, though it was the last sound I wanted to make. "You can't come with me. I just said I have to protect you."

He shook his head, rising on his knees to meet me. "That's not how it works." He tucked my hair behind my ear. "I protect you."

"How very archaic," I drawled, hoping to anger him. Anything to pull him away from me. "How very civilized. How very..."

Human.

It wasn't a fair accusation. My mother had witnessed, firsthand, a time in history when men didn't control women under the guise of protection. But that wouldn't make sense to him, and it did little good for me, either. After all, *I* wanted to protect *him.*

Why shouldn't we be equals, protecting each other?

"Let me finish the story," I said.

"Fine." He pulled away from me, letting the cold move in.

"Where are you going?"

"I can't sleep next to you," he said, sliding off the bed.

"Why not?" I asked, suddenly angry. The thought of being without him tonight opened a chasm inside of me. "Are you such a slave to your impulses that you can't be near me without having me completely?"

"It's not about that!" He spun around, and the anguish in his voice astonished me. "It has *nothing* to do with that. Don't you realize how you make me feel?"

"Taylor."

"Stop. I don't need to hear why you can't be with me

again. I don't need to hear you reject me over and over again. I get it."

"All right. I'm sorry." I could not tell him that my coldness was not intended to be a rejection. I could not tell him that the very reason I pushed him away so hard was because I cared about him. "But Taylor?"

"What?" He stood halfway across the room, facing the wall, but I could still see the side of his face.

"What if tonight were the only night we could lie together?"

He closed his eyes. "Don't say it."

"I haven't said anything, not plainly."

"You've said enough. Why are you going back?"

"I have to."

"Why now?"

"Because I've learned what I needed to learn," I said carefully. "Now I can face them. Possibly defeat them."

"Alone?"

"I need you to let it go. I'm here now, and that's all I can offer. And if you would have me, as I can give... "

He didn't think about it. He moved so fast, he couldn't possibly have had time to think. But when he lay upon the bed, he kept his distance, facing away from me. He waited for me to come to him.

"All right," he said as I curled into him, "tell me the rest." His voice was sullen, but he molded his body to mine the moment we touched. I slid my hand up to his chest and he held it close to his heart.

"Please don't hate me," I said, murmuring close to his ear. He said nothing. I sighed. "The princess traveled to the Seelie Court and sought an audience with the Bright Queen."

I paused, waiting for the back-and-forth I'd come to expect. He didn't disappoint me. After a quiet minute, he said, "Why would the Queen help her?"

I held him tighter. "The princess was offering the one thing the Bright Queen wanted: the destruction of the Dark Court."

"But wouldn't the Bright Court still reign? Their Queen could seize control—"

"Ah, the princess thought of that as well. Really, the destruction of both courts had been necessary all along. But it was not until this point that she knew how to destroy them. Thus, she offered to take down the Dark Court herself, if the Bright Queen agreed to disband her own court in response. She let the Queen point out that the Dark Lady was too powerful for the princess to defeat. She let the Queen offer to bind the Dark Lady herself."

"Brilliant."

I blushed, wishing more than ever that I could kiss him.

Who am I kidding?

I wanted to do much more than kiss, and he was willing. But soon, I would be out of this place, and these unnatural feelings would leave me.

They had to.

"So the Bright Queen just agreed?" Taylor asked, wholly unaware of the places my thoughts had traveled to.

"She was skeptical, but she was also intrigued. She knew it must not have been easy for the princess to have such a cold, uncaring mother."

Taylor twisted a little, to face me. It was almost as if he knew I was talking about myself. "Don't worry," he said, holding me in that piercing gaze. "I just wanted to see you."

And I, you.

I traced my fingers along the muscles in his arms. Memorizing him. "But the Bright Queen was no fool. For all she knew, the princess was merely a Dark-Lady-in-training. So she came up with a way for the princess to prove her loyalty *and* provide a proper offering."

"An offering?"

I shrugged. "Faeries rarely do anything for free. They like trades."

"Interesting," he said, his voice growing groggy. But in spite of his fatigue, he was trying not to fall asleep. He kept blinking to keep his eyes from closing.

I had a feeling neither of us would sleep tonight.

"What did the Bright Queen do?" he asked.

As I spoke the last line of my story, the moonlight filtered in, framing his face in soft light. He looked so sincere then, I almost believed it was natural to want him. "She gave the princess a riddle and sent her on a quest."

20

TAYLOR

Lora dressed in black, to match the night. From where I stood, in a velvet vintage tux, the inky blackness started at her chest, where a corset possessively hugged her curves, then crept down her hips like clinging smoke and spread out into forever. It was impossible to know where she ended and the darkness began.

All I could see for sure, as we hurried down the pathway toward the ballroom, was the glow of her arms above her full-length gloves, her seductively enticing décolletage, and her mischievous, grinning face. She also wore a crown—Kylie's self-proclaimed greatest creation, made of glass berries woven through wires. It looked like jeweled branches were rising out of her head.

Keegan danced alongside us in a 1920s pinstripe suit and matching hat. Kylie trailed behind. Pausing for the third time, she hitched up her black satin mini dress. Her gray suit jacket wouldn't stay buttoned, and, although she'd slicked her hair away from her face, a strand kept breaking free, tickling her nose.

She sighed. "Whose idea was this?" she asked, pulling a tube of lip balm from her pocket.

The response was swift and unanimous: "Yours."

She brushed past us, wheels spinning. "I seriously doubt that."

As we passed clusters of trees and antique patio furniture, I chewed on my nail and thought about the closeness of the hotel room she and Lora had discussed yesterday. For the past hour, Kylie had been hinting that the room could be used for more than an after party, but I couldn't even think about trying to seduce Lora tonight. Everyone would be around, and besides, to think about that was to think about the fact that Lora was leaving.

I needed to put it out of my mind. I needed to put one foot in front of the other and try to have a good time.

Kylie snapped her fingers, bringing me back to the present moment. Mostly. "Can we just do this and get it over with?"

"I thought you couldn't wait to do this," I said.

"You *have* been blathering about it all month," Keegan agreed.

Kylie rolled her eyes. "All part of my light-hearted façade. I just want to prove it's as bad as I think it's going to be, so I can feel justified in scorning a normal teenage existence."

Keegan pinched her shoulder. "You're such a liar. You know you're going to love it, and you're terrified."

Her lip quivered as she said, "Yeah. Right."

"Sure you're not going to burst into flames?" I asked Keegan.

He turned, his cheeks round above his joker's grin. "I get it. Prom is for people who have pre-marital sex after covering the undesirables in buckets of blood. I'm not scared." He raised his eyebrows twice. "It's all about perspective."

"Meaning?"

"Meaning…" He tipped his hat at a slant. "I'm not attending this party. I'm crashing."

———

The crowd outside the ballroom was unreal. It looked like none of the outcasts were being let in. Dressed in fairy wings and fancy crowns, party dresses over ripped jeans, and suits from every possible era except our own, they stood in a haphazard line, girls holding hands with girls, and boys holding hands with boys. I was content to hang back and wait in line, but Lora had other plans. Pushing her way through the crowd, she led us to the great double doors of the ballroom. She marched right up to Principal Jade, cutting in front of Alexia Mardsen in the process, and boomed, "What's the problem?"

Principal Jade tucked a strand of orangey-red hair behind her ear. She must have borrowed her dress from a friend. In my four years at Unity, I'd never seen her in anything but a neutral-toned pantsuit.

Tonight, she wore sequins.

"Well, hello to you too, Miss Belfry," she said. "I'm happy to see you're participating in student events." But the principal didn't look happy. She looked exhausted. There were dark patches under her eyes, and her shoulders hunched toward the ground.

"Well." Lora linked arms with Kylie, causing Alexia to raise her eyebrows. "I'm *trying* to participate. But it seems that a small minority have taken it upon themselves to discriminate against me."

Principal Jade's face crumpled. "Miss Belfry, I—you— I'm happy to sit and talk with you during school hours about your ideas. But this is not the time."

"You've been conspiring with Mrs. Rosencart," Lora teased, a comparison the principal obviously did not like.

Her lips formed a very thin line. "You well know that Mrs. Rosencart and I differ on many things. But when it comes to order in my school, I will not—"

"Forgive me for interrupting, Camilla—"

"*Principal* Jade."

"Principal Jade, this is not about order," Lora said smoothly. "This is about justice, fairness, and doing what's right. You, of all people—"

"I'm warning you, Miss Belfry—" The principal's face was suddenly burning. It looked like Lora had struck a nerve. "I would like nothing more than to permit this group into the building, but unfortunately several students—in fact, the parents of several students—have made it clear they are not comfortable with the promotion of certain lifestyles at school events."

"Interesting," Lora said, turning to the rustling crowd. "Do any of you have parents?"

The response was a resounding *yes*.

"Right." Lora touched her lips, catching the principal's eye. "So, as far as I can count—and, as you well know, I do excel in math—there are far more students outside than there could possibly be inside. Which means," she said, holding up her fingers and counting in silence, "that the students outside have more parents than the students inside. Isn't it rewarding when the education system does its job?"

Principal Jade lost what little steam she had. She squirmed as if her dress were shrinking. "I'm happy to see you taking an interest in mathematics. And social justice, for that matter. But that doesn't change the fact that tonight is not the time."

"Sounds like an argument the Nazis would have made," I said, taking my place at Lora's side. "Terrible things have happened throughout history because people were convinced to be quiet."

Several students yelled in agreement.

"Mr. Alder," the principal began. "Please."

"I don't know about you," Lora said to the people behind us, who were pushing themselves forward. "But I'm sick of being told to keep quiet."

The crowd erupted. Screams and applause ripped

through the night and Principal Jade stumbled, falling against the building.

For a second no one moved.

Then Lora held out a hand. "You all right?"

I watched the shift in the principal's features as she took Lora's hand. I couldn't say what it was, exactly, that I saw in her eyes, but I knew she'd changed her mind.

"Well." The principal spoke so that only those closest could hear. "I would certainly hate to have to refund all these tickets."

Lora nodded solemnly. "That would be too bad."

"Oh for godsakes." Alexia rolled her smoky Cleopatra eyes. "Just let the kids in already. If we stand out here any longer, I'll be dressed for last season."

Naturally, everyone's eyes fell on her dress. Red. Strapless. Skin-tight.

How can she breathe in that thing?

Principal Jade smirked. "That would be a tragedy," she said, then turned back to Lora. "You've made your point. Even if you did cut in front of everyone in line to do it."

"Forgive me," Lora replied. She held the principal's eye, her lips curling, and moved to the back of the line. We followed.

When we reached the double doors again, a more relaxed Principal Jade took our tickets and waved us inside.

———

My head swam with visions of sugarplums and other delectable things. In spite of the second-skin nature of her dress, Kylie had managed to smuggle a flask of whiskey into the ballroom, and its contents were currently swirling in three separate stomachs. Only Keegan had declined, saying a clouded mind would give him more reason to tell his classmates what he really thought of them.

He wanted to take the high road.

Too bad.

I watched Lora spin in circles around a wildly flailing Kylie. Her crown had fallen off twice. Now it hung around my wrist, the inner plastic spikes poking my skin. As for the rest of my body, it was planted against a wall on the far side of the refreshment table. The circular room glowed with the light of a dozen chandeliers. Up above, the domed glass ceiling revealed a sky dotted with starlight. For a high school prom, the whole thing was surprisingly romantic.

Not that it would do me any good.

On the other side of the room, Alexia and the other Prom Court princesses (minus Lora) had positioned themselves on the stage where the coronation of king and queen would take place. A herd of guys stood below them attempting to dance, with varying results. Every few minutes one of the guys would try to sneak onto the stage, only to be shut down by the dancing princesses. I kept looking for a sign that said, "No boys allowed."

Alexia probably tattooed it on her inner thigh.

I laughed a little at that. Still, underneath my laughter, I felt nervousness unfurl inside me like a wave. Any minute it would rise up and I would drown. I was determined to accompany Lora when she went back home, but how could I do that when I couldn't even ask her to dance?

Yeah. I was that pathetic. At this point, I'd been watching her dance for half an hour. But now I was going to do it. Now was the time. My body buzzed with excitement and whiskey, and the pathway to Lora was suddenly clear. Even better, she was heading in my direction, her hips rocking as she walked. A slow song blared from the speakers.

She was mere feet away. Her gaze landed on my face.

And then she passed me by. "Hello Bradley."

I turned around in time to see Brad glide across the floor. Dressed in black jeans and a tuxedo T-shirt, he was all too smug. "Hell-o, sexy."

Now she was coy. "Are you ready to dance?"

"Hell yeah." He slid an arm around her waist and led her back to the dance floor.

My heart dropped to my feet and was stomped by passersby. The slow song seemed to go on forever. In that eternity, I grew to hate every clichéd lyric. I watched, and tried not to watch, as Lora held tightly to Brad. Burning remnants of whiskey crawled back up my throat.

Then, just when I thought I could no longer endure this torture, something strange caught my eye. Next to the stage, a girl with sugar-white dreadlocks was dancing with a boy from my gym class. Her eyes glinted red as she scanned the ballroom.

Who is that?

I shook myself, shifting my gaze. There were lots of people I didn't know at this school. Besides, we were allowed to bring guests to prom.

A new face was no cause for alarm.

Then, on the other side of the room, I saw a guy spinning a hazy-eyed junior. The guy's muscles were so big they stilted his movements. His mouth was stretched into a deranged smile.

"Monsters," I mumbled, and then laughed at my drunken revelation. "There are monsters at this party."

A flash of red caught my eye, and again, I followed it without much thought. Lora was leading Brad in small circles, the way someone might dance at a medieval ball. When her hand slid up his shirt, I thought I was going to throw up. But when she pulled down his collar, I caught a glimpse of a yellow baby's bib.

How did she do that?

I wasn't the only one who'd noticed. Other people were pointing and whispering behind their hands. I watched the trail of whispers leap from one ear to the next, traveling around the room. I followed it all the way back to—

"Lora. Hi."

"May I?" she asked, holding out a hand.

I blinked. The strange series of events flashed like memories of a dream, but the images couldn't hold my attention. Lora was in front of me now, giving me exactly what I wanted. Who cared that Brad was suddenly nowhere to be seen?

I pulled her close. "I missed you," I said, unable to stop myself.

She laughed into my neck. "And I, you," she whispered, wrapping her arms around me. It was perfect. I wanted it to last forever.

So, of course, after a minute she said, "This is unnerving."

"What?" I inhaled her scent. Even now, she smelled like evergreens.

"This." She gestured with her hand. "Pilfering moments of intimacy beneath the watchful gaze of strangers."

"I'll take moments of intimacy over nothing."

She hugged me close. "Do you like this?"

I laughed, suddenly dizzy. "Not the dance." Brushing a strand of hair behind her ear, I let my hand linger. "But I like you."

"I feel suffocated," she said.

I jerked my hand away. Too late, I realized she wasn't talking about me.

She spoke into my ear. "I think that if we started to devour each other right now, they would look upon us as if we were a show. Nothing feels real here. Everything is plotted out."

I struggled to make sense of this, wondering if the alcohol was contributing to the shifting patterns of her speech. It was as if she was seeking a union between who she was and who she'd been pretending to be.

"What can I do?" I stepped back, giving her room to breathe.

"Indulge me," she said wryly, as if apologetic. "Your drink has broken down the walls I built to keep the anger out. And the fear. The lust."

I exhaled sharply.

"And yet, you must know what I feel for you is more than that." She placed a gloved hand on my neck, sliding her fingers into my hair. "Would you escape with me, for a few moments, to get away from all this?"

"We won't be able to come back in."

"We could if we really wanted to."

"What about Brad?"

"What about him?"

I smiled at the dismissal. I couldn't help it. "You know what I mean."

"We will worry about that after the coronation. His room is right next to ours. I arranged for it to be so."

"How did you get that bib on him?"

"I'm good with sleight of hand."

"Lora."

"Don't ask me, Taylor. Just be with me while there's still time. Please?"

I ran my hands down her arms. "I know where to go. But we'll have to tell—"

I wasn't able to finish. The screech of microphone

feedback filled the ballroom and the music stopped. Up on the stage, Principal Jade was adjusting her sequined dress.

No.

She held a golden envelope in her hand.

Not now.

"May I have your attention?" she asked over the rising din. "Will the members of the Prom Court please join me on stage?"

"Meet me at the doors," Lora said as she started toward the stage. "I won't be long."

Of course you will be, I thought. But I just waved.

I was right. It took several minutes for the members of the Court to assemble. On the principal's left, Alexia towered over the other princesses in impossibly high heels. On her right, Brad stood awkwardly beside four other guys. He had his arms crossed over his chest like he was protecting himself.

"Any guesses?" Kylie asked, coming up beside me.

"What's the point?" Keegan replied from my other side. "Queen B is a shoo-in. The B stands for—"

"Lora might win." Kylie squeezed my arm.

Keegan shook his head. "There is no justice. Only the illusion of justice."

"Lora will win," I said.

"I hope not, for her sake," said Keegan. "Everyone in the Alliance voted for Brad."

"What? Why?"

He laughed, but Kylie grimaced. Clearly she wasn't happy with the way things were going. "We're hoping to get another glimpse of the bib," he said.

I didn't have time to answer that. Principal Jade was speaking into the microphone: "Ladies and gentlemen, your new king and queen are ... " She tore into the envelope and pulled out a card. For a second she just stared at it, narrowing her eyes to slits. Then she spoke with forced excitement. "Brad Dickson and Alexia Mardsen!"

The crowd erupted in catcalls and cheers. If anyone was angry with the outcome, I couldn't tell. Everyone was staring at Brad, waiting for something to happen. Even Lora was watching him, her eyes glistening hungrily, like she was actually impressed he'd been crowned King.

It gave me the most terrible feeling.

"Thank you, Principal," Alexia said into the microphone, breaking whatever spell Brad had on us. "Thanks, Brad."

Brad, too, seemed like he was under a spell. But he managed to lumber off the stage, to the crowd's disappointment. Then it was just Alexia up there.

She'd already taken off her crown.

"This is such a beautiful gift," she said. "I know just where I want to stick it." She glanced at the crowd and we stared back, transfixed. "But I don't really deserve this. There's only one person in this school who does. She's the only reason I'm here tonight. She's probably the only reason I'm alive." She shifted her gaze, searching the crowd of faces. "Kylie

Angelini, you're the love of my life. Would you please join me on stage?"

The crowd stared, speechless, as Kylie rolled up the ramp. When she reached the center of the stage, Alexia placed the crown on her head and kissed her lips.

———

"Are you ready?" Lora laced her fingers through mine, pulling me against the crowd. All around us, people stood like zombies, staring at the couple on stage. The vast confusion, which had reached the chaperones as well, allowed for a moment of lax security, and Lora and I were able to slip out of the door unnoticed.

The wind grabbed at our hair as we ran across the grounds. Within minutes we'd reached the outskirts, sheltered by clusters of trees. In a way, it reminded me of the area where we'd first met: the swing-set hidden by trees.

I didn't want to think about what that meant.

Lora pulled herself onto a low branch. I knew that if I stood right in front of her, she could wrap her legs around me.

But would she?

"I don't believe it," I said, taking a step toward her. "I really thought you were going to win." I meant it as a compliment, but the second it was out of my mouth, I realized it might hurt her.

Her laugh surprised me. "Maybe I did." She took hold of my tie and pulled me closer. "I'm here with you, aren't I?"

I removed the jeweled crown from my arm and placed it gently on her head. "Are you having fun?"

"Surprisingly, yes." She reached out her arms like a child. When she spoke, the words were too wonderful to believe. "Come closer."

I stepped between her thighs. And then I was staring at her blatantly, at all that skin above the binding tightness of her corset. The tops of her breasts were smooth; her neck curved like a reformed vampire's kryptonite. I wanted to trail my lips over the nape of her neck, inhale the woodsy scent of her, but instead I tilted my gaze up, to her eyes.

"I feel like you've drugged me," I said. "Put me under a spell."

She leaned toward me, gripping a branch above her head to keep from falling. Our lips were inches apart.

"Definitely a spell of some kind," I murmured.

"Do you doubt the authenticity of your feelings?" Lora let herself slip down, dangling that much closer to my mouth. She was playing with me, the way a kitten toys with a combative mouse, but I couldn't stop leaning into her.

I wasn't kidding about feeling drugged.

"No," I told her. "But there's something about you … "

She shook her head. "It is you who have enchanted me, ensorcelled every inch of my being. But … "

"What?"

She gripped the branch above her head with new-found conviction. "I must not succumb to it."

"Hasn't anyone ever broken the rules?" I brushed her cheek with my hand, refusing to give up. I wanted to see if she would lean closer.

She did. "With affairs of the flesh, certainly. But affairs of the flesh do not last."

"What about love?"

"On occasion. We thought them mad."

"Is that how you feel?"

"I feel as though I am seeing clearly for the first time. And yet..." She searched my eyes. "What is the fate of the perennial blossom who gives her heart to the ephemeral butterfly?"

"*What* are you talking about?"

"We are beyond star-crossed. We are fatally mismatched. Even if we could delude ourselves into chasing fleeting moments of joy, we are destined to lose—"

"How can this possibly be losing?"

"I would be leading you into danger. Infringing upon your free will—"

"I choose this."

"It goes against my nature."

"I choose you." I wrapped an arm around her waist.

"We could lose everything—"

"I'll take it."

"—and compromise the future for both of our families. Taylor, you don't know what you are playing with."

Using my free hand, I trailed up her arm, toward the branch that she was holding. "I'm not playing with anything." I tried to push my fingers into the palm of her hand, to loosen her grip. She held tight. "You can doubt your feelings all you want. But don't ever doubt mine."

The air between us stilled. I lifted my face until I could taste her breath. "Let go."

Lora fell into me. Her hand slipped from the branch, tangling with my waiting fingers, and she wrapped her legs around me. I caught her mouth with mine. I wanted to drink from her forever and never seek another form of sustenance.

She tasted so sweet.

Loosening the hand that held hers, I slipped both hands beneath the folds of her skirt. My fingers crackled with electricity as they slid over her skin. I was running them over the tops of her thighs when she broke away, barely, leaning against the tree to create distance.

Her movements didn't faze me. I lowered my lips to her ear, listening to the sound of her breath to discern what brought her the most pleasure.

I realized I was straining to see clearly. The sky, which had been mostly clear all day, had in the past few minutes grown increasingly dark, and I looked up to see purple clouds gathering. Then the clouds began to spill warm rain.

Lora gasped as lightning streaked the sky, and she pulled my hands from her thighs. It seemed like she'd taken the darkening sky as a sign, a warning against our closeness.

Again, she'd found a way to pull away from me.

My heart cracked. I lifted my hand, my body panicky with want, and let the pads of my fingers linger half an inch from her cheek. "Please let me touch you."

"Taylor."

"I won't hurt you," I promised.

"My sweetest salvation," she said with a smile. "I don't think you could." She smoothed the hair from my face. Her touch was like white heat, like crackling lightning, and my body lurched forward, pulled in by the feel of it.

She realized what she'd done. As she slid down to the ground, I stepped forward, pressing her against the tree.

"Do you want me to back up?" I asked.

Her gaze traveled down my body, to where my leg slid between hers. I got the distinct impression she could slip out of my grasp with the tiniest of efforts, but I waited, in reverent silence, for her reply.

As she spoke, she closed her eyes. "No."

I waited another minute, wary of angering her or giving her a reason to pull away. "Do you want me to kiss you?"

"Always." She looked at me, and the urgency in her eyes mirrored my own feelings. "And you don't even know it."

"What do you mean?"

"All this time, you have revealed yourself to me. In spite of pain, and terror, you have revealed yourself to me. And still I keep myself hidden."

"But I know you."

"You can't," she said, smiling sadly. "I haven't let you."

"Lora."

"I haven't told you the true ending of the story. Please…" She slid out of my grip, just as easily as I'd thought she could. One second she was there, pressed so close to me, and the next she was gone. Her gaze darted about fearfully, reminding me again of the day we'd met. Was it a sign that things would begin and end the same way? Would she now disappear as quickly as she'd arrived?

"Come with me," she said. I took her hand, and she led me across the grass to the hotel. We climbed two flights of cement stairs and followed the outdoor hallway to our room.

Lora stepped inside first, letting me pass her as she locked the deadbolt and latched the chain. Slowly, as if barely awake, she lowered herself to the edge of the bed. I knelt on the floor in front of her.

She was shaking. "My body, spirit, and heart are drawn to you, almost as if bound. But my mind is in turmoil. How can this be, my greatest desire? How can that which is against nature feel to me like a force of nature? Nothing has ever felt so right. Nothing."

I watched her intently, aware that something had changed. Maybe everything.

"I have always trusted myself without question," she said. "So now, when my spirit moves toward you with every breath, who am I to let some story keep me from trusting myself? You are a force of nature, and I know that in spite of my efforts to keep my distance, nothing in this world can change the way I feel about you."

"What are you saying?"

She leaned back, fumbling with the pouch around her neck. I waited for her to pull out the blood-spattered dandelion. But the object she removed was fuzzy and green, coiled tightly like a cocoon.

"I'm saying our story isn't over yet." She held out her hand.

21

ELORA

My hand shook as I clutched the riddle. My entire body shook, wracked with the fear of how much he could hurt me now that I had admitted to needing him. I had never needed anyone before. Now I felt I would wither and die if he rejected me. But he had kissed me, held me, maybe even loved me... could I really risk all of it by revealing my true self?

I looked into his shining, leaf-green eyes.

Yes.

I had no other choice. If he rejected me, I would know his adoration had been an illusion. But if I did not give him the chance to see me fully, he would not have the opportunity to truly love me.

We cannot love that which we do not know.

I had to risk it.

"Taylor," I began, my fingers tracing the edges of the Queen's riddle.

"Lora," he said, and I started to shake.

"Elora." I closed my eyes to match my clenched fist.

Even as I said, "My name is Elora," I couldn't open my hand. "I told you a name that would seem common to you, to hide my difference. Every deception, I made to hide my difference. To keep myself safe from you."

"Why?" Taylor placed his hand over my fist, as if to soften my grip.

"Because to admit that we can be … together, without breaking some great universal law, is to leave behind the person I was and the person I've been pretending to be. It is to become something else entirely, and that, more than anything, is what scares me. I do not so much fear my world changing as I fear changing myself, admitting that everything I've believed about myself is untrue. I would have to become something previously unimagined to make room for this one, unbelievable truth. The truth of how I feel about you."

"How do you feel about me?" All this time, his eyes had never left my face. A lesser being might have let his gaze stray down, thinking of the earthly delights he was sure to receive when I finished talking. But this story—the first completely honest story I had given him—was all he cared about. I could see it in his unflinching gaze, feel it in the way his fingers kept gliding over mine. Soothing me. Guiding me.

He is so kind. The Seelie Court would love him.

I opened my mouth to tell him the feelings I had kept guarded, even from myself.

His phone rang.

Is it a sign?

"Sorry," he said, fumbling to pull the phone out of his pocket.

I watched in silence as he rejected the call.

"My mom," he said. "Probably just checking in."

"She loves you."

He dropped his gaze.

"I know you don't believe that, but she does," I said. "Taylor?"

"Hmm." He kept his gaze down, trying to ride this moment out. Waiting for me to invite him back into my thoughts, and maybe my embrace.

The Seelie Court would love him, I thought again. *But why would the Unseelie Court hate him? Especially enough to consider him their bane?*

The phone rang again. Again, he silenced it.

It is a sign, I realized as his hand explored the spaces between my fingers. The riddle had already been solved. I was just trying to twist its meaning to get what I wanted.

I cannot have him.

"Taylor. Look at me," I said, taking advantage of the opportunity created by his mother's call. His eyes glistened, hopeful. "I know you believe that your family's abandonment means they don't love you, but I believe there is more to it than that. They kept their distance for their own reasons, not because of you. Do you understand that?"

"I don't want to talk about this now."

"You need to talk about this now. Now is the only time we can talk about this."

"Why? I'm coming with you. I already know that."

"Taylor. My sweet." I kissed him because I could. Because I needed to. And because, as I had told him, our time was running out. "I'm not telling you the truth because I need you to come with me. I'm telling you because you need to understand that sometimes, when people leave you, it isn't because they don't love you. It's because they are trying to protect you."

"What are you saying?"

His phone rang a third time. This time he just looked at it, forcing me to talk above the sound.

"If things remain as they are, you will not understand why I must leave," I said.

"You can't be serious. I—"

"Taylor." I spoke over him. I had to get this out before I caved and convinced myself I could be with him. "I cannot have you thinking that I'm leaving because I don't care for you."

The phone rang and rang, and he just stared at it.

"It's because I care *too much*. I will not risk your life by bringing you into danger. And I will not let you live as someone's plaything—"

"Stop." His harshness startled me.

My heart jostled around in the sea of my chest without his sweetness to anchor it. "Please, understand—"

He lifted the phone to his ear. "Hello?"

His mother's voice exploded on the other end.

"Mom?" he said, trying to get a word in. "Mom, calm down. Are you okay?"

Another pause. I leaned in. In the midst of her hysterical crying, I made out the words *found, body,* and *Lora.*

Me.

My heart thundered so loudly I could hardly gather my thoughts. Still, over the hammering, I realized what had happened. I had lingered in the human lands too long. My glamour had worn off. And Laura Belfry, the girl whose life I'd borrowed, had been found.

Her body, that is.

And now Taylor's parents believed I was dead. His poor mother had been assigned the task of informing him.

I touched my fingers to his lips, closing my eyes for only a second. A moment later, my arms were wrapped around him, stifling his efforts to listen to his mother. He didn't hug me back.

He didn't hold me or kiss me or tell me he loved me.

My foolishness had stripped him of the chance.

"I am so sorry for all of this," I whispered, moving toward the back balcony. "I'll give you some privacy."

Taylor tried to protest, but I would have none of it. Opening the sliding glass door, I slipped into the dark, delicious night. Brad's balcony was merely a leap away.

I closed the door behind me.

22

TAYLOR

Beneath Mom's muffled sobs, words were hard to distinguish. I could only make out the bones of it: *girl, missing, dead,* and something I didn't understand: *clothing.* But the trigger word, the one that made me want to pick up my things and run, came hard and fast:

Police.

"What do you mean, Dad called the police? Mom, *calm down.* You're not going to help me if I can't understand you."

"Help you? I can't help you!" Mom shrieked. "Why did you do this?"

"What did I do?" I strained to see through the glass door to the balcony. The darkness swirled like a mirage, teasing me. The curtain was partially closed. I would have gotten up to open it and bring Lora back inside, if only my legs worked.

Mom's voice was a whisper spoken through fabric. "Your father was watching the evening news. There was a special about a girl—a girl who went missing. They've just found her body in the woods outside of town."

"That's terrible, Mom. But what does it—"

"Laura's body. Your friend."

What?

"It's a mistake." It couldn't be Lora. *Elora.* She was sitting right in front of me a minute ago. And now she was out on the balcony. I could prove it.

I tried to stand.

"Honey, tell me you didn't do anything," Mom said frantically. "Please tell me you didn't hurt that girl."

"Hurt her? Why would I—" My legs buckled. "Oh my God. You think I killed her?"

"It must've been an accident. An argument, or maybe she fell." Mom was babbling, talking to herself in a way that only sounded like she was talking to me. My mind was babbling, too, telling me to stop thinking about that picture I'd seen on TV.

The picture of Lora.

At least, I'd thought it was Lora. The girl had her face. Her name, with a different spelling. But it couldn't have been—because that girl was dead, and Lora was here with me. I'd seen her. Talked to her. Kissed her. And you can't kiss a dead person. Well, you can, but it's pretty messed up, and—*Oh God.* What had they found?

Who had they found?

I launched myself toward the balcony, learning that my legs worked just fine if they were struggling to catch up with the rest of me. I caught my balance on the wall by the door and pulled the curtain aside. Why was it so dark?

"Mom, it's a mistake," I said, my hands fumbling over the painfully simple latch. It shouldn't have been locked. It *couldn't* have been locked from the outside. I thought of that night in the parking lot after the soccer game, how my car door wouldn't open.

"Mom—"

"Please stop lying to me."

"I'm *not lying*."

"Taylor, we went into your bedroom."

"What?"

Flip the latch, flip the latch. Wipe the cold sweat off your hands and flip the latch.

Finally, I got it. I slid the door open.

"Your father took the hinges off the door."

"What? How could you—"

"It was an emergency, Taylor! We found her clothes."

"I can explain that," I said. "She came over before prom—"

"We found blood on the sleeve!"

"Blood?" I stepped onto the concrete.

"Your father wouldn't listen to reason."

"I don't understand," I said to the darkness. The empty darkness.

Yes, I was finally on the balcony.

Alone.

Alone with the darkness and my mother's panicked voice.

"He's called the police. Honey, I'm sure you have a good explanation. Just keep a clear head and explain to the officers that it was an accident. A mistake. I know it was a mistake."

"They're coming here?"

"It would be best if you surrendered yourself to them. Don't make yourself look guilty."

Guilty?

The phone dropped from my hand. I didn't throw it; I just loosened my grip. I'd loosened my grip on reality and everything was spinning.

Lora was dead, but I'd just seen her. Now she was gone and I was about to go to jail for her murder. All of this was impossible.

I closed my eyes. Behind my lids I saw her body, lifeless and bloodied. Laura's body. Elora's body.

How had the girl died? The girl who was and wasn't the one who'd been living in my bedroom. In my life.

In my heart.

I felt my way back into the room and sat on the edge of the bed. I knew I couldn't lie down and rest. I had to get the hell out of there.

Get the hell out of hell. That's a funny one.

Clearly I was losing my mind. Maybe *that* was the explanation for all of this. I wasn't dreaming, I was just insane, and I'd imagined the whole damn thing. Imagined the girl living in my room, a girl whose face I must've seen on TV in passing. Anything could happen in this moment. The hotel room could turn into a forest. In fact, wasn't that a leaf I was sitting on? It was already happening!

Wait.

I stood up. I wasn't going crazy. That *was* a leaf beneath me, but it hadn't crumpled under my weight. A magical leaf?

Sure, that wasn't the least bit disconcerting.

I unrolled the leaf and held it in my hand. My brain started registering the words before I'd fully accepted that there was writing:

> *"Bane of the darkness, perfect for light,*
> *Steal him away in the dead of the night.*
> *Bind him with blood, this young leader of men,*
> *And bring him to Court before Light's hallowed reign."*

"What the hell is this?" I yelled, as if someone might answer me. For all I knew, Mom was still babbling into the phone. But she wouldn't have the answer to my question. Nobody here would.

Except me.

Because I did know the answer to my question.

It had been dancing on the edges of my subconscious for three weeks. And as I stared at the riddle given to Elora by the Bright Queen, all my confusion fell away. I saw Elora appearing to me in the darkness that first night. I saw her disappearing into the darkness when I'd tried to follow her to the park. She was always one step ahead of me. She was always one step ahead of all of us. And the riddle she'd given to Brad ... that may have been her cleverest trick.

"Oh, God."

Bind him with blood ...

"This can't be happening."

Bring him to Court ...

"No, no, no."

But in my head, all I could hear was *yes*.

I took a breath, my body filling with newfound resolve. In that moment, I was acutely aware of three things: One, Lora was the princess from the story. Two, she'd taken the place of a human girl who was now dead. And three, she'd gotten the answer to the Queen's riddle wrong.

I grabbed my bag and left the hotel.

23

ELORA

"Come now, little beastie." I should have brought a leash. Brad stumbled along, drunk on liquor and magic. Tree trunks, brambles, bushes—all of these things jumped out at him. It seemed that the forest itself was attempting to block his passage.

That, like the call from Taylor's mother, struck me as a sign.

But it wasn't. It couldn't be. Brad was simply out of his wits, and wasn't I the one who had made him that way? Certainly, I had not asked him to ingest half a bottle of tequila in his hotel room, but the magic... well, who else was to blame for that? I knew that as long as I held those drops of blood in my necklace, he would follow any reasonable command from me. Humans had little concept of the power of blood, or, for that matter, of names. If I'd asked for his middle name, the boy would not have stood a chance.

He would have cartwheeled through the forest at my command.

But as I had only his blood, his heart was still his own.

"Bradley. Do a cartwheel over that log."

He lifted his arms, poised to act, and paused. A hint of clarity came back into his eyes. "Why?" he asked, challenging me.

See?

"Let us just walk, then."

He nodded, his eyes clouding over.

There's a good boy.

Did I feel remorse at stealing a human away from his family and his home? Well, to admit that would be to allow remorse for other things. And if I allowed myself remorse for those things…

I had to be strong. Magic is funny in that way. The moment you lose control, your power slips away.

I traveled on. I couldn't help but be grateful that the prom organizers had taken us to such a remote location. The hotel rested on the edge of a forest, much like the one I had traveled through to get to Unity. Or, I should say, *the one I had traveled through to stumble upon Unity.*

All of this had happened by chance, hadn't it?

"Not long now," I promised, veering away from the highway. For the first few miles, we had traveled parallel to the speeding cars, to muffle the sound of our footsteps. Now we turned away from the din, into the dark parts of the forest, toward its heart.

Soon the terrain began to rise. Legs tired more quickly this way. After the first upward mile, I found myself half-carrying Brad. My wings were twitching, begging for use. I knew flight would be beautiful, even while carrying Brad's weight. I had yearned for it for so long now, it almost seemed unreal that I was so close to returning to the sky's embrace.

This is the time. I have waited long enough.

Still, I led Brad deeper into the woods. Over time, I'd let my glamour slip away from me, but in the dark, with my wings tucked neatly against my back, my little offering was none the wiser. A great nervousness unfurled in my stomach, opening like wings. I could not tell if the feeling was fear or excitement.

This is the problem with heightened emotions: one feels so like its opposite. To a lover scorned, passion can bleed into fury.

Is that what Taylor is feeling?

I had to stop thinking about him.

I paused, listening to the sound of the forest settling. Branches scraped against each other. The wind whined, and was silenced. A hundred subtler sounds went unnoticed, drowned out by the distant cars and the rain. For a moment I wondered if my efforts to muffle my footsteps would work against me.

After all, if others could not hear me, I could not hear them. Cold trickled over my neck.

That was a sign. But I missed it.

I unfolded my wings.

"No fucking way."

The voice was not mine. Nor was it Brad's. He was

standing to my left, staring dumbly at a branch as if I did not exist. I turned around slowly, willing the voice to be a manifestation of my fear.

No, no, it cannot be. With the exception of Taylor, this was the absolute last human I wanted to encounter.

The one who could thwart me.

She stepped out of the shadows, no longer taking care to quiet her steps. In spite of the three-inch heels, her feet were adorned in slashes of red. Her floor-length gown looked as if the forest had tried to eat it alive. But every scar and tear she wore proudly, and her eyes never left mine.

"And where do you think you're going?" asked Alexia Mardsen, reigning Queen of Unity High. But she wasn't wearing the crown the students had given her.

She was wearing mine.

"I wasn't going to keep it," she said when she noticed me looking. She held it out for me. Her hand shook, just a little. "I found it outside your room."

"How thoughtful of you." I took the crown and turned it over in my hands. Kylie had spent days creating it. The artistry was beautiful.

I placed it on my head.

Alexia gasped. "She's a demon. She's a princess. She's a demon princess!"

"I'm glad you're having a good time."

She smiled. The movement was stilted, a puppet's mouth jerking up on the sides. But at least she was keeping up the act.

Back at the Dark Court, she'd be right at home.

"What are you doing here, Alexia?"

"I followed you."

"There seems to be a lot of that going around."

"Then you should've been prepared for it." She was circling now, taking in the sight of me. Sizing up her opponent.

Her enemy.

I shuddered at the thought that I might have to hurt her. Even Brad was to remain unharmed.

"But why did you follow me?" I asked, turning with her so she could not catch me off guard.

"I saw you leaving with Brad, and I went looking for everybody else. But no one was where they were supposed to be."

"What do you mean?" Another shudder ripped through me. Another sign?

"They weren't in the room! They weren't at the dance. They weren't anywhere."

The words scraped my heart, leaving scars.

Unanswered questions.

They cannot be in danger.

"I was hoping you'd lead me to them," she said. "I thought maybe you were going to have some sort of ritual in the forest. You know, banish Brad from this realm or something."

It was startling how accurate her suspicion was. But I didn't tell her that.

"They're not here," I said. "Surely, you noticed that after the first *mile*."

"I did, but by then I was committed. Besides, once I figured out you were the bad guy, I knew the others were safer away from you."

"The bad guy?" I raised my eyebrows. "What made you think I was the bad guy?"

"Oh, please. Mysterious girl arrives in town and leads Prom King into the forest? He appears to be drugged? I've seen this movie." She chuckled, a sound born more of shock than acceptance. "At least, I thought I had, until the whole *wings* thing happened. So you've got to help me out. What movie is this?"

I gave her a genuine faerie grin. The kind that stretches the mouth far wider than a mortal's mouth can stretch.

She stopped circling.

"Perhaps the movie where terrible things happen to mortal girls who follow the bad guy into the forest?" I said.

"Mortal girls?" She touched her lips, clearly disturbed by the word. "Oh, God, are you a vampire? Tell me you're not a vampire."

"Don't be ridiculous."

"Good. I hate the smell of garlic."

I stepped closer. Alexia inhaled sharply, like she wanted to move back. But she didn't, and I respected her for that. "You're either very stupid or very brave, you know that?" I told her.

"Thanks," she said, but she was shaking. When she dropped her hand from her lips, I saw the blood blossoming there.

She'd bitten herself.

"Are you afraid of me?" I asked, reaching up and touching the blood. She froze, not even breathing, as my fingers trailed her skin.

She shook her head, barely. The blood smeared on her lips.

"You should be afraid of me." I let my pupils overtake the color in my eyes. "I could kill you in an instant. Make a palace of your bones. I could destroy everything you love right in front of you, and—"

"Stop." She stumbled back, trying to tear her eyes away from mine. My gaze was strong when I wanted it to be. Hypnotic.

I blinked, and I waited for her to run away.

Yet even backed against a tree, with me closing in, Alexia did not break. "You swear to me you haven't taken Kylie?"

"Where would I have taken her? You've watched me the whole time."

"Not the whole time." She shook her head. "Everyone got away from me." She seemed to be remembering, or trying to remember, something that was dancing on the edges of her mind.

I caught her eye again. "You have to go back. Back to

268

where the mortals are. I didn't take them. They won't be harmed tonight."

A voice pierced the darkness. "I wouldn't be so sure of that."

24

TAYLOR

When I pulled into the parking lot of Whittleton Cemetery, all of the spots were empty. The clock on the dash read 12:38 a.m. Technically, it was Sunday morning. It helped me to think I was sticking to my Sunday routine, since everything else in my life was starting to feel like a nightmare.

Says the guy heading to the graveyard.

Still, the place didn't scare me. I'd been there a hundred times. And even though the faeries of the Dark Court were apparently very real, that didn't mean other things were out to get me.

That's what I told myself as I opened the big metal gate. It didn't even bother me that Eddie, the night guard, wasn't sitting in his post. Yes, this place was so fancy they had a security guard working nights.

Graveyard shift at the graveyard.

These kinds of thoughts kept my spirits up.

Spirits. Get it? A definite chill was creeping down my neck. I followed the little stone paths like I always did, between the gargoyles that kept evil out and the angels that kept goodness in. A breeze drifted past me, cool and potentially soothing, but it carried the scent of death. Maybe this doesn't seem strange, to smell death at a cemetery, but usually it just smelled like grass and flowers.

Tonight it should have smelled like spring.

But it didn't.

It smelled like autumn.

Like leaves drying.

Like decay.

Stop.

I'd been here a hundred times, but never at this hour. Why were things different now? What was it about the human mind that feared the dead coming back to life?

Dead is dead. The soul leaves. There's nothing in there to come back to life.

I knelt before Aaron's grave. Instinctively my hand fumbled for that patch of dirt, the one I kneaded nervously whenever I visited, as if I could somehow reach his hand that way. Even in the cool midnight air, the dirt felt warm, like maybe he was reaching for me too. But thoughts like this, however comforting, would do me no good this time. I couldn't hold on to the idea that he was lingering in the land of the living.

I had to let go.

Words poured from my mouth, the way they always did here, but this time they had a greater meaning. "Aaron, I want you to know I'm sorry. I know I've said it a million times, but I am. Dad's sorry too, he told me. Can you believe that?" I paused, looking at the ground, the distant trees, anything. "You probably don't believe it. But it's the truth." I squeezed the dirt so tight. "I love you, Aaron. I'll never stop loving you and I'll never forget any of it."

That wasn't entirely the truth. Some memories were as clear as yesterday; others were fuzzy, like they'd happened in a dream. But it was okay to say it. Some lies were okay, if they were what you really wanted. And if he could hear me, I wanted him to believe that his memory would never fade in me.

I wanted to give that to him.

"I have to go away now," I said, still squeezing the dirt, squeezing like I had the power to give life to it. "I don't know when I'll be back. But that's okay too. Adventures are like that. You might never come back, but you have to go because it's what you're meant to do. I have to go, and you … " I bent over, touching my hands to my lips. "I don't want you to be afraid." Tears spilled over my hands, blending with the dirt. "No matter where I go, I'll still be with you. No matter what happens, I'll always be your brother."

I stopped, tilting my head. I thought I'd heard a car door shutting in the parking lot. For a minute, everything was quiet. Then, from the other direction, I heard an impossible sound: the not-so-distant sound of a kid crying.

It sounded so much like Aaron, I couldn't breathe

for about three seconds. Who would let their kid wander around the graveyard in the middle of the night?

Who would let their brother climb to the top of a fifty-foot tree?

"Are you okay?" I called, and the crying stopped. I almost convinced myself that I'd imagined the whole thing. It would have been so easy to return to the parking lot and see who'd arrived.

But I didn't.

Instead, I walked toward the sound, and in that moment the universe made its little alterations. What might have been different if I'd chosen the parking lot over the darkness?

What might have been different if I'd never gone to the swing-set that first night?

Our choices change us, every one of them.

I went looking for the kid, and the course of my life was forever changed.

I caught a glimpse of him as I reached the back end of the cemetery. At least, I thought it was the back end, but through the trees I saw no sign of the fence. What I did see was a boy's head—a young boy, with hair a shade darker than Aaron's had been. It was the exact same shade as mine. This similarity struck me as significant, but I couldn't figure out why.

I was too eager to catch him.

I'm not sure when things shifted from "find" to "catch," but it was clear he was hiding from me. And it wasn't like I was going to hurt him, or even detain him unless he was in some kind of danger. I just wanted to look at him, face to face, and maybe bring him home to his family.

"I'm not going to hurt you," I called, stepping into the space between the trees. No matter where I went, I couldn't get away from trees. It seemed like the trees here outnumbered the graves, and that couldn't be right.

None of this is right.

The thought sent chills up my spine. I told myself to stay calm. I hadn't exactly spent a lot of time exploring the outer edges of the cemetery, and I certainly didn't know every inch of the place.

As I ducked under a branch, I misjudged its height, and spindly branches trailed across my neck. I had the strangest impression that the tree was tasting my blood, and then I knew my imagination was getting away from me. But my neck burned, and I held my hand over it to calm the sting. When I took my hand away, it was covered in blood.

Covered.

I started to panic then, pushing through the branches even though it only led to more cuts. I'd never been overly sensitive to blood, but seeing myself lose so much—at a cemetery—had a bad effect on me. My stomach churned.

Only the whimpering of the boy kept me from giving up entirely.

"I'm coming; just stay where you are. It's going to be okay."

But was it? My heart was beating really fast, and that couldn't be good for slowing the flow of my blood. I put my hand back on my neck and it felt wet, sticky. I could have sworn that blood was dripping down my back, but that wasn't possible. It had just been a little scratch.

I wasn't going to die or anything.

I whipped around when I heard the boy behind me. Laughing, like we were playing a game. But it wasn't a game I wanted to play, because I'd suddenly realized why the cemetery smelled like autumn. That smell wasn't crumbling leaves—it was freshly turned dirt. I'd smelled it on days when someone needed to be buried. But no one needed to be buried in the middle of the night, and even if they did, it wouldn't explain the strength of the smell. It smelled like the entire place had been overturned. Like every grave in the cemetery had been freshly dug up.

I stepped out of the trees, out of the darkness, and found that my eyes had adjusted to the night. Now I wished they hadn't, because the things I saw shouldn't have been seen by any human.

I saw the boy skittering up the back of a gargoyle, his nails so long they could slit your throat and bleed you dry.

I saw so many crows flying overhead, their bodies blotted out the moon and the sky.

And when I looked down at the freshly turned dirt of the cemetery, I saw dead things crawling out of the earth.

25

ELORA

At the sound of the voice, I whirled around. The darkness shifted and two creatures stepped into the moonlight, wearing the shadows the way a lady wears a dress. Dark things. Unholy things.

Unseelie.

"Lhiannon and Lamia," I snarled, unable to hide my displeasure. "I might have guessed. What brings you to these forbidden lands? Hungry for a snack?"

Lhiannon lingered in the shadows, too proud to answer, but Lamia stepped closer. Her angular horse's body shifted with each step. Her coat was black as coal, and her eyes resembled the heavens at the darkest part of night. But if it suited her, she could transform to reflect a man's deepest desire, and in that form she could make him crumble.

Or kill.

"And now we're talking to horses," Alexia said beside me, but her voice was pinched and shaky. Clearly she was aware that these creatures were more than they appeared. Those sharp edges, jagged as bones; those eyes that had witnessed the beginning of the earth—even the dullest of humans would have been afraid of them.

"Answer me," I commanded the faeries, ignoring the mortal girl who was anything but dull. At least Brad was keeping himself busy. He sat in the dirt building a mud castle. "Or was I not painfully clear that I wasn't to be followed?"

Lhiannon snorted, and the movement revealed what I had not been able to see: the little creature perched on her back, webbed fingers splayed out in welcome. So familiar, my heart went a-flutter in my chest.

My old friend.

My dearest companion.

"Illya!" I rushed to her side. It struck me as odd that she hadn't flown to me already, but up close, I saw the reason.

"Oh, Illya."

"It's nothing to worry about," the marsh sprite replied, ducking away from my gaze. "It doesn't even hurt anymore."

I leaned in, surveying her wings—what remained of them. "Naeve," I whispered, my fingers hovering over the damage.

"He burned them. Curled them up like paper."

"Brave Illya." I held out my hand, and she wrapped herself up in it. "I'm so glad you are alive."

"As am I. Most of the time."

My heart broke at the words. But wouldn't I have felt the same way? I had hardly been able to bear the past few weeks, bound to the land like a human. How would I feel if I actually lost the ability to fly? Forever.

"Maybe there is a way to heal them," I said as Illya stepped out of my embrace. But even as I spoke, my throat constricted.

"Perhaps in the old days," she said softly. Who hadn't heard stories of such things? Of magic healing all wounds, and gardens springing up at the hands of the faeries. "But power is weak now among the fey. Unless something changes . . ." She glanced at the humans, unable to mask her disgust.

I reached for her, but for the first time in our long friendship, she pulled away.

"There will be time later for conciliation," she said. "We must return to Court before Naeve discovers where we have gone."

"What do you mean? Where is Naeve?"

"Too close for us to linger. He nearly caught up to you at the ball. He has probably captured the boy by now."

"Captured the boy? *What* boy?"

"Just one of the humans."

"One of the—" I couldn't breathe. I felt as if my chest were caving in. "Tell me what you saw. Did you *see* Naeve capture a human?"

Say no, say no, please say no.

"No."

My breath rushed out in a whoosh. Still, my heart screamed.

"His beasts infiltrated the dance," she said. "I would not have thought it possible for a dark faerie to dance so closely with humans, but then, you have been doing it all along, haven't you?" She paused, a shudder ripping through her small frame. "They followed you out of the ballroom, but they lost track of you at the bedchamber. When the boy came out alone, they went in after you. You know what they found there."

Nothing.

"What did they do next? Please, Illya, this is important."

"They followed the mortal. Well, three mortals, actually—"

"Three? *Three mortals?*" I glanced over at Alexia, who was trying to light a cigarette. Tears had blossomed beneath her long, dark lashes, and her teeth drew fresh blood from her lips.

She couldn't get the cigarette to light. "She took my best fucking lighter," she said, flicking the wheel over and over. "I have to get it back."

"I could get it for you," I said, hoping to reason with her mad ramblings. She glared at me like I had offered to twist a knife in her back.

Maybe I had.

"Tell me what happened next," I said to Illya.

"The boy climbed into an iron chariot," she said, watching Alexia's breakdown with detached interest. "And two others followed him, in their own."

"A boy and girl? Brother and sister?"

"I don't know! They were humans."

"And you followed them?"

"Yes, for a time."

"Did you see where they went?"

"No. But we saw signs, along the path, for a cemetery of all places. That's when I offered to look for you in the opposite direction, in case you tried to slip away while Naeve tracked the humans."

"And he allowed you to break away?"

"He knows of my bond with you. He thought that if I happened upon you, my story would convince you to rescue the humans. What a fool he is, thinking you could care for them."

"Illya…"

"We must return to Court while his back is turned."

"I am not going back to Court."

"You must."

"I can't. Not yet." I struggled to find a way to explain things to her. "I must stop them from interfering with the mortal world. The courts may be at odds, but we agree on one thing: humans are off limits."

"Except to you?" Illya glared pointedly at Brad. His hands were covered in dirt, his eyes still glazed.

"That remains our secret," I said. "But if the dark faeries slaughter three humans, everyone will know of it. It will give the Bright Court power over us. We will have to allow *them* three humans, and what do you think that will do to my pact with the Bright Queen?"

Illya turned away. Alexia had taken a seat beside Brad on the ground, still flicking the lighter. Her thumb had started to bleed.

"Let me put it this way," I explained. "If the Bright Queen gains three humans *for nothing*, why would she want one *for something*?"

Illya looked up at me. "You will be putting us in danger," she said.

It pained me to see how much she'd changed in my absence. How much she had hardened.

Or maybe she just didn't recognize me anymore.

"I'm not asking any of you to help me save the humans." I knelt before Lamia, holding her gaze. "But I am asking for your aid." I glanced toward Alexia, who was trying to open her lighter with the heel of her shoe; toward Brad, whose cruel existence meant so much to my revolution. "I know it's a lot to ask"—I returned my gaze to Lamia's dark, fathomless eyes—"but would you take this boy somewhere for me?"

Lamia did not merely shudder. Her skin rippled, like water breached by a stone. She brayed and stepped away from me, but not far enough to indicate refusal. Even though I had promised her freedom at the end of things, she was still in my service.

I was still her princess.

"You need only to take him to the borderlands," I said. "Members of her court can meet you there." I did not say *the Seelie Queen*. I dared not even speak her title to Lamia. It would have been enough to change her mind.

Her great head dipped, and I rose to my feet. "Thank you, friend," I said, praying she would not attempt to suck out Brad's soul on the way. But when I turned back to him, more pressing concerns were brought to my attention. In the moment I'd turned away, Alexia had slid her arm around Brad's neck. Now the sharp edge of her heel was pressed into his skin.

"I'll slit his throat if you don't take me with you." She caught my eye, and she did not look scared. She looked angry and perfectly in control. "You know I will."

It took me a moment to understand. The cigarette, the fit she'd thrown over the useless lighter—it had all been a distraction.

"You are quite the little actress," I said.

"And you are easily fooled."

"It won't happen again."

"It won't have to," Alexia said. "After we rescue Kylie, you will never have to see me again." She tightened her grip on Brad. My stomach tensed as blood smeared his neck. I knew the blood was hers—crimson remnants from the thumb she'd sliced on her lighter. But the sight invoked all kinds of images; images of blood pouring down his neck. Images of him taking his last breath.

I had no time to argue, or even to think. Brad was in danger. Taylor was in danger, as were the twins. Nodding to the faeries, I said, "A detour, then."

26

TAYLOR

The dead things didn't come for me right away. They were too busy celebrating their resurrection. They licked the dirt from their fingers and grabbed each other's hands, dancing in clothing that looked like it came from the circus. Stripes and top hats, fluffy skirts; everything torn and muddy. I thought, for a second, that one of them looked more like a rabbit than a man, but when I looked again, I realized it was a mask. Whatever these creatures were, wherever they had been, they were back for blood.

I stepped backward, my eyes scanning the grounds for Aaron's headstone. For the moment, his area of the cemetery seemed relatively empty. I had a pretty good idea that these creatures were looking for something alive to eat, but I couldn't stand the thought of them digging up my brother's body.

I crept along the outskirts of the grounds, feeling with my hands so my eyes could keep watch. The night was dark, which should have been a relief; already I was seeing things that made me want to claw out my eyes. But the lack of light was worse than seeing, because they could come up behind me and slide their fingernails over my neck. They could reach out of the ground and pull me under. Gnaw off my limbs. I knew if I felt those cold, cracked lips on my skin I would go crazy, and then they would be able to do whatever they wanted to me, and to Aaron.

I had to escape them.

Already I'd bypassed *how can this be happening?* and moved right into *how can I survive this?* I had no time for disbelief. If faeries could exist, so could these dead things. And if I sat around trying to understand the universe, I was going to end up dead.

Or worse.

My fingers fumbled over the bark of an oak. I looked up, calculating how easy it would be to climb it. I didn't fully understand my logic in that moment; I should have bolted to the parking lot and driven until the gas ran out. But the parking lot felt miles away, and I couldn't leave Aaron until I knew he was safe.

Even now, my darkest fears were being confirmed. They were creeping toward his grave.

I pulled myself into the lowest branch, moving as quietly as I possibly could. The second a twig snapped, they'd be alerted to my presence and they'd surround me. That's how it always happens in the movies. The hero thinks he's finally outrun the villain, and then one stupid twig snaps. Next thing he knows, the villain's sucking his soul out through his lips, leaving him a husk of a man.

I wasn't going out that way.

In *my* movie, I'd set the entire graveyard on fire before I'd let these fuckers mess with the bodies of people's loved ones. Everyone would rest in peace: the dead, the undead, even me. Maybe that's why Elora left me right when I'd lost the option of going back home. Maybe my purpose was right here, defending good from evil in a fight to the death.

At least I could go out with a bang.

But how?

I looked down, though it was the last thing I wanted to do. A big fat group of them were gathering around my brother's grave. I couldn't read his gravestone from here, but I knew it was his. Why wouldn't it be? They probably heard me pouring my heart out to him.

They probably fed on my despair.

I did my best to stay positive.

It was a challenge. They were digging now, some of them, with those long nails that kept growing after death. They were licking at the ground, too, or eating it. Anything to get at my brother's body. I had to find a way to distract them, to offer them something else to chase.

That's when I heard the scream. I recognized it, though I didn't want to.

I turned just in time to see the dead surround Kylie and Keegan. It happened quickly, like ants covering a carcass. They didn't have time to fight back.

I'm not sure what was worse: witnessing the capture of the twins or realizing they'd come here looking for me.

No, the former was worse. Of course it was worse. But the guilt was sharp and all consuming.

No matter what I do, I end up putting people in danger.

I was a mess. Useless. How could I help them? I started to wish for divine intervention then, instead of the wicked universe taunting me with its sense of irony. I wished for angels to swoop down and save all of us. That's what you needed when you were dealing with demons.

And that's what they were. I could see it, now that they'd neared the light of the parking lot. Their wings were black and slick as bats' wings, and some of them had horns coming out of their heads. I realized, in the darkest moment of my life, that fire wouldn't hurt these creatures.

Where they came from, fire was everywhere.

It was home.

Please, God, send us angels. I will never disbelieve in you again.

I felt like a fool. I'd prayed to God so many times since Aaron's death. Prayed that I was dreaming. Prayed that I wasn't to blame. Why would a divine being listen to me now, after all this time? It was clear I'd been forsaken, again and again.

It was clear God was no friend of mine.

But wait—there in the distance, something was approaching. Something grand and beautiful and winged. Those wings could have been white; they glowed, silver-tinged, in the moonlight. But of course they were black.

Don't take her away from me, God. Do not take Elora away.

But there was no one who would hear that prayer, because she was already lost to me. She'd been lost long before she came to the human world. Lost from the moment she'd been born. My God, she was one of them.

She'd always been one of them.

That's when it hit me. *They* weren't dead things. They weren't even demons. They were dark things. Dark faeries.

They were her family.

Now they'd come for me. Now they'd make me dance until my feet bled and all the bones in my legs were broken. They'd scald the flesh from my body and make me smile through the pain. They'd bury me alive and have a tea party on my grave, sipping my blood from little cups.

They were the cruelest creatures on the planet, and they were going to punish me for loving their princess.

27

ELORA

When my feet hit the ground of the graveyard, I did three things to prepare for my confrontation with Naeve. I kicked off my shoes. I took off my gloves. And I tucked my wings into my back.

I'd be using them plenty by night's end.

For now, I would use my eyes and my wits. The grounds were overrun with dark beings. Through the fog of their glamour, I checked off the list of the usual players: the Headless Hags, rolling in the muck like pigs; Carnivorous Jack, gnawing on his own arm to satisfy his bloodlust; and a host of would-be changelings: small, shriveled creatures we might've traded for children in the old days, before the rise of the courts.

Before the dark faeries' hatred blossomed into something ugly.

Now I could see the ugliness, but it was too late. The twins were being held captive, and I could not free them by convincing the dark courtiers of their merit. I would have to fight, and that, too, would be ugly.

At least Taylor was nowhere to be seen.

I stepped closer to the fray. At my back, my servants prepared to depart, Brad in tow. Only Alexia was permitted to remain, and I prayed she had the good sense to stay out of the battle.

But good sense goes out the window when love is involved.

Alexia dove into danger, the pointed heel of her shoe held out like a knife. I could not hold her back.

Now she was being surrounded by a host of feathery wings and sharpened nails. Now she was trapped, along with the twins. Humans might have knives and guns at their disposal, but faeries can walk into a battle unarmed and win. All we need to do is summon the elements to do our bidding.

I watched as vines encircled the humans' wrists. The faeries were tying them to a statue of an angel, no doubt to add insult to injury. *Where are your angels now?* the gesture seemed to say. *Where are your gods and your free will and your protection?*

My heart went out to the mortals, and not only because their world had been turned on its head. The faeries were putting on a show for them, intuiting their darkest fears and using these to dominate them. So here came the spiders, here came the snakes.

The faeries were playing Wicked Circus, one of their favorite games. Rather than sporting their garments of shadow and brambles, their necklaces of thorns, they now dressed as if they were a caravan of circus performers who had fallen into the gaping mouth of a grave, and died, only to rise again on this very day.

It's a good show when your life isn't at stake. I walked across their stage with purpose. But whether I was to be the Surprise Act, or the acrobat who slips and falls to her death, I did not know. My survival depended on my ability to balance and never slip.

To never look behind my back.

Soon I entered their inner circle. *Center Stage, where the magic happens.* But before I could get to the Ringmaster, I would have to pass by the two main acts.

If humans tame lions, what do faeries tame?

We all knew the answer to that.

Olorian held a whip, not that he would need it. His muscles could serve as an advertisement for magical performance-enhancers. But he wanted a weapon that matched the circus theme, and the whip would do perfectly.

"Well, well, well," I said, dipping my head as if to show respect. Really, I was shaming him, exposing the fact that he should have been bowing to me. I was his princess, heir to the Unseelie throne. Or had he forgotten?

He stepped forward, a good little bodyguard. His inky black body was difficult to make out in the darkness. It didn't help that he used glamour to flicker in and out of substance. One moment, his body was like an obsidian statue; the next, he was a shadow. Smoke.

He was also an idiot.

One flick of the whip, and I was yanking it out of his hands. "You're swinging it like a toy," I scolded. "Try circling next time. Back-and-forth is easier to catch."

Olorian sneered. In the space where his teeth might have been, there was an abyss, and his eyes burned like coals. "If I wanted to hurt you, I would have," he growled.

"Maybe so." I stepped closer. "But I doubt that very much."

He snarled and lashed out with that bear claw of a hand. But he never quite made contact, and that told me all I needed to know. Naeve had ordered them to scare me, nothing more. He wanted me all to himself.

What a sweetheart.

I approached the next of Naeve's underlings with little fear. Like Olorian, the Lady Claremondes need not utilize whips or chains to scare people. All she had to do was swing the noose she had grown out of her sugar-white dreadlocks, and wag her tongue. Even now, that tongue hung from her lips in warning, venomous drops laying waste to the flowers on the ground.

One moment, alive. The next moment, dead.

I'd never really understood how quickly things could end.

I'd never had to. But as I approached the Ringmaster, passing *through* the Lady Claremondes's ethereal lower half, I understood many things.

Naeve sat beside the great stone angel—and thus, the humans—on a throne his underlings must have thrown together on the spot. *Mud and animal bones. What clever little beasts they were to think of that.* A mile or so down the road, at the pet cemetery, someone's darling Fluffy would be missing from her grave.

Her limbs would be, anyway.

The humans knelt in a half-circle before him. At the sound of my approach, they began to squirm. Yet try as they might, they could not turn to look at me. Vines and dark magic had them rooted to the spot.

The beast requires an audience, I mused, looking coolly at the creature seated before me. With the greatest look of disdain, he met my gaze. His bulbous body was so large it oozed over the edges of his throne. A thin coating of hair covered him like dust. He had the appearance of a long-forgotten thing, something better left buried.

I wondered at my decision to dig him up.

"Pretty mask, brother." I tugged at the strings of black hair that hung from his head like mold. "Pity it does not mirror the aberration within."

Naeve let out a sound like choking and a rat crawled from his mouth. "Welcome to the Wicked Circus, *princess.* Is the reception to your liking?" His face housed a family of boils, and when he smiled, they blended with his lips.

"Utterly delightful. It's clear you have gone to so much *trouble.*"

He rose languidly from his throne. "Trouble?" he intoned, as the air around him began to shimmer. "Don't be silly, child. You practically led us right to you."

I grinned, refusing to show weakness. "Wasn't it nice of me to give you a fighting chance?"

"That *would* have been nice," said Naeve, his body undergoing a curious transformation. Pounds of flesh dripped from his frame, dissipating in the air. Golden wings unfurled behind his back. On another sort of creature, such wings would have been prismatic, reflecting every hint of light, yet from Naeve they cast elongated shadows. "But you have never been nice."

He circled the humans, his eyes never leaving my face. Waving a pale, gold-flecked hand, he twisted their bonds, and like pieces on a carousel they turned with him.

Keegan's terror transformed to awe. "He's—"

"Beautiful," Kylie breathed, staring into Naeve's golden eyes.

"Am I?" Naeve asked, flashing a grin. It was the kind of look a snake gives before unhinging his jaw and swallowing you whole.

"I bet you're ugly on the inside." That was Alexia, looking to get herself killed, no doubt. But I couldn't really blame her, could I? If I were in her place, I would have said the same thing.

I should be in her place.

Naeve knelt before her. Bless her little soul, she didn't blink. Not until his blue-black hair began to writhe like serpents and a line of blood trickled from his lips. "You reveal more than you realize. Be wary of that."

"I'll write it down," she snarled. "If you'll just loosen my bonds..."

"Little lies, easy lies."

"It's called sarcasm," I said, stepping close enough to draw Naeve's attention. "If you had any insight into the minds of humans, you would know that."

"And yet even I am smart enough to know that an unexplained meteor shower would attract their attention," he replied.

My heart skipped. His words were little claws in my chest.

"I had my reasons," I said flippantly. "But how would you know of my glamour's effect on humanity? Have you been sipping tea with them? Sharing a bit of gossip?"

"We came upon a group of them in the mountains, after that stupid little marsh sprite spoiled your secret." Naeve laughed. "Surely you must have known that humans notice strange movements in the stars? Even the foulest, most inbred of the lot knew something was amiss. They pointed my courtiers in the direction of your little town. That is how you think of it now, isn't it? Your town?" Naeve spat the words as if they had poisoned him.

I wish they had.

"What happened to you?" he asked. "How did you fall so far?"

"I woke up," I said.

"And you thought you could live out your days in

the wasteland? You did not think that we would come for you?"

I shrugged with the careless expertise of a human teenager. "Doesn't this all work out in your favor? You acquire your birthright, the position I *stole* from you. You become the Dark Lady's one and only child."

"Ah, if only it were so simple," he said. "But unfortunately, the Dark Lady has grown attached to your presence. She does not eat, she does not sleep."

"She always was good at keeping up appearances."

"Oh, what a tragic story! Poor neglected princess, who had everything she could ever want. But that wasn't enough for you, you wicked little wretch. You had the Court, but you wanted the world." He lashed out, barely missing my neck. Those long, spindly fingers curled in the air. "You insult your family. You insult your queen. You insult your people, and for that you will pay."

"You will have to catch me first." I opened my wings. Naeve may have been cunning, but I had always been the better flier.

"Oh, little Elora. I've already caught you." He crouched down, laying a hand on Kylie's cheek. Like a lion stalking its prey, he had sniffed out her sweetness. And he would use that sweetness to subjugate me. To try.

"What do you want?" I asked casually, hoping he could not hear the hammering in my chest.

"Not a big thing," he said. "Just your life."

I rolled my eyes. "You would trade my life for the lives of humans? Are mortals more valuable than the fey, now?"

He scoffed. "You misunderstand me. The lives of mortal babes are all but worthless. And yet, they seem to hold some meaning for you."

He bowed a little, as if to say: *Your move.*

"And if I refuse?"

Naeve beckoned the Lady Claremondes. "Won't you give us a demonstration?"

The Lady cackled, slithering across the ground. Before I could reach the humans, she had lowered her lips to Kylie's neck. "One little lick makes baby sick," she hissed, revealing her tongue. "Two on the neck means baby's death."

"No!" Keegan screamed, but it was too late. The Lady slid her long, venomous tongue up Kylie's neck. For a moment, everything went silent, and I thought this was some sort of trick. Then all the blood drained from Kylie's face.

The scream that followed did not sound human.

"You've made your point," I said, my voice trembling. Down in the dirt, Kylie was convulsing as black bile dripped from her lips. "But I will not succumb to a simple game of trades. You must fight me, and you must agree to my terms."

Naeve looked at me coolly.

"First, tuck the humans away." I nodded to the tree nearest to us, a great sprawling oak with claws for branches. "And tuck your beasts away as well."

He raised his eyebrows.

"I cannot fight you fairly with them hovering about," I explained, my stomach turning as Kylie begged for relief. "And I am not foolish enough to believe you will exclude them."

"Tuck them away how?"

"Let me bind them to the trees with magic. They will not break my spell easily. And *you* will not release them."

"Very well," he said after a moment. "This could prove to be very entertaining."

His courtiers laughed, but the laughter died the moment I took to trapping them. The surrounding trees bent to my will, extending long branches. Then, when the faeries were close enough to touch, the branches curled around them, dragging them into the air. The dark fey shrieked and screamed, but the trees showed no mercy. Soon the lot of them were trapped in makeshift cages high above the ground.

I whispered a soft chant into the wind, strengthening the branches. Now they would be as steel, and the faeries would need to be clever to break them. When Naeve copied my movements, binding the humans in the nearby oak, he failed to duplicate the spell. Clearly, he thought he would not need it. Humans couldn't break such thick branches without help. They would need an ax or a chain saw to get out.

They were helpless.

Or so they seemed.

"Ready to play?" I asked, taking to the sky. In spite of the danger, I could not help but feel that familiar thrill. Too long my wings had been bound, by glamour and by apprehension.

Naeve rose effortlessly into the air, matching my pace, and pulled a pair of thick gloves from his cape. By the time he was level with me, the gloves covered his hands. His heavy wing beats roused the stagnant air.

It gave me an idea.

Focusing my attention on the air itself, I warmed the space around me. When my warm air collided with Naeve's cold air, the force of it shook his body. Thunder crackled around us.

I laughed openly. I was only toying with him, giving him a taste of my abilities, but the gesture pleased me. It had been a long time since we had played this game.

He appeared less entertained. Drawing a whip of liquid from the clouds above, he cracked it in my direction.

The whip encircled my neck, solidifying. Naeve yanked me forward, cutting off my ability to breathe. Just as I reached him, I lashed out with my left foot, catching him in the temple. The whip leapt from his hands.

Naeve sneered, but I was already planning my next move. Focusing on the symbols that pulsed beneath my skin, I began to recite a spell. Darkness curled out of my body until it surrounded me. Still, I chanted quietly, and that darkness filled up the entire space. The humans whimpered in their cage. Even Naeve, a child of the Dark Court, would have trouble penetrating this vaporous cloud.

I slid through the air, navigating easily. How could darkness blind me? I was a part of it.

Giddily I neared Naeve, sending the vapor into his mouth, his eyes, his pores, until it choked him from the inside. He reached up, grabbing at his throat, but he could not break free, the poor baby. His wings fluttered weakly. The more he struggled, the weaker he became.

He began to fall.

Naeve was inches from the ground when the darkness disappeared. There was not enough time for him to gather his wits, and he fell into an open plot. Before he could climb out, piles of dirt poured over him.

"Don't be upset," I called as he fought to avoid a premature burial. "It's a great color on you."

The plot began to shake. A shower of dirt burst forth and I darted upward, evading the arc.

"Ready to stop playing around?" I asked.

Naeve pulled himself from the earth. "It would be inhospitable," he spat, "to intimidate you." Frustration was plain on his muddy face. Within seconds, he had risen into the air and was hovering beside the tree that caged his favorite courtiers.

I feared a breach of our terms.

"If you free them, you will prove your inferiority," I warned.

Naeve only smiled, reaching through the branches to

stroke the Lady Claremondes's face. She leaned into his touch, shuddering in pleasure.

I followed his lead, nearing the tree that held the humans, though I kept my back to them. Naeve already knew I shared a bond with them; I could not reveal my true attachment. "Everyone here will know I bested you," I called. "Is that what you want?"

Naeve eyed me for a moment, lips twisted in a peculiar grin. "No," he said, still touching the Lady's face. She was practically purring, pushing herself against his gloved hand.

My stomach turned as she kissed his fingers. "You gave me your word you wouldn't release them."

"And I intend to keep that promise. Now I want you to do something for me."

His courtiers snickered, but I did not understand why. A train of whispering circled the grounds, skittering from tree to tree.

"What?" I asked.

"Turn around."

The hairs on my neck stood at attention. "I will not turn my back to you."

"I will not attack you while you are turned."

"And your—"

"Nor will my courtiers. And if I go back on my word, our deal will be null. You can take the humans and be out of our lives forever."

What could possibly be hiding behind my back? Some monster I had never even imagined?

I turned around.

Oh, Darkness.

I turned, and I wished for a monster.

Please, no.

No monster can destroy us like love.

He had made his way to the middle of the tree. Now he was pulling at the branches that encased the other humans. In the chaos of my battle with Naeve, I hadn't heard him working. Or maybe I hadn't wanted to.

"Oh, Taylor."

Suddenly the branches opened, the tiniest bit, and he was reaching for our friends. But the closer he got, the wider the opening became. Until he was slipping into it.

The branches closed around him.

Naeve.

I spun around just in time to hear the sound. The sound of *tearing*, of flesh being separated from flesh. Then came the shrieking, the guttural moans. I knew someone was choking before my eyes could register what was happening. But they did—all of me registered the sight—and bile rose in my throat.

"You gave me your word," I said as Naeve grinned, clutching the Lady Claremondes's severed tongue. Blood poured over his gloves, black and thick.

No, not blood. Venom.

One little lick makes baby sick.

"You cannot use your courtiers against me," I said.

Two on the neck means baby's death.

"This is not for you," Naeve said, drawing back his arm. "It's for him."

He let his weapon fly. I had little doubt his aim would be perfect. Without even thinking, my arm shot up to stop the poison from reaching Taylor.

Instinctively, I chose love over life.

Sticky venom oozed over my skin. I had taken off my gloves, hadn't I, to be able to fight with my bare hands? I had wanted to feel Naeve's skin under my fingernails as he took his final breath.

Now my lungs suffered a spasm as I fought for breath. Black spots loomed before my eyes. They blotted out everything. My love. My life.

I screamed.

I fell.

28

TAYLOR

My scream reverberated off the cage. I clawed at the branches, trying to break them apart with my hands. Splinters slid into my skin, making a home there, but it didn't matter. Nothing mattered except Elora.

I have to save her.

At least she was alive. That much was clear in the way she writhed in the dirt, her fingers curling as she tried to push herself up. She fell back against the ground, blood shooting from her mouth, blending with her hair. Dark symbols pulsed under her skin, and her wings, black and tattered like clawed curtains, shielded her from nothing.

Now I was seeing her in her faerie form. Now, when she was so close to death.

Why now?

Naeve descended like he had all the time in the world. When he passed by our cage, I pressed myself against the bottom branches. I wanted him to think I was cowering, maybe passed out from the fear. It was better if he thought I wasn't a threat.

Down on the ground, Elora pressed her knuckles into the dirt, pushing herself to her knees. Blood dripped from her mouth when she said, "What now?"

She's taunting him.

Warmth flooded my chest. I almost smiled, until Naeve touched down beside her. "Now," he said, "we discuss your limited options."

"Out with it," she spat. "The wait … is killing me."

"How delightful." He stroked her hair, and my stomach churned. "You joke even upon the cold threshold of death."

"The threshold is wider than you think." She paused, licking her lips. "I don't believe you have what it takes to get me there."

The crowd snickered at that. They didn't seem to care who was winning, as long as there was a bloodbath.

Naeve stretched his arms like a cat. I thought of how it would feel to wrench those arms from their sockets. Then he walked to the back of the throne and lifted something from the ground. "Oh, but I do have what it takes." He showcased the object to Elora.

Blood rushed through my ears.

"That sword has a metal blade," Elora said.

"Indeed. A special kind of metal."

"Iron is forbidden, Naeve. Even to you."

"You would lecture me on the laws of Faerie?" He lifted his chin toward the tree that acted as our cage. I pressed my stomach against the bottom, flattening myself.

Still, I could see over the edge as he said, "If you lie here before me and weep, I will carve into you only a little."

Elora laughed.

"Fine." He lifted the sword over his head. "We'll do it your way. You have forsaken your people for the company of mortals. May the punishment fit the crime."

He brought down the blade.

"No!" I screamed, but he didn't look at me. He didn't even care that I existed. Holding Elora up by her hair, he sawed back and forth across the base of her wings. Even then, she refused to cry out. But her pain was a tangible thing. It filled up the graveyard like thick, black smoke, seeping into my nose and mouth. Choking me. I wanted desperately to break the branches of our cage, leap to the ground and gather her into my arms, kissing her until she was healed, the way kisses healed in fairy tales.

Then it came to me in a rush. This was no fairy tale. This was real. I was caged. Elora was suffering. Soon we'd all be dead.

The end.

Maybe.

"We have to get out of here," I said, as much to myself as to my friends. I didn't expect the words to come out so shaky. "Please look at me. Please listen to me. We're going to die in here."

It was Kylie who responded. Her lips were cracked and bleeding. I would have done anything to get her a drink of water. She said, "Safer here."

I shook my head. "They're dark faeries. They'll find a way to kill us."

Now she was laughing. Her eyelids fluttered like she'd gone a little crazy. I guess I couldn't blame her if she had. "Not faeries," she said.

Alexia turned, just barely. "She thinks faeries are little babies with butterfly wings and magic wands. Love spells, that kind of shit."

"But you believe me?" I crawled over to Alexia.

She shrugged, looking at anything but me, or Kylie, or the ground. She was avoiding all of it. "Why shouldn't I?" she said. "She told me they weren't vampires."

"Stay with me, please," I begged. Down below, Elora was crying, a high, muffled sound, like she wanted to hide it.

"I'm here," Alexia said. "I am. *I am.*" She tried to steady her hands.

But her devastation was nothing compared to the sweat dripping down Keegan's face. He looked as sick as Kylie did. Saliva slipped from his lips. He dipped his head down, close to her neck.

He's trying to suck away the venom.

"Oh, God." I tried to pull him away from her. He was cradling her like a baby. "Don't do that. Don't do that, please. She won't die from it."

I didn't realize the truth of my words until I spoke them. But I'd seen the faeries surround Kylie at the cemetery gate, and she hadn't tried to fight them. They couldn't take her life unless she had.

"They can't kill you unless you enter the fight *willingly*," I explained, recalling Elora's story. "Those are the rules. The venom is temporary."

Keegan glared at me like I was the one who'd put it in her veins.

I reached for Alexia's hand. "I'm going to need your help with this. You're the only one who can."

"No, I can't. I can't look, Taylor." She covered her face with her hands. Tears were sliding down her fingers, but she wiped them away quickly. "I thought I could handle anything. But this is too much—"

"We need to get Kylie to a hospital. You know that, right?"

"Taylor, I can't."

"Yes, you can. We can figure this out. We can save them. I'll help you if you'll help me."

She stared at my outstretched hand.

"Come on, please?" I said. "We can do this."

Alexia took my hand. Together, we peered through the bars of the cage. Naeve had released his grip on Elora. Now she lay slumped on the ground. Two jagged black stumps rose out of her back, one trailing a long, dark vein.

He'd really done it.

He'd taken her wings.

They lay in a heap in the dirt.

"Oh, God," Alexia said beside me. I tightened my grip on her hand.

Naeve tossed his sword into the air. It circled slowly,

catching the light. As he chanted under his breath, I prayed that my intuition was wrong and he wasn't going to hurt her anymore. The sword fell into the stone angel and shattered. The shards glittered in the air like stars.

Then they fell.

Naeve picked up a piece and knelt beside Elora.

"No, no, no," I said.

He didn't listen. Instead, he slid the shard into Elora's back. That's how it looked to me, effortless. He was destroying her without even trying.

Her skin started to hiss.

"Does it hurt?" Naeve asked, picking up another shard from the sword. He turned it over in his hand, toying with her. "Not nearly as much as it should."

I turned away as it pierced her skin. Alexia was running her hands over the wood of the cage, like maybe she could break it. Even Keegan was starting to pay attention.

"What are you doing?" he mumbled.

"How alive do you think this is?" She pulled a leaf from a nearby branch. The tree shuddered a little. "Jesus."

"What are you doing?" Keegan laid his sister down gently. He crawled over to us. "Don't do it."

Alexia reached under her dress and pulled something out of her thigh-high.

"*Don't do it.*" Keegan was shaking, but his eyes had cleared.

"What are you going to do?" I asked. But I'd already

recognized the object in Alexia's hand. I'd seen it before, in Kylie's possession.

"You're going to get us killed," Keegan said, raising his voice, but nobody outside the cage could hear us. The dark faeries were cheering too loudly.

Alexia held the lighter up to a branch.

"We could fall to our deaths," pressed Keegan. "Burn up—"

"I'll take that over the alternative," she said.

We looked down. Naeve had stopped torturing Elora for the moment, but almost all of the shards were sticking out of her back.

I turned to Alexia. "Do it."

She flicked the lighter.

Nothing happened.

"No. No, damn it." She flicked it again. Barely a spark. Then nothing. "Damn it, damn it. Help me!"

"What can we do?" I asked. "None of us has another lighter."

"I do."

We turned. Kylie was holding out her hand.

Another flash of gold. Another lighter.

"Oh my God, baby. Thank you." Alexia cradled the lighter in her hand. "You're perfect. You're the best."

Kylie smiled sleepily. Her eyes were clearing, just like Keegan's had. But I wasn't about to ask her to get up and see Elora writhing on the ground.

She needed her strength.

Once Alexia had the lighter upright, she unleashed its flame. The tree shrieked and pulled back a branch. For one beautiful moment a window opened for us. A window of opportunity. A window of escape.

Then it closed.

"No. No, damn it!" Alexia was cursing again. She kept lighting the branch, then watching the opening close before we could get through it.

"Empty your pockets," Keegan said.

I could barely keep my hands steady, but I did as he asked. Half the contents of my pockets spilled out into the cage. But the branches were pressed so close together, only a few pennies fell through. The rest of my stuff was still within reach.

"What are you thinking?" I asked as Keegan sorted through my things.

"Small flame, small opening. Big flame … you follow me?"

"Dutifully."

He smiled. It was so good to see, and I needed it. I needed something good in all of this darkness. "Got any kindling in there?" he quipped.

God, we laughed so hard. We were being held captive by *a tree*, yet we couldn't get to any of the smaller branches to gather kindling. Our laughter died down quickly, but hope remained.

"I'll make some," I said, picking up my keys. "I'll figure it out." From the corner of my eye, I saw Elora moving. She was crawling in the opposite direction of our tree. The movement forced Naeve to follow her, keeping his back to us.

She's distracting him.

I took the largest key and started sawing at one of the branches. I knew I wouldn't be able to sever it completely. I just needed to fray the sides. While I worked, Keegan handed a piece of gum to Alexia, taking one for himself. Then he pulled the bills out of my wallet. "Ten, twenty, forty, fifty. Why the hell are you carrying around fifty-three bucks?"

"In case of emergency."

"These branches are too big," Alexia said. "They won't burn."

"We never should've left that flask in the car." Keegan started sticking bills onto the branches with the gum, right beside the pitiful strips of wood I'd managed to fray. "Hiding anything in your panties?" he asked Alexia.

"What panties?"

Kylie laughed. "I have stuff," she mumbled, pulling what looked like a pile of lint out of her jacket pocket. But hidden beneath the lint was a tube of lip balm.

Keegan snatched it up. "Bingo!"

"Big deal," I said, lining up more bills along the branches.

"This crap's loaded with petroleum." Keegan slid the

tube over the bills before applying the lip balm directly to the branch. "Petroleum and fire are total BFFs."

"Thank you, disturbed teenager," Alexia said.

"A Boy Scout is always prepared."

"Oh, God."

"This is good." I stared at the piles of money stuck around the branches. "This could work."

"If only we could get Lora to help us," Alexia said.

"She's trying to distract him." I didn't want to look down. I'd been trying very hard to focus on my task and block out the rest. But now I let my gaze flicker down, and saw Elora lying on her side. Her eyes settled on me.

Alexia ran her thumb across the lighter, showing Elora what we were planning. Elora's hair darkened until it was black. She looked frightening, severe. Then she did the strangest thing.

She pulled Naeve down and kissed him.

Alexia unleashed the lighter's flame. At first, nothing happened. My heart sank like a rock. Then the first bill began to curl, and within seconds the bills were glowing with orange and blue flame. The tree started to shudder, then shake. It was like it knew what we were planning.

And it was afraid.

"It's working, it's working," Kylie gushed. Then, "He sees us!"

It was true. Naeve had noticed the burning tree and was striding in our direction. Elora did not try to follow him, but watched in silence. It seemed she was summoning her magic, summoning her strength. And when the tree began to scream and pull back its flaming branches, she blasted a gust of wind into Naeve.

God, it was beautiful. Naeve's body made a perfect arc through the air. When he slammed into the big stone angel, I resisted the urge to laugh. A trail of blood stained the marble as he slid to the ground. Within seconds, he was trying to push himself to his knees.

"Now," I said to Alexia, and she helped Kylie out of the opening. Already the fire was dying down. Keegan was next; I ushered him along, then watched for three eternal seconds as he climbed down the trunk of the shaking tree. All eyes were on us now, and the faeries in their cages were shrieking in fury.

"I probably deserve to die for the things I've done," I said softly, to the wind. "But if you let me live, I'll do everything I can to make up for it."

I pulled myself through the opening and crawled around the backside of the trunk, where I wouldn't be seen. But I didn't climb down slowly after the others.

I jumped.

There came a whoosh of air, and I was flying. Then I was falling. The shock of my landing knocked the breath out of me. My leg muscles screamed for relief, but I couldn't rest.

Quietly, I picked up a branch that had broken away

from the tree. My friends were nearing the bottom of the trunk. "Run to the parking lot," I told them. "Let them see you after you've created some distance, but don't wait for me. Get yourselves out of here."

"No," said Kylie. "We're not leaving you."

"I need you to," I said. "I need the distraction. Please."

She bit her lip. "Taylor. I—"

"I know." I reached for her hand. "I love you guys too."

"What are you going to do?" Alexia asked, gathering Kylie in her arms. She'd noticed the branch in my hand.

"I'm going to save her," I said, tightening my grip. "Now go."

She touched her hand to her lips, and then to my cheek. Keegan was nodding, holding my gaze. Then they were running as fast as they could, sticking to the outskirts of the cemetery so Naeve wouldn't know I'd stayed behind. As they reached the far side, they started screaming so that he could hear them.

They were doing exactly what I wanted.

I crept along the outskirts in the opposite direction. Toward the angel, where Naeve had fallen. He was standing now, laughing openly as they passed through the cemetery gates.

They made it.

He towered over Elora. "Such cowards," he said, kicking her in the ribs. "This is what you have chosen over the Unseelie Court?"

Elora opened her mouth, but only blood dripped out. I watched her as I passed between the trees. It was clear she'd used the last of her strength to summon that gust of wind. Now her eyes fought to stay open.

No. Not now, please.

It wasn't supposed to work this way. The closer I got to her, the better chance she should have of surviving. But now, as I neared the back of the stone angel, Elora's body started to shake.

Not now. Not now. Not now.

"I suppose it's poetic," said Naeve, "that you should live long enough to see them for the curs they are. Now you know the mistake you made in choosing them over us." He knelt to stroke her cheek. But the movement wasn't meant to be comforting. It was a violation, just like everything else he'd done.

Something cold and gray opened up inside me, swallowing the parts that were able to feel happiness. Swallowing the parts that were able to feel compassion. I welcomed it, reveling in the numbness.

"Don't worry," Naeve said, pressing his lips against her cheek. "I'll take good care of your mother."

I touched the sharp tip of the branch I carried. With Naeve almost within my reach, my gray thoughts darkened to black. I didn't just want to hurt him. I wanted to kill him. I wanted to slide the edge of the branch across his neck and feel warm blood ooze over my hands.

Who am I?

I didn't recognize the person having these thoughts. I wondered if watching Naeve torture Elora had changed me. Made me into something darker.

But maybe that person had always been inside me, resting beneath the surface. Maybe the things I'd witnessed tonight had simply uncovered my true nature, the one I'd buried my entire life. I'd never had thoughts like these. Not even when my father had ripped out my heart and blamed me for the loss of it. Terrible thoughts raced through my mind, beckoning me to act.

I stepped up behind the angel as quietly as I could.

From above, the dark faeries tried to warn Naeve—at least, those who weren't trying to copy our escape and burn their way free. But they'd made a mistake by screaming all night. How was Naeve supposed to know that this moment was different?

"The Queen will be devastated when she hears of your downfall," he said to Elora, shaking his head. "Her only daughter, defiled by humans."

"Lies," Elora murmured.

"I won't have to lie. That's the beauty of it." He leaned in. "From the moment you were born, I warned her you would be drawn to this place."

"Why... would I be drawn...?"

Naeve laughed, the sound cutting like glass. "Why do you think your wings grew in so wretchedly? Why do you think I had to take them away? Unfortunately for your mother, you've always been your father's daughter." He lifted a final, glittering shard from the dirt. "A pity you won't live to spill that secret."

"Oh, I think she will." I slammed the branch into Naeve's head.

There was a sound like bones cracking, and then he slumped to the ground. I stared down at him, triumphant. But the triumph bled out of me quickly, replaced by something colder.

Oh, God.

Naeve wasn't moving. A thin line of blood trickled away from his head. I watched it, mesmerized, as it meandered across the dirt.

He's dead.

But he couldn't be dead. He was a supernatural being.

I killed him.

Seconds ago, I'd wanted to kill him more than anything. Now I felt the burden of his death pressing into me. I felt his blood on my hands.

I looked at Elora, begging silently for forgiveness. But what could she give me now? And how could I ever look myself in the face again?

"I didn't mean to," I whispered, though it was a lie. "I'm sorry."

Elora's eyes struggled to open.

I brushed the hair from her face. "I'm sorry for what I did. I'm sorry for wondering if you hurt that girl."

She narrowed her eyes.

"The real Laura Belfry. But you didn't, did you? You never would have done that."

She shook her head, barely. "But I might have stopped—"

"Don't say anything." I pressed my face into hers, lending her warmth. "Just let me take care of you."

More blood slipped out of her mouth. Some of it was darker, almost black.

"God, how could they do this to you?"

From the direction of the parking lot, I saw light. I turned, blinding myself for an instant. I realized my friends hadn't listened to me after all.

I realized they were waiting for us.

"I'm going to get you out of here," I said, looking to the trees. The dark faeries were still captive, for the moment. "But I need to know if I should take these out first." I gestured to the iron shards in her back. I had to force myself to look at them. "I know it's poison, but I don't want you to bleed to … " I stopped, wiping my nose with my sleeve. "I don't want to hurt you."

She opened her cracked lips. "Yes."

"Yes, take them out?"

"Yes."

"Okay." I got down on my hands and knees, surveying the damage. Naeve had covered her upper back with the shards, everywhere her corset didn't cover, but I told myself I just had to take out one after the other. Eventually, they'd be gone. I circled the first one with my fingers.

Elora gasped. Even this caused her pain. The tiniest of movements.

"I'm so sorry," I said.

I pulled.

Her body seized as the shard came loose. Blood-tipped and jagged, it fell to the ground. I made myself think of nothing but making a pile of them. I let no other thoughts get in.

Two, then three, fell beside the first. Then five. Then ten. Elora was still breathing; I knew because of the crying. I could hear footsteps approaching, and I hoped they were the steps of my friends.

But I couldn't focus on it.

Then I heard wingbeats, and I looked up. The faeries of the Dark Court had managed to break free. At least, one group had, and they were using branches burning with purple fire to free the rest. But the dark fey weren't the only ones with allies. Keegan and Alexia were now kneeling next to me. Kylie had her chair, and she was unscrewing a water bottle for Elora.

"Get the wings," I said.

I don't know why I said it. But some part of me knew what would happen if we left them here, knew they'd be ripped to shreds or hung up in the Unseelie Castle in celebration of what Naeve had done.

Alexia grabbed them as the last of the shards from Elora's back hit the ground. The wings were covered in blood and dirt. So was Elora.

I picked her up as carefully as I could. "We're getting you out of here."

She tried to wrap her arms around my neck, but they slipped away. Then she was just hanging there in my arms, not even shaking anymore.

"Let's get her to the car," I said.

"And then what?" Alexia asked, following. "We can't take her to the hospital."

"We'll figure it out."

"I'll catch up to you." That was Keegan.

I turned to find him kneeling next to Naeve. "No," I said.

Keegan's fingers slid over Naeve's neck. "He's got a pulse. Barely."

I closed my eyes. I felt relief, then fear. "There isn't time," I said, eyeing the gates. I couldn't explain to him how it felt to have someone's death on your hands. He wouldn't know until he was crushed by it.

"He hurt my sister. I'm going to kill him."

"I wouldn't blame you if you did. But not today."

Keegan stared at Naeve's body, his hands clenched so tight I didn't think there was any blood left in them. Finally, he stood up. "Fine. Let's get out of here."

The dark faeries were closing in. We had very little time before they reached us.

We raced across the grounds. I tried to keep Elora warm by holding her against me. I didn't want to think about how quickly her body was losing heat.

When we reached our cars, Keegan started opening doors. "I'll drive. You take care of her."

"Okay," I said.

"Where are we going?" asked Kylie. She and Alexia were throwing stuff off the seats of Keegan's car to make room for us. "Should we go home? Keegan? We could take her—"

"No," he said, catching his sister's eye. "We can't involve our families. Those *things* could come after us, and ... "

I closed my eyes, waiting for the truth to sink in, the *pain* that came with realizing you couldn't go home. But when I opened my eyes, Kylie was nodding. "We'll go to the coast," she said. "Alexia's mom has a house there. If we drive fast enough, maybe—"

"It won't work," said a voice from behind us.

Together, we turned.

Two massive black horses stepped toward us, unfolding feathery wings. Dark faeries. Enemies.

"Stay the hell away from here," I snarled. I tried to lay Elora down in the car, but something stopped me.

Alexia stopped me.

"It's okay," she said.

"Are you kidding me? How could you possibly know that?"

"Because we've met before." She turned to the horses. "You came back?"

"We could not abandon her," the closest one replied.

Her body appeared to be more vapor than substance, and her edges blended with the landscape.

Everything here is edged in shadow.

Looking at Elora, I saw the shadows clinging to her as well. But these shadows were hungry. They curled into her skin as if tasting her.

She was dying.

No.

"You can take her to safety?" I asked.

"Yes," the horse said.

"Where? Not the Dark Court."

"The Dark Court is our home." As she stepped closer, I recognized the figure clinging to her back. Brad. "It is where she should be laid to rest."

"Laid to rest?" My stomach dropped so hard I almost fell to my knees. "You're not even going to help her?"

"She is beyond help. We know of no magic that can heal this."

"You're giving up?" Keegan asked, his eyes flicking warily to Brad.

"She has been poisoned with iron."

"We can't just give up!" Kylie took Elora's hand. We all would have given her our warmth, if it came to that.

"There has to be something we can do," I said, running Elora's story through my mind. There had to be an answer in there, buried like treasure in the sea. But each time I dove under the waves, I was tossed out.

"There is nothing," the closest horse said. Tears formed

in those big black eyes. She was crying. The twins were crying. God, even Alexia was crying.

"There has to be *something*." I slid my sleeve across my face, trying to center myself. "Iron. Iron is poison to faeries. Iron is starlight. We have to find the cure for starlight. No."

I lowered my head to Elora's face. I knew I was getting further away from the answer, but I didn't know how to focus. The horses peered at us. There was no color in their eyes. No tiny spark of light.

Probably due to a lack of iron, I mused, feeling delirious. My grip on reality was slipping away. Biting my lip to keep from drifting, I stared into Elora's now-open eyes.

For a second, I thought she was dead. My heart stopped. My breath. Everything.

Then she blinked, and I looked at those eyes again, really looked at them. I was startled by the amount of light in them.

Must be because of the iron, I thought, and shook my head at my own stupidity. Her eyes had always been bright—it had to be something else. Sunlight?

The sun is a star, you idiot. You absolute, complete—

"Oh my God." My thoughts spun too fast to hold on to.

Iron comes from stars. Stars create light. The iron from stars poisons faeries. But without the sunlight, everything on earth would die.

We needed that light to survive.

"Light," I mumbled, remembering the part of Elora's

story that I'd been trying to find. Her words about the Bright Queen danced through my mind:

She was known as the greatest healer in Faerie.

"I know where to go." I kissed Elora's forehead as her eyes fluttered closed. I waited for them to open.

And I waited.

29

ELORA

I was seventeen when death crossed my path. Before that, I'd only felt her cool breath on my neck as she passed me by. But late one night, death offered to take me home. She kissed my cheeks and told me stories of a land where I could fly without wings.

"*Come*," she said, and beckoned.

I recognized her voice then. I knew exactly who was leading me into the darkness.

All I had to do was follow.

30

TAYLOR

When someone dies, you lay her bones to rest in the earth and say a prayer. You scatter dirt and roses over her coffin. You don't carry her out of the cemetery and out of the known world.

But we did.

So Elora couldn't be dead.

This was the way I rationalized it as the six of us traveled over the ocean, huddled together on the backs of the horses. But she felt so cold, and her body felt rigid in my arms, paralyzed by the poison. If she wasn't dead, she was very close.

I chose to believe she had more time.

We flew for hours, Elora held tightly against my chest, Alexia clinging to my waist. I saw the sun rise and set. Then we passed through a strange, rolling fog that made me think we were entering Faerie. I kept my face close to Elora's, whispering promises I couldn't possibly keep. "I'll give you my blood, my breath, my life. Just don't leave me." I didn't even need to open my eyes. I just needed to feel her chest rising and falling.

But something happened that forced my eyes open: a sudden onslaught of light. I blinked, expecting to see the Seelie Court in all its glory.

Instead, I saw the borderlands: the place where Bright and Dark Courts met. What fascinated me, more than the glowing light coming from the east, was the contrast of light and dark battling it out for everyone to see. From the western side, shadows tried to swallow the world, but the light wouldn't let them. As we swooped down, under a patch of cold, wet clouds, I saw another sign of the battle between Bright and Dark: thin, black trees rose up in a line, stretching over what must have been the length of the borderlands, while long, green vines from the Bright Court tried to choke the life out of them. Still, those trees kept growing, and still those vines reached, forever battling, never able to rest. It must have been so tiring, devoting every waking moment to that kind of hatred. And Elora had been raised to hate the bright faeries *and* humanity. No wonder she was so tired.

No wonder she wanted to rest.

"We're almost there, baby," I promised, calling her the sweet things I'd never had the courage to say before. It all seemed so stupid now, my reservation. My fear. Back then, the worst she could have done was reject me. Now she might die in my arms.

"I love you," I whispered in her ear.

She said nothing.

We arrived. Our flying horse reared back in midair, like she wasn't able to fly past the border. I knew, or thought I knew, that her aversion was based on fear rather than a physical barrier, and I stroked her neck with my hand, though it only made her feathers drop.

"Please," I begged, loud enough for her to hear me over the rush of the wind. "Please do this for Elora."

She brayed loudly, but in a rush of speed burst past the border. Feathers were dropping freely now, and her coat looked paler than it had before. I wondered if the light was causing her to *fade*. But I didn't know what I could do about it, because I didn't know where we were supposed go. Should we just drop down in the middle of the forest and expect the Bright Queen to *know*?

Then out of the forest came a doe, the largest doe I'd ever seen, and though I had to assume they'd never met before, the horses seemed to recognize her, and followed.

When our horse dipped down to the tops of the trees, she practically flickered out of substance. For a second, I actually thought she was going to disappear.

"What's happening?" Alexia hissed into my ear. Her grip tightened around my waist, making it hard to breathe.

"It's a trick," I said, twisting around as much as I could. "It has to be a trick."

"Why?" Her voice was too loud, after the hours of silence.

"Because this horse isn't disappearing. I can *feel* her. Can't you?"

"Yeah," she agreed, her grip loosening the tiniest bit. "But I still don't like it."

I didn't like it either. I wanted to tell the fey horse she'd done enough, but there was no way I would be able to catch that doe on foot. She was bounding between trunks, over brambles and through gales of light. It occurred to me, then, that the light might be hurting Elora; I looked down and saw that the symbols on her skin had faded completely. Her hair was practically ablaze, the red strands laced through with gold. But the rest of her was just as visible as always, and the light didn't seem to bother her at all.

Why would the Bright Court's light have so little power over the Dark Princess? Did it have to do with what Naeve had said to her in the cemetery?

You've always been your father's daughter.

I didn't have time to wonder. I only had time to be thankful, because now we'd reached a patch of trees so guarded that there was a canopy of leaves blocking us. The deer had gone in and not come out, so we needed to go in too. There was only one problem—the horse either wouldn't or couldn't enter.

We were stuck.

"Please," I begged, though I hated to say it. Would the light be brighter beneath those glowing leaves? Would it hurt her?

I started to panic, trying to figure out how possible it would be to carry Elora from the horse onto the branches. Never mind that between Aaron's accident and the oak in the cemetery, the branches of a tree were the last place I wanted to be. If it was my only choice, I would take it. I would risk my own death to save her.

I reached out for the nearest branch.

"Ouch!" the branch squealed, peeling away.

Great. The trees can talk here.

And the branch had bent in an entirely unbranchlike fashion. It moved like an arm.

"Show yourself," Kylie said, coming up beside us on the other horse. Keegan sat behind her, and Brad, dazed and useless, was strapped to Keegan with a vine.

The branches shook like they were snickering.

"Please help us," I said. "Please. She's dying. I'll do anything."

"Ooh. You said the magic words," trilled a voice close to my ear.

I turned my head.

There, sitting on a branch, was a girl who wasn't a girl. Her skin was the color of bark and leaves grew out of her head like hair. She had teeth like sharpened twigs, and when she grinned, I thought she might eat me.

She peeled herself away from the branch that had appeared to be a part of her.

The horses snorted and reared back, but now more creatures were slinking out of the holes in the tree and crawling out from between the branches. Creatures who didn't bother with clothes, who had hair like vines or knotted branches or brambles. Without a word, they took Elora out of my arms. Others circled Brad, whispering about "the mortal offering" with his horse.

I'll deal with that later.

The faeries led us down the tree, but they wouldn't let my friends into the space where the doe had gone. They only let me, probably because I'd offered to give up *anything* to help Elora. Now the light was so bright I wanted to sew my eyelids shut. I couldn't see anything, but using my hands, I found my way to the place where they'd laid Elora on the ground. I heard them disappear back into the tree, or into their glamour, or wherever they went to spy on visitors.

"Where are you?" I said, blinking as if my eyes could ever get used to this brightness. "I can't see—"

Then, just like that, it was gone. It felt like all the light had been sucked out of the room, and in its place, black spots loomed over everything. I was defenseless. Anyone could have come at me. I understood, in that moment, the brilliance of the Bright Queen's power. People could use whatever weapons they wanted, but if they were accustomed to sight, they would be useless the minute it was taken away.

And I felt useless. Maybe that was the idea. But I would still protect Elora with my life.

I draped myself over her, trying my best not to touch any of her wounds.

"Show yourself," I said softly, imitating Kylie.

Laughter filtered over me like light, and behind the black spots I could make out flashes of the doe's body. Then, before my sight fully returned, the doe began to change. But unlike Naeve in the cemetery, her body did not melt away. Rather, it grew, until a creature three times my size towered over me. She was frightening but beautiful, soft but strong. She was everything I expected, and nothing I could have imagined.

"Your Grace." I bowed my head. It hurt to look away from her, from skin that was the color of earth and eyes that were so like mine, but brighter, almost blinding. She'd bound her body in a gown of glowing green, and the tops of her breasts spilled out over the top, but any sexuality was cancelled out by the feeling that I was looking at my true mother.

The mother of everyone on earth.

"Take heart, child," she said in a gentle voice, "And look at me."

I did. But suddenly that light was back, and I threw my arm across my face.

"Forgive me, young one." Her laughter trickled over me. "An old joke."

"Hilarious." I struggled against the brightness.

"I thought it would be," said the Bright Queen. "Now, give an old woman some room."

Her words seemed to amuse her. Another joke? Sure, she was ancient, but she looked everlasting. Leaves and vines grew out of her hair, green to match the forest, and her lips were stained like she'd been eating berries.

I hope they were berries.

I gave her the room she asked for, but only a little. Elora lay in the grass, curled up in a fetal position, her chest barely rising and falling with each breath.

"Thank you for doing this," I said.

"I haven't agreed to anything yet." The Queen's skirt billowed around her as she knelt, trailing a hand across Elora's forehead. It should have been a soothing movement, but her nails were long, like sharpened knives, and I thought I saw the thinnest trail of blood.

"I understand," I said, only partially lying. "What would you ask in return?"

"A simple token of your loyalty." She touched her bloody finger to the earth and a drop of water sprang up. Soon there was a pool there, sinking into Elora's clothes. Washing the blood from her skin.

"Just a little, to draw out the poison," said the Queen. "Blood holds such power."

"Is that what you want?" I asked, horrified at the possibility of Elora bleeding out right in front of me. But the Queen wouldn't let that happen. She hadn't invited us in here just to murder the daughter of the Dark Lady.

My heart started to pound.

"I can give you—"

"Your blood?" she asked. "Oh, Brightness, no. As you can see, I have plenty of blood."

She gestured to the pool, where the water had turned from crystalline blue to magenta.

My heart screamed for relief, but I couldn't backtrack now. Whatever the Queen was planning, I had to try to save Elora. I had to believe it was a possibility.

"Let me make this clear," I said as Elora's breathing softened. "And I say this knowing full well it's a foolish thing to offer. But I would give you anything to save her. Whatever you want for her life, just ask."

The Queen's smile grew so big it almost eclipsed her face. Sharp teeth slipped out from between her lips. I wondered, in that instant, if her lips were dark because her teeth were constantly cutting into them. What would happen to a person who'd spent centuries in that kind of pain?

"I'm at your mercy," I said, in spite of the danger. "I'll do anything so that she can live."

"Isn't that sweet? But I would only ask for a very small offering. And, after you give it, you get to keep it."

Another riddle?

"Tell me," I said, creeping right up to danger and calling out to it. Even kneeling, the Bright Queen could crush me in an instant. Her light could burn me up.

Turn me to ash.

"I ask only one thing," she said to me. "A name."

I looked down at Elora. The bloody water was sinking away now, crawling back into the ground. "I don't know her full name." I cradled Elora's head in my lap. She was still breathing, but it was even harder to detect.

"I'm not asking for her name," said the Queen.

"You want my name?"

Elora sighed, and my heart leapt. My body started buzzing. But maybe it was a warning of some kind.

"You just want my name?" I repeated.

"A simple token."

It's a trick.

I don't know if the words came from me or from somewhere else. Holding Elora in my lap, I could feel her energy. Maybe I was tuned in to her thoughts somehow; I didn't understand how I could intuit such a thing about the Queen on my own. Then again, maybe a part of me was remembering Elora's story.

What did she say about names?

It didn't matter. I would give the Queen my life if it meant saving Elora's. "My name is Taylor—"

Elora's lips parted, and I leaned in. Was she trying to tell me something about giving away a name? After all, she'd only given me her first name, and that had taken weeks.

It doesn't matter.

"Taylor Christopher—"

This time, Elora shook a little, and moaned as if in the throes of a nightmare.

Don't give up your name, warned a voice inside my head. *Names are power. Giving a name is giving up power.*

I looked down at her one last time. She was so pale, she looked like she'd never be warm again.

"Remember that first night in my bedroom?" I whispered. "When you promised me my heart's greatest desire? My desire is you, safe and alive. That's the only thing I want."

I lifted my head. "Taylor Christopher Alder."

31

ELORA

Back in the human world, my heart had made a promise before the rest of me knew what I wanted. The promise had been foolish; the boy could have asked for anything. And after I said it, I was certain I would be harmed by it.

I was right.

The light from the Bright Queen's bower was so bright that it reached into the land of the dead. It bled into the darkness and, as light will, obliterated it.

Everything was revealed then.

I saw the universe. I saw the nearly infinite number of spirits. But I did not see Taylor, the boy whose greatest desire I had pledged to give. And before I even decided to keep my promise, my heart knew that I was choosing him.

So I did.

My spirit slammed back into my body so hard I forgot how to breathe. The poison still swam in my veins, but it was different now. The knives and claws of it had been replaced by needles, tiny and only scraping my skin. I knew then that I could withstand the pain.

I felt Taylor holding my hand.

Love flowed into me as light did. The Bright Queen and Taylor—together, they healed me. Together, we make our way from pain to peace.

Only, always, together.

Taylor leaned over me, fingers touching me so lightly, like feathers. Like wings.

His voice drifted into my ear. "I'm here," he said.

I opened my eyes to him; they struggled against the brightness.

I opened my lips. "Kiss me."

He did. Lips warm and soft. Breath rushing into me.

"You saved me," I murmured, remembering how to breathe. I was as a newborn again, and I hadn't even been born that long ago.

Who else can say that?

"Who would have thought it—the mortal saving the faerie?" said a rich, pleasant voice. A voice I had only heard once before.

"Lady," I breathed, looking to the back of the bower. "My deepest appreciation ... " I fell silent. The Queen's magic danced in my veins, drugging me gently, blotting out the worst of the pain. Blotting out the memory of all that had happened to me.

The Queen glared down at me as if I were a naughty child. *Bad Elora.*

A giggle escaped my lips.

"I did not do this for you," said the Queen, as the trees

bent down to whisper in her ear. "You have disappointed me. You failed to complete your end of the bargain."

"Failed?" I mumbled. "But I brought..." I glanced around the bower, half expecting to see Brad tied to a tree, vines circling his wrists and flowers in his hair.

"I'm sending him back."

"What?" I tried to sit up.

"Relax." Taylor brushed his lips against my cheek. It felt so amazing—every touch, a quiet ecstasy—that I wanted to climb over him right then and there.

Rein it in.

"I did not want something spoiled and rotten," said the Queen as I fought to collect myself. "You knew that. You must have known that."

"But... the riddle."

It was Taylor who answered me. "I think I understand."

I looked up at him, and saw that he looked perfectly at home. His golden hair was adorned in leaves. Light curled around his limbs, clinging possessively. Did he even know it was there?

"You thought *bane of the darkness* meant the most horrible human," he said.

Well. Obviously.

"So you twisted the meaning of *perfect for light* to mean someone the human world wouldn't miss. Someone like Brad."

I shook my head. "I didn't twist..."

Did I?

I could hardly remember it. Wait, there it was, flitting in front of me.

Catch it, Elora. Catch it!

I reached out my hand.

Gotcha.

"*Perfect for light* meant a perfect, mindless toy," I said slowly, as if relearning to use my lips. "Someone *she* wouldn't feel guilty about keeping."

"Look at it the other way around." Taylor's eyes never left my face. His hands stayed in constant motion, stroking my hair.

What a sweet devotee. Perfect for light?

No. Perfect for me.

"*Perfect for light* means the best kind of human," he said. "The kind that proves the Seelie Court right about humanity. And the riddle didn't say 'horrible for the darkness.' It said 'bane'—someone who has the power to thwart you. In other words, *the bane of the darkness* is a human who thwarts the dark faeries. Who proves the dark faeries *wrong* about humanity."

The sweetest kind of human.

"Oh, Darkness…" I murmured. Taylor leaned into me, thinking I was in pain. In truth, I felt tingly all over. *Happy.* The strange fact that the Queen's light hadn't killed me didn't even concern me. Nothing could concern me here in this happy, lovely place.

Nothing except…

"Taylor." I looked up at him, trying to understand the unpleasant, cold feeling in my chest. It wasn't just the wet clothes.

There was a danger here that I was not quite grasping.

"Don't try to talk." He lowered his forehead to mine. He felt so warm against me; he was practically radiating light. "You're shivering."

"I am?" I lifted my head. "Well, look at that."

He laughed like I'd said the funniest thing.

"Such things do happen when one is draped in the water of a pond," said the Queen. "I shall take my leave of you for now. Let her rest, and perhaps free her of her garments," she said to Taylor.

I opened my mouth, but nothing came out. My mind had gotten stuck on the thought of nakedness, and Taylor, and being *alone*. Never mind that I needed to rest.

The Bright Queen began to transform into a deer. I clapped, utterly delighted at the show. I had seen the leaves of her hair darken with her moods, but not this. This was fantastic. My mother might transform into a wolf or raven, but never something vulnerable.

I wished she would.

Wearing her animal disguise, the Bright Queen bounded out of the clearing. The sight almost made me laugh. But my shivering had worsened, and now I could feel it.

"Taylor. Something feels wrong…"

"It's okay." He kissed my cheeks. "Everything's okay. You're just cold."

I couldn't help it. I believed him.

"Should I ... can I undress you?" he asked.

I suppose I should have felt shy.

But I didn't. "Yes."

Yes, please.

I was eager to get these suffocating clothes off me. Eager to feel his hands on my skin. Hidden in the land of the human-loving Seelie fey, I allowed myself to feel the things I could not accept before. I felt bold. Desirous, though I was much too weak to engage in anything too strenuous.

Or am I?

I touched the knee of his pants. "It seems I'm not the only one who is wet."

He looked away for the first time since I'd awakened.

"And the air might be pleasant, if I was not so near to freezing. Would you consider undressing along with me? My body could use your ... heat."

Taylor blushed red. But when he'd finished undressing me—*slowly* unlacing my corset, guiding my skirt over my hips—he set to work unburdening himself of his clothing.

He was beautiful. Strong bones. Soft skin. Everything was as it should be.

Except ...

"You're glowing," I breathed, staring at him unabashedly. Behind his back, great beams of light unfurled like wings.

He laughed, his eyes darting away again. "I think the forest likes me."

"More than the forest," I said, though I couldn't track the

comment to its source. There was something strange about the way the light was responding to him, circling his arms like darkness circled mine. It was as if the Bright Court had claimed him.

"Taylor…"

"Don't worry," he said, taking my hands. "Let me take care of you."

Who could argue with that?

He drew me into him. His body was warm, and mine grew hot in every place that his touched. I found myself crawling over him, my thigh sinking between his, my arms pinning him to the ground. He lifted his head and gave me the softest, sweetest kiss. And he guided me down to his chest. There we lay, in each other's arms, skin pressed against skin, hands cradling, holding, until my eyes closed and I fell into pleasant dreams.

32

TAYLOR

The mortal saved the faerie. That's what the Seelie Queen said. But the truth is, Elora saved my life long before I ever saved hers. She saved me that first day in the park.

She gave me a reason to live.

For seventeen years, I'd only gone through the motions, never letting myself love someone completely, and never really feeling loved.

Now I could feel everything.

Her love had opened me up, made me whole where I'd been fragmented like Humpty Dumpty. Like a puzzle missing half its pieces. Maybe she was love embodied. That's how she felt to me, lying on my chest. She felt like happiness, like safety. And I'd never felt so alive.

There were only a few problems left. My friends and I had been brought into a world we knew little about. Without really asking to be a part of it, we'd been drawn into a war between two rival faerie courts. Oh, and I'd given my name to the Seelie Queen.

She owned me. And Elora didn't even know that yet.

As I lifted my gaze from the love of my life to the ancient trees of the Seelie Court, I realized my dance with death was just beginning.

Acknowledgments

Thank you to the fabulous Sandy Lu, for taking a chance on a faerie story and for taking a chance on me. I will forever be grateful. Thank you to Brian Farrey-Latz for being the brilliant, funny person that you are, and for bringing order to the madness of this story. Thank you to the wonderful Sandy Sullivan, the magnificent Mallory Hayes, the amazing Kevin Brown, and everyone at Flux for your insight, dedication, and all-around awesomeness. And thank you to Marwane Pallas, for taking the photograph I couldn't get out of my head.

To my family, in the Pitchers and the Hauths, for your continued support and encouragement. I thank you muchly.

To AdriAnne Strickland, for being an amazing writer, reader, supporter, friend. (And for reading eighteen billion emails from me each week. You are truly the awesomest.)

To the Lucky 13s, or as I like to call them, the best people in the world. You have saved me, supported me, defended me, befriended me. I love you so much, it's making me rhyme. Someday I hope to hug each and every one of you (except one, for whom I will curtsy).

To the #WeNeedDiverseBooks team, for literally changing the world and for letting me be a part of it. I am in awe of you every day.

To the critters: Maegan, Cassie, Krzysztof, Jon, Jefferson, LaShenda, Quin, Elizabeth, Jan, Amanda, John, Carole, Kara, Sarah, Stephanie, Kim, Jacqueline, Mike, Dylan, Neil, Blakely, Kathy, and Hannah. You are irreplaceable, and this book wouldn't be nearly what it is without you.

To Evil Editor, Phoenix Sullivan, and minions, who read through countless queries for this novel and never told me to get lost. Without you, my journey would not have begun.

To you, the illustrious, fantastic readers, who make all of this possible.

And to Chris Hauth, my unstoppable force of nature. Thank you for inspiring this story and changing my life.

© www.cameronbrowne.com

About the Author

Chelsea Pitcher is a karaoke-singing, ocean-worshipping Oregonian with a penchant for wicked faerie tales. She began gobbling up stories as soon as she could read, and especially enjoys delving into the darker places to see if she can draw out some light. She is also the author of *The S-Word* (Simon and Schuster, 2013). You can visit her at chelseapitcher.com and follow her on Twitter at @Chelsea_Pitcher.

Taylor and Elora's story
continues in
The Last Faerie Queen,
available Fall 2015.